W9-ALV-509

THE RADICALS

ALSO BY RYAN McILVAIN

Elders

THE RADICALS

DISCARD

RYAN McILVAIN

HOGARTH
New York

Copyright © 2018 by Ryan McIlvain

All rights reserved.
Published in the United States by Hogarth, an imprint of the Crown Publishing Group, a division of Penguin Random House LLC, New York.
crownpublishing.com

HOGARTH is a trademark of the Random House Group Limited, and the H colophon is a trademark of Penguin Random House LLC.

Library of Congress Cataloging-in-Publication Data
Names: McIlvain, Ryan, author.
Title: The radicals : a novel / Ryan McIlvain.
Description: First United States Edition. | New York : Hogarth, [2018]
Identifiers: LCCN 2017032393 | ISBN 9780553417883 (hardback) |
    ISBN 9780553417890 (ebook)
Subjects: | BISAC: FICTION / Coming of Age. | FICTION /
    Literary. | FICTION / Cultural Heritage.
Classification: LCC PS3613.C535 R33 2018 | DDC 813/.6—dc23
    LC record available at https://lccn.loc.gov/2017032393

ISBN 978-0-553-41788-3
eBook ISBN 978-0-553-41789-0

Printed in the United States of America

Jacket design: Rachel Willey
Jacket photograph: Glenn Glasser/Gallery Stock

10 9 8 7 6 5 4 3 2 1

First Edition

FOR SHARON

THE RADICALS

I t didn't feel quite right that Sam should be there in the first place—Sam Westergard, clearly fish out of water in our graduate course in Marxist theory. He didn't look the part, anyway. He wore stretched-out polo shirts to class, or old road-race T-shirts, an almost constant smile. He intrigued me. On the night Sam showed up in an oversize Roger Federer shirt, I rustled enough to pay him my compliments on it. I was a fan myself. "Hey, really? Hey, *cool*," he said, with startling enthusiasm.

Pretty soon Sam and I were playing tennis together most Friday mornings and whenever else we could get away from the city and classes, the teaching, underpaid, the life, underpaid. Tennis was a balm and a crucible all at once. We each wanted to win, obviously, very badly, but we also wanted to maintain the illusion that our "practice sets" were only that—a little practice, a lark, a pair of pale intellectuals disgracing the game with our play . . . It wasn't an easy false premise to keep up: The sweat started pouring off me usually in the first game, or else I'd notice Sam's jaw, strangely squarish for his face, jutting out like an old cash drawer after he sent a ball into the net or sailing long. I started calling him Lockjaw. Or Little Lockjaw—a reference to his tall, lordly stature. I probably didn't know Sam well enough to joke with him like this, not at first, but what else could I say? I couldn't have known I was standing across the net from a murderer, and neither could he.

"M or W?" I said one morning in April, the cruelest month, apparently. I had my Wilson Pro pinned, head down, to the grainy green of the court, the frame making its thin crackling music as I rotated the handle between thumb and forefingers, ready to spin it loose.

"No, no, no," Sam said, smiling at me. "Do the thing." He saw my face and said again, "Do the thing. From last time? The one about the revolution—right, comrade?"

In the last few outings he'd started calling me *comrade*. I didn't know how to read it, or what he wanted from me now. His face was simple and expectant, eyes gray—neutral eyes. A little curl still hung around his light brown hair at the sides and bottom, but at the top, all wispy like smoke, all you saw was the sun on his broad forehead.

"'Up with the revolution, down with capitalism'?" he said. "Wasn't it something like that?"

"Oh, yeah. Well, so you know it already."

The racket spun and clattered to rest, the white *W* of the Wilson logo pointing up. "Up with the revolution it is," I said.

"I forgot to call it," Sam said, looking guilty.

I let him serve first, suddenly impatient to be back at the baseline. Was I a performer to him, a bearded lady? I couldn't read his smile. We played to four–all in the first, all my slices coming back with interest. I'd noticed Sam was weak coming over his two-handed backhand, so I swallowed my pride and kept it high and to the ad side, looping the balls high over the net, Nadal-like, the yellow orbs rising and falling like suns. At the zenith of a shot you could see the ball freeze-framed against the Hoboken trees, tall beeches, and the power lines beyond, the rich brownstones with the wrought-iron balconies and the zigzag of fire escapes—the playground of the gentry, and we were crashing it. Anyway, we were graduate students, de facto experts in our contradictions: squeamish adjuncts, fake-casual athletes, complicated atheists. Sam was once a Mormon, he'd told me, and come to think of it he still looked the part—blond, looming. For my part I looked like my Russian Jewish father— dark hair, easy five o'clock shadow, a certain basset hound wariness about the eyes. And the old man's paunch, too. Tennis was supposed to be my exercise.

By the second deuce of the four–all game, our play had devolved into clay-court bullshitting, lob after yawning lob, a game of chicken more than tennis. A pair of seniors warmed up on the next court over, looking askance at us in their golf shirts, high shorts, stinging white socks, their rally balls ticking back and forth metronomically, and low over the net, like grown-up shots. The next ball to land at all short I took early, ginning myself up for a crosscourt screamer. Good knee bend, snapping the racket up and over, the ball buzzing the net cord—I was in my prime again. I followed the shot to net, split step, lunge, and fuck if the ball wasn't by me. The passing shot landed an inch from both lines; I stared dumbly, panting, my racket puddled at my feet.

On the next point, advantage Westergard, I sent a flat serve halfway to the back fence. The second serve came off my racket like a badminton birdie, floating to the middle of the service box, sitting up a foot above the net for Sam to angle easily away.

"Fuck," I said, loud enough for Sam to hear me across the net—his sudden chagrined downcast look, the disapproving stares of the men on the next court.

Sam held to love in the next game to take the set. When he started his lope toward the water bottles sentineling the net post, I intercepted his path with my outstretched hand. I was done for the day. Tapped out.

"You're sure, comrade?" he said, and that same gnomic smile again. He held my handshake a beat too long, my hands wet and red at the extremities. A crescent of sweat glued my shirt to my upper chest, a spidery network of perspiration lines ran down my forehead and into my eyes. Yes, I was sure. And why did he keep calling me *comrade*? What was that about?

"You okay?" Sam said.

I was staring at him.

" 'Comrade'?" I said. "Am I a comrade to you?"

Sam's face changed so suddenly, eyes wide and adrenal, I knew I'd let in my Trotskyist street voice, my meanness. I hadn't meant to.

"I wasn't trying to offend," Sam said. "I was just kidding."

"I'm not offended."

"Oh . . . good . . . I just—"

"It's okay," I said. "I just wasn't sure what you meant by it."

I went over to my racket bag, arranging my gear just so: spare balls, grip tape, shock absorber, keys, phone, wallet. Tinkering, really. Sam stared at his feet as he fingered loose the laces of his tennis shoes, taking out of his bag the faded brown loafers he usually shuffled into class in, like moccasins he'd worn them so thin. Tall guy, tiny shoes—at least in that he followed the uniform of the day.

"I mean," Sam finally said, his voice upcurling in a gesture of détente, an olive branch, "I guess I thought I was using the word like you use it when you talk about your friends, your 'comrades' in the East Village? Not much of a proletariat around NYU, I wouldn't think."

"You'd be surprised. You can have a trust fund and still care about social justice," I said. "And most of my comrades live on the Jersey side or in Queens."

"You're serious, then? You're a believer?"

I bristled at Sam's choice of words—it wasn't the first time, it wouldn't be the last—but yes, I said, I was a socialist. You couldn't sit through hours-long ISO meetings without a certain conviction to gird you, and you sure as hell couldn't stomach five years of reading in abstruse Marxist polemics. It did matter to me. It mattered a lot. It took up a lot of my time, but I gave it gladly.

Sam Westergard blinked at me. He looked chastened and sensitive, his pale face rounding into some kind of recognition, but I wasn't sure of what, and I don't think he was either. He looked like he wanted to ask me something but stopped short, tentative now.

"Take last month," I said. "Some of my ISO comrades at NYU—that's the International Socialist Organization, by the way—do you know it? Well, they were organizing a sit-in to put pressure on the university administration. The university wouldn't disclose their real estate holdings, didn't want to admit to the embarrassingly large swath of lower Manhattan they either own or have investments in. Classic sign of corporate excess: Shut the blinds, turn the lights off. The monopolist doesn't take kindly to people asking about his monopoly—cramps his style. The sit-ins were entirely peaceful, laid-back, no destruction of precious NYU property, nothing like that, but they weren't going to move until their demands were met.

Finally the campus security got called in, people got dragged out of the building by their hair in the middle of the night. It got ugly. The administration showed their true colors, and it was all on TV. Anyway, those were some of my comrades."

"Did it work?" Sam asked.

"Did what work?"

"Did the university disclose its holdings?"

"Not yet," I said.

We passed out of the park on the west side, where Sam's tan spreading Buick sat in the canyon shade of more apartment buildings, more wrought-iron balconies, dappled shadow high up on the dun-rose brick—it was a beautiful spring morning. I didn't like the thought of going into the city that afternoon, descending into the close fetid caverns of the PATH, rising up into the noise and hurry of Sixth Avenue. Is it heresy to say that I sometimes tired of New York? That the streets and crowds and great vanity of the place could jump-start the blood as well as sap it? Not to mention the ungraded papers that waited for me in my office, the endless papers ... It was still early—too early to think about the city, the papers; I supposed I could grade them over the weekend if I needed to, or early Monday. In the clear morning light you could see why the earliest base-ballers took their city game across the Hudson, crossing over to the relative green and space of Hoboken, getting away for a few hours. Somewhere nearby was the home plate they'd laid for that genesis game. A monument now. I'd never seen it.

In the car I rode on a towel, over Sam's objections. He really didn't care, he said. What did he care? His upholstery dated to the Reagan administration. I'd heard these protestations before, kind, gentlemanly ones—Sam was often a gentleman around me—but I suppose I knew enough not to take them at face value. Sam had a new pine-tree air freshener twirling from the rearview mirror, for one. And I think I'd begun to notice other cross-hatchings, the little complications that shaded Sam's gentlemanliness. He drove aggressively this morning, as he always did, riding the bumper of a tall black Range Rover, rushing a pair of yellow lights. Warehouses, gas stations, abandoned grassy lots shot by my window. When another car inched out from a side street, Sam hit the brakes to let a woman in a hijab pull slowly, slowly out into the opposite lane—a little selective in his doing unto others, but I did note it. It was one of the few things he'd held fast to when he jettisoned the faith of his fathers, he'd told me. I'd noted the phrase: *hold fast*. Something antique about it, touching. He was quoting Paul. Myself, I've always preferred Hillel's negative version of the Golden Rule: "What is hateful to you, do not do to your neighbor." More realistic, more manageable. More humane. It's never been clearer to me that the lessons of history and economy combine to shout: *Modest, be modest! Baby steps, baby steps!* All we can hope for, really. The human stuff is too fragile, too fallible.

"These *lights*," Sam said under his breath, stopping short at a clear red. A sudden jolt threw us forward, the whole car, with the dull staccato crunch of broken glass coming from behind us. Behind us, a dark-haired wide-eyed boy, late teens at most, stared openmouthed through the broad scuffed windshield of a brown Jeep Cherokee. The car couldn't have been more than a few years newer than the ancient Buick we rattled in. Sam asked if I was okay. He put his right blinker on, pointing largely and elaborately for the teenager's benefit to a garden center's parking lot to the right of us, nosing the Buick right.

"The fucker's making a run for it!" I said.

The Jeep whirred in reverse and pinched high on its back tires, pivoting and peeling out into the left-turning traffic of the opposite lane. I tried to get the license plate but a gray sedan, honking and braking, blocked the back of the Jeep as it sped away.

"That little *fucker*," I said.

"Did you get the plates?"

"I was about to but—"

Sam whiplashed the car around into the oncoming lane. Another horn was blaring, a quick, bending Doppler howl as a car ran up behind us and just managed to swerve around. Sam spurted away after the teenager, separated now by the gray sedan and the other car, a low-slung black sports job that didn't appreciate Sam's jockeying and tailgating. The car flashed its brake lights in warning when we came up too close on a turn, the brown Jeep hinging visible three cars ahead like a boxcar that segments and breaks from a turning train. When Sam got to a little turnoff in the lane, he threw the car left and floored the gas, the big beleaguered engine responding like a crazed bathroom fan, slingshotting us forward. We split the two lanes for several hundred feet—corridor of cars, horn fanfare—then jerked back into the right lane, cutting off the black sports car and its mutely shrieking driver. I realized from the mounting pressure in my forearms that I was squeezing either side of the worn leather seat, my veins rippling and cording, corrugating. Up ahead was one of the lights Sam had rushed a few minutes before, and now as the gray sedan braked at the end of another yellow, Sam threw us left and right again, button-hooking the sedan and shooting the intersection just ahead of crossing traffic.

"Jesus!" I said, almost laughing for fear.

Sam was silent, his gray serious eyes straight ahead, his sickle jaw slicing the air, pointing *avant*, *avant!* With the fan of the engine whirring crazily, factories gas stations abandoned grassy lots blurring by, we managed to get within tailing distance of the Jeep. I kept one hand anchored to the leather seat and with the other snapped a cell-phone picture of the license plate, blurry but discernible.

"I got it," I said. "Got it."

"You got it?" Sam said.

Up ahead another traffic light loomed, stubborn red, with a line of three or four cars brooking no escape. When we pulled to within rear-ending distance of the Jeep, I took another picture of the license plate for good measure. We sat there idling, watching the teenager's dark motionless head through the glass.

"Well, this is awkward, isn't it?" I said.

Sam put on his right blinker again. He rolled down the window and hooked his pointing hand over the roof. He honked the horn once, a restrained, staccato beep, almost polite, continuing to gesture with his other hand.

"I can only assume he's hard of hearing and seeing," I said. "Wait, what are you doing? I got the license plate!"

Sam was up and out of the car, striding up to the driver-side window of the rusted brown Jeep. My breath caught in the sudden dinging, in the wan overhead dome light of the Buick. Sam, in reed-thin loafers and baggy shorts, a pair of stork-like pasty legs stretching in between, Sam in his sweat-grayed tennis shirt, the incipient tonsure of his bald spot catching the light—Sam knocked slowly and deliberately on the teenager's window. He spoke in a loud, slow voice. "Excuse me, but you hit my car back there. Will you please pull over to the side of the road so we can talk?" Then he stepped back a pace, held both hands up, palms out, at shoulder height, as if to show the young man that he wasn't armed, or maybe to baptize him into the proper repentance. In any case, it worked: The Jeep's right blinker lit up, ticking audibly, and the car rolled over to the shoulder of the road.

Sam trotted back to the Buick's open door, slid into the seat and into gear. Somehow the light had stayed red—no angry honks pierced the air, no sounds at all, really. The air inside the car felt close and gauzy as we pulled up behind the Jeep, and Sam's sly voice sounded distant as it said, "Good, right?"

Good. Right. A man of action, apparently. A complicated man of action. I stood at the right front corner of the Buick's spreading hood as Sam again approached the driver's side of the Jeep. The teenager stayed inside his car, rolling down the window and speaking softly, apologetically from the sound of it. Sam's voice carried back to me—variations on I understand, I understand but damage has been done. He'd heard the crack of glass himself. At one point he called out to me ("Comrade? Damage report?") and I went around back to inspect Sam's car: a rubbery stain on the bumper, black streaks like frozen current, and a good-size jagged hole, vaguely New Jersey–shaped, punched out of the left brake light. I took a few more pictures with my phone. By the time I got back to the front of the car the teenager's hand was holding what looked to be twenties out the window. Sam slowly shook his head. He stretched his long crane-like arm onto the roof of the Jeep and patted it twice in benediction.

"Go and sin no more," he said to me, showing a wry little smile as the Jeep pulled away behind him.

In the car Sam said, "Probably on his phone—saw him try to hide it when I came up to the car."

I stared at him, waiting.

"Which isn't actually his car. It's his older brother's—so he said. Anyway, he did apologize to me."

When we came to the scene of the accident a few minutes later, another red light stopped us. The giant Legoland of the turnpike and Route 9 tilted up to the right of us, the ramps rising and curving away. In the shadow of the freeway was the garden center Sam had tried to turn into, its white wooden trellis hanging rows of round flowering plants, pinks and yellows, like pixie wigs. Closer by, I thought I saw red brake-light glass scattered in the road, glinting.

Finally I said, "Speaking of confrontational politics . . ."

Sam laughed a little, blushing. "Yeah," he said. "Sorry about all that."

I held up a clement hand. "Can I ask you a question, though? I've been meaning to ask it for a while. Deeply invasive, deeply personal . . ."

"Do your worst," Sam said.

"Why are you in a Marxist theory class? Not that you don't belong there. This isn't a purge. It's just that, well, I'm curious. I'd always heard you guys were above theory, or you thought you were."

"You mean poets?"

"All you MFA types."

Sam nodded his head in time to the road's vibrations. We were moving again, crossing the great highway plaza. "You first," said Sam.

"Why am I in the class?"

"You're ABD. You already know the stuff cold. Why go into campus when you don't have to?"

"Boredom," I said. "You get really bored. Do a doctorate, you'll see—boredom, isolation. Alienation. The dissertation cuts you off from your 'species being.' You remember that one—comrade?"

Sam smiled, shook his head.

"Well, it's an embarrassment of jargon, isn't it? Especially in Hahn's class. I sometimes think she should have a translator."

"She should," he said. "You."

I laughed.

"Why not? You TA one of her classes, don't you?"

"An undergraduate class. A general ed class."

"A general education is what I need. It's decided. You shall intercede with the Mother," Sam said, turning onto my street, the caged pin oaks and ivied fences, the painted garages and porches and stoops. When we pulled up to the clapboard row house I rented a room in, Sam held out his hand. "You were soundly beaten today, sir. Until soon?"

"It's your turn," I said. "Why are you in the class?"

"Ah, yes." Sam repeated the question to the windshield, smiling. His gaze slid down to the empty air around the old slotted tape deck, the grimy knobs and buttons going soft at the edges like rounds of cheese. "Same reason as you, I guess. Boredom. Or I don't know. I went to a few Occupy marches when all that was going on. Were you involved with any of that?"

"When there wasn't real activism to do, sure. It was a good party."

"Can of worms?"

"Not really. That's the extent of it for me."

"I guess for me, with the class, I was just tired of poetry workshops, and maybe a little curious. It's been a good vocabulary builder if nothing else."

"Here," I said, "hold on a second."

I ran upstairs to my room, four walls, three of them covered with jerry-built bookshelves, pine planks and cinder blocks, books on labor history, civil rights, the Marxist canon, the smattering of poetry and prose that I'd kept from my undergraduate days, Continental philosophy, science fiction, a little fantasy, architecture, art, a clutch of Audubon guides, my swollen backlog of *The Nation*, a long, low, wall-hugging shrine to literature, books like wainscoting, a cluttered riot of books—better that than IKEA shelves. I plucked a narrow reed from the bulrushes, took the stairs two at a time back down to Sam.

"What's this?" he said when I handed the slim volume through the window, his voice mock scandalous.

"Oh it's dangerous all right. Few things more dangerous than a lucid Marxist."

Sam was holding the book up to the light, turning it sideways, squinting. "Looks a little thin—I don't know. Not much chance of the kind of Stockholm syndrome *Capital* gives you. This won't hold me captive for more than the weekend."

"Read it slowly," I said. "And don't worry about *Capital* for a while. Hahn never makes good on her threats of reading quizzes—and socialism has evolved. Callinicos is good, up-to-date, a proper introduction. I'll be curious to hear what you think."

"Okay," Sam said, "I'll read it. And tell you what I think."

One other thing I remember from that morning—not a particularly proximate start to my story, but somehow it feels like the start: a tennis match, a car accident, a car *chase*, a loaned book in the aftermath.

I waved Sam goodbye telling him I was sorry about the fresh damage to his car. He stuck his face out the window, as if he could crane around to see the punctured brake light, and gave a full-faced shrug. "The things of this world, right?"

That was typical of Sam—always signing off with some cryptic biblicalism, as if we'd all spent our formative years in a seminary. We were worldly-wiser now, of course, wry and unillusioned and yet still beatific enough to believe in causes. Or something like that. I've since had plenty of occasion, urgent occasion, to think of what that particular quip might have meant to Sam—something about the transience of all earthly things, wasn't it, but what did that transience mean to *him*? Was it a good thing? An enabling thing? The more I think about the phrase in Sam's mouth the less it sounds like a quip at all. Maybe more like a prophecy, or a threat.

Anyway, I shouldn't get ahead of myself, or not more than two or three days at this point—skipping ahead to an elevator ride up to Dr. Hahn's office, late Monday afternoon, and where the hell had the weekend gone anyway? What to say to the good *Frau Doktor*? Hahn and I were relaxed enough around each other, and I was certainly seasoned enough in the academic game, that I felt I could dispense with the tepid, transparent excuses for why the batch of twenty essays still lay on my office desk, inevitably, ungraded. Not a family emergency, no—my folks sat quietly in suburban Massachusetts like little Matryoshka dolls, tidy and neat: Take off their shells, they'd keep surprising you, but the calm lacquered exterior was calm indeed. And no mononucleosis either—no one to give it to me. No crippling depression (no chemical depression, anyway), no psychotherapeutic Rolodex to flip through and pluck from. I was a hale, hearty, well-adjusted child of loving, educated parents— one of the lucky ones. I just couldn't bring myself to give a shit anymore. Was that an admissible excuse? Dear Dr. Hahn, I feel my veins fill with lead at the prospect of reading another paper about checks and balances, or the shameful Three-Fifths Compromise. My limbs like salami, heavy and dead. It's the same with my own work. It's a sort of soul-soddenness, the weight of waste. What did it really matter *what* thirties-era radicals did to try to disrupt the New Deal? Why history? Why yesterday? Wasn't Time's winged chariot assembling now, and now, and now? Randolph's famously open curriculum, a doctorate in Politics, simply, had given me so much rope to hang myself with that I'd now collapsed under the weight of it, crushed under the coiling coils of it, the pile rising on top of me like toxic soft serve, or a funeral cairn, like the brainy abstract involutions I'd once plunged into headfirst. Theory! Ideas! The dialectic! It was Alex who'd cut to the quick of it all a year ago—had it already been a year?—when she dropped out of her fancier program at Columbia, ABD. *I could jerk off to Deleuze and Guattari for two hundred pages . . . or I could actually do something.* We were lying in bed when she said it, in a Florence *pensione*, no covers, no cover at all. She'd made the lazy masturbatory hand gesture, the wet raspberry sound to punctuate the pause. I looked down at my bare flaccid penis, father to none. Alex and I broke up a month later.

Did I miss her? Of course I did. But what I also missed was some dimly remembered sense of purpose, the orientation toward *doing* that Alex had apparently reclaimed. Dear Dr. Hahn, is it too much to ask that my life be more than the sum of its little routines? Dear Doktor, what should I do about the sense of hollowness that overtakes me, spreading inside out until my skin feels like a mold?

The elevator dinged and in walked a pretty girl.

A redhead.

Short. Shortish. Not tall, in any case.

Small freckles on her face, light brown, massing at her cheekbones and nose bridge like the drips in a Pollock painting.

She pressed her lips together in a thin smile, acknowledging me. I gave the same look back. Her red-brown hair was long and thick, loosely ponytailed, piled into the hood of a navy blue Randolph sweatshirt, her skin that much whiter by contrast, a little waxen in the pallid chrome elevator light. She hit the Lobby button and swung a leather knapsack around to her front, rummaging around in it—scent of vanilla on the tiny breeze, and what else? She'd installed herself in the right front corner of the spacious elevator, weirdly empty, I realized, though it was late in the day. The twin rows of descending silver buttons were partly covered by her body, and as the doors drew shut she turned her head and asked was I going to street level? Did I need something else? Her thin auburn eyebrows stretched in the most modest solicitude, and I couldn't contain a wider smile. A slight quirk in her look, brown crescent eyes pulling narrower as if by drawstrings, little lines, the faint parentheses appearing at the corners of her face. I was staring, obviously.

"Was that eleven?" I said.

The floor began to move underneath us.

"Yes," she said.

"Ah."

"You needed eleven?"

"I needed eleven."

"I'm sorry."

"What for?" I said.

She was half facing me now, one hand on her bag strap, the other burrowing into the sweatshirt's hand warmer. The eyes were narrow, lightly brown. She had light brown freckles like a pale constellation across her narrow, smooth, slightly waxen face. She could have been ten years my junior, and she was beautiful, the kind of beauty that stands just around the corner from typical, traditional beauty, the kind of beauty that forgets itself on a tired Monday afternoon and is all the more striking for it. These impossibilities free you up to be yourself. I complimented her sweatshirt. Very germane, I said. The sartorial laws typically frowned on the wearing of a Randolph sweatshirt, say, on the Randolph campus, but she was obviously above all that.

She looked up and down my outfit, slowly. "Sartorial laws, huh?"

Tan canvas shoes, black jeans, a T-shirt, French style, white with gray horizontal stripes—I eyed my reflection in the dull mirror of the elevator doors. A passable build, ignoring the slight swell of my stomach. My flop of late-period John Lennon hair, a little raggedier than usual today.

"Well . . ." I said.

The floor kept falling beneath us, lifting us back down to earth and the bright Formica expanse of the lobby that looked out on Twelfth Street, the trees outside giving off a greenish glow. When the elevator slowed and dinged again, the doors opened onto this scene, prearranged, and the beautiful girl stepped out into it.

"Better luck this time," she said, smiling the same curt smile over her shoulder.

I saw that the button for eleven was already lit.

When I got upstairs I knocked a brief apology, a lilting little knuckle tap at Dr. Hahn's office door. It was ajar. I was told to come in, sit down. I was asked how I was. It was a rhetorical question.

Hahn sat with her arms crossed in front of her on the table, holding court at the small, Arthurian slab in the near corner of her office, a sort of breakfast nook, really, one of the petit bourgeois touches that belied her fierceness and endeared her to me. Around the table sat the two other graduate students I shared the TA-ship with, Greg Baxter and Tiffany Wong. Our work together amounted to a batch of sixty papers split three ways three times a semester. The study sessions we led didn't hurt much; office hours were barren, paid reading time, really—but the papers hurt, the papers cost. Greg with his round fleshy face and staunch eyebrows, from the Sociology Department, known to wear bow ties, like today, liked to dock his students for split infinitives, prepositions at the end of sentences, all that Strunk and White bullshit. Tiffany was more sensible. A casual friend from the Politics Department, she studied race theory and Asian American solidarity movements and had picked up the extra course, I assumed, for the same reasons I had: money first, money second, money third. She was watchful and precise, always soft-spoken, the skin of her face smoothed back as if by a permanent gust of wind. She once referred to a movie that had "chinked out" white actors in Asian roles, a trick of makeup and lighting that she described through gentle scoffs. A sharp, unsentimental mind. I suppose I was a little cautious around her.

And then there was Hahn—grumpy, graceful, small-toothed, bob-cut, lithe, bespectacled Hahn. In her office she wore the white blouse and gray sleek pants, matching coat draping the chairback, that a lesbian friend of mine had once apostrophized: "Oh how I love you, Professor Hahn's pantsuits!" But she was fierce, a Stalinist, unrepentant, known to challenge her students, as she'd once challenged me, if they recited the well-known crimes of the Maoists. *Look, famines do happen, don't they?* She didn't hesitate to criticize her former employers, either, the bosses at Princeton who'd accused her of goading her students to riot in the protests around the U.S.–Contra collusion. She left Princeton before they could force her out, drifted for several years, organized, wrote. Among the talented misfits and castoffs at Randolph College she found safe harbor. Twenty years later I drew on her work on Ralph Ellison in my senior thesis, the cream of which I submitted to graduate schools. It couldn't have been my undergraduate GPA that got me into the program Hahn more or less ran now. It might have been pure luck.

"Did you get a chance to average out your papers?" Hahn said, looking sidewise at me.

"You mean the grades?" I said.

"Do you have an aggregate? Greg's hard to please, Tiffany's on the cusp I'd expected for a second paper—B, B minus. How did your students do?"

Idiotically, I reached into my backpack, shuffling around for the papers that weren't there. I must have left them in my office, I announced. I stepped across the hall to the windowless room with the gray felt walls and the quartet of thick metal desks, each of them shared by two graduate students—the Animal Cubicle Farm, we called it. There was the untouched manila folder, thick with papers, lying brazen on the far desk.

I tried to keep the folder close to my body as I settled back down next to Hahn, the papers like a losing hand at her table. When the manila cover bent and kinked open against me, Hahn eyed the first essay as I pushed the cover shut. Traitorous reflex! With a curdled expression she removed my hand and the first essay from the folder, flipping through the unmarked pages. "You need to make more marginal comments than this," she said. She flipped to the last page, also bare—no marginal comments, no terminal comments, no grade, nothing. Greg and Tiffany tipped their eyes down in concert, suddenly very interested in the grain of the table wood. Hahn took me in with her lips turned inward, a faint white pressure line where the mouth used to be. Her eyes were flat and dull under the slanting bangs.

"Can an atheist make confession?" I said.

Hahn took out another paper, lifted the pages, let them drop. She took out another.

"I was in bed all weekend," I said. "I'm sorry."

"You were sick?" she said.

"I wasn't feeling well at all."

Hahn sighed into the silence of the room. She reached into the stack of ungraded papers, adding two more to the pile in front of her. She dealt them all together, rapped them smartly on the table. "I can do these five," she said. "Anyone else feeling charitable?"

"I'll do five," offered Tiffany, faithful Tiffany. Blessings on the hand that received the stack across the table, blessings on the eyes that smiled at me, a little mischievously.

"Greg?" Hahn said.

"Sure," he said, though he mirrored Hahn in the turn of his lips, his fat fusilli eyebrows rising—a curse on those eyebrows.

"Which leaves five for ailing Eli," Hahn said. "Do you think you can handle that?"

"Of course," I said. "Thank you. I am sorry, guys."

"We need to have these back to the students by tomorrow's class," Hahn said. "Greg, if your papers are that bad, they're that bad, but take another look and consider curving up. Like I said, B, B minus is more or less where I'd expect the second paper to be. Thanks everybody. See you tomorrow."

I thanked Greg and Tiffany again on their way out, keeping my seat. When Hahn and I were alone, her mouth reappeared and drew lopsided, winching up into a head-shaking almost-smile. She nodded at the plusher seat across from her desk and I dropped into it heavily. The office window brightened with a sudden swell of sun through the clouds, the white fine horizontal slats of the blinds glowing orangely at their bottom tips. Hahn's curt blond bob was backlit too—there couldn't have been ten windows on the entire street that got light at this hour, but she was blessed. I would have to make my intercession.

"Well?" she said.

"I don't know. I don't know what's wrong with me. I'm sorry."

"Why do I think you really were in bed all weekend," Hahn said.

"I was."

"But you weren't sick."

"Not strictly speaking, no."

"Am I going to have to find a replacement TA in the middle of the semester?" Hahn looked at me levelly through her glasses, reflecting the room at me. "I'll withdraw the question for now. But you need to carve some time out of your standing existential crisis to get your papers done, understand? Either that or I'll have to start quoting Mao to you on work and solidarity."

"God no," I said.

"Or I'll have to replace you. Clear enough?"

With her fingertips, absently, Hahn slid a photocopied flyer back and forth across her desk, and suddenly there she was again, smiling out at me: the same round pretty face, slight eyes, the constellation of freckles in the mounting cheeks, the long hair done up into a sleek chignon to match the sleek sleeveless dress she wore, a formal photograph. In black-and-white the auburn hair looked charcoal-dark, the skin of her arms lightest gray. Below the photograph in a large fine font were the words *Jennifer Daugherty, Senior Piano Recital, April 9, 7:30 p.m., Church of St. Joseph.*

"Ah, yes," Hahn said, "that was the other thing I meant to tell you. Our friend"—she turned the flyer toward her—"our friend Jennifer Daugherty came to see me just before the meeting you were late to."

"Daugherty?" I said.

"She came to complain about the grade on her first paper, which she said she just got back. A C plus."

"I remember the name, but I didn't know who she was. Why didn't she come to me?"

"I told her that. I held the line," Hahn said. "I looked through her paper and more or less echoed what you'd said— descriptive, not argumentative. Not that you'd said much. You really do need to mark up these papers more, Eli."

I tried to picture where she could have sat in the sunken amphitheater hall. If I'd seen her coming into class or leaving it, I'd forgotten. Which seemed unlikely. She must have sat near the front, or it could have been the middle, or anywhere on the left side of the room, really. I tended to slip in late, perch at the right back corner of the room, and slip out early. I supposed the remarkable thing would have been if I *had* seen her. A senior. Jennifer Daugherty . . .

"I might go a bit easier on her in the future," Hahn said. "The prose was good, good organization. If an argument shows up, she's a top-of-the-stack writer."

I remembered the papers under my hands and flipped through the five remaining to me. Jennifer Daugherty's wasn't there. Probably for the best.

"Her senior recital?" I said, nodding at the flyer. "What's a senior doing in Poli Sci 110? She's a music major?"

"It happens now and then," Hahn said. "You leave the required courses you're dreading for last. That way they don't impact your GPA as much. You never tried that? She told me it was writing-heavy classes she dreaded. I told her she didn't need to, her grade on the first, late-returned paper notwithstanding."

"I know," I said, "I know." I was penitential now, Christian, bowing my head all the way to the wood-warm desk. I was generally unworthy.

Hahn stood up, pulled the coat from her chairback, and slung it rakishly over her shoulder. With the other hand she closed down her computer, replaced a pair of pens in a garish red coffee mug that asked, in loud white capitals, TWO PARTIES FOR THE BOSSES, BUT WHO'S FOR US?

"Where's your next stop?" Hahn asked me at the door.

She'd added my ungraded papers to her shoulder bag, and Jennifer Daugherty's flyer too.

"Home, I guess."

"Your undervalued student here is playing Mahler tonight. I told her I might just stop by. Have you eaten?"

Outside on Twelfth Street the trees moved gently in the wind, the wind turning the leaves matte-side, then shine-side, shimmering them light against the dark-shaded backdrop of the brownstones. The wind made no sound, or only the sound of the cars and trucks and taxis motoring past, the horn peals, sirens, the great windy rustle of pedestrians, crosswalk signals, music floating down from upper stories—nature's lip-synch. Turning onto Fifth Avenue, Hahn and I passed the bus stop just beyond the college's main entrance where a group of mostly students, I assumed, waited. Bohemian in dress, concerned in their unconcern, they talked a little, flirted, tipped their faces down for sly glances at their glowing phones—the politer ones were sly, anyway. I'd half expected to see Jennifer Daugherty waiting there in her Randolph sweatshirt, casual and pretty, though by now she was probably at home getting ready for her recital.

Which meant what exactly? Doing warm-up scales? Meditating? Doing her hair? O brave new world that has such music majors in it! Or maybe she was brooding on the overhasty C plus I'd given her first paper. I remembered her curt smile in the elevator. Did she know who I was? But she must have known. I felt the urge like a stinging cattle prod to ask Hahn if I could see the flyer again—and for this reason I resisted it.

We'd decided on a Moroccan restaurant. Hahn knew a great place right on her street, with a great wine list. She deserved some alcohol, she said. Apparently Mondays were her new Fridays.

"I just need to stop off at home for a few minutes to check in on things," she said. "You don't mind?"

I said I didn't mind at all.

Hahn continued down the sidewalk at pace, leading just slightly, leaning into her steps, a toe walker.

Suddenly she slowed. I watched her face cloud over.

"Or if you'd rather wait for me at the restaurant . . ." Hahn said. "You could get us a table. It shouldn't be too busy at this hour, but you never know."

The sun-split Arc d'Washington Square grew large at the end of the avenue, and we were in NYU territory. We turned left onto Eighth as a pair of students swung by us on swan-necked rent-a-bikes, the Citibank logo running down the blue center tubes. This was Soc territory to our Greaser, though of course we all swam in the same money, most of us. I knew Hahn certainly did, and she knew I knew. Why was she suddenly so shy of her apartment? Or was it her husband?

I'd actually visited Hahn's apartment once before, and met her husband, though maybe she'd forgotten. It was in my second year of the program, an end-of-semester party for her Labor History seminar, and I can tell you that Hahn's sixth-floor penthouse was nothing, but nothing to be ashamed of: It was huge, bright, high-ceilinged, with a view of the Tompkins Square trees at the end of the street, though you saw them through a warren of scaffolding on the next building over. There were fine paintings on the apartment's white plaster walls, fine rugs on the hardwood floors, recessed lighting, a fireplace, you name it. During the party Hahn's husband, Stephen, had come out of his study to tell us hello and to make ourselves at home. He was a tall, frail, stately man, a retired ophthalmologist, with a shock of white hair and a genial wave as he stepped back behind the whitewashed door. I'd heard about the minor tremor that put an end to his career as a sought-after surgeon, but I understood he still consulted, and that the condition was manageable. I retained in my mind the image of George Plimpton, a slender, sad-eyed, harmlessly patrician old man.

At First Avenue we stopped for a traffic light, cars and buses sliding by in the fading day, a little drained of their color, a little depleted.

"My place is just on this next block," Hahn said. "The restaurant's a few doors down from it on the left. Cafe Mogador. Why don't you go ahead and get us a table. I'll just be a few minutes."

"Whatever you prefer," I said.

"It'll just be a few minutes. Tell them Linda will be joining you if there's any trouble getting a table. I've practically moved in there in the evenings—I'm like Sartre at the Café de Flore. Well, a little better than Sartre. Sartre used to take up a table for the entire day, and he'd only order a single cup of tea. That's how he wrote *Being and Nothingness*, did you know? That massive doorstop?"

"There's your brief against the existentialists," I said. "Table hogs. Hogs at life's table."

"I'm sure I tip better than Sartre did too."

I added, apropos of too little, probably, "Did they ever get rid of that scaffolding on the building next to yours? I remember it was bugging you and Stephen when I visited with the Labor History seminar. Do you remember that party?"

Hahn said, "We're on the ground floor now."

The traffic light changed. The little white man of the crosswalk signal bade us come, chirping. Over the chirping came a car-horn beep, and another, high, polite. A dark-haired woman in a gray sculpted minivan was waving at us, nosing slowly onto St. Mark's Place from First Avenue, smiling and waving.

"Do you know that woman?" I said to Hahn.

"Oh," she said. "Oh." She lifted her hand in a wooden wave. "Well."

"Neighbor of yours?"

"Nurse," Hahn said. "That's Renilde. That's Steve's nurse."

When we got to the red-brick building where Hahn and her husband lived, the van was already unfolding itself onto the sidewalk, the large black metal tray lowering itself down, coming to rest with a long hydraulic hiss. Hahn stopped just short of where Renilde operated the controls at the side of the van. Renilde, olive, plump in a blue windbreaker, her brown hair in a loose bun, turned to Hahn in greeting. I was introduced as a young colleague from the college, a gross overstatement of my position, though later, thinking of it, it made my heart swell a little. They'd gone up to the West Side marina,

Renilde said. To take the boat out a little. Did Hahn still need her tonight?

The ramp ground down into the sidewalk pavement with a low dull scrape, anchoring itself.

"All ready, Steve," Renilde said.

Out of the shadowy maw of the van came Hahn's husband, pivoting, in a motorized cart, cresting the top of the ramp. The thin whine of the motor preceded him down into the last light of day. He moved slowly and steadily down the ramp, not nodding, not smiling at us, but acknowledging us with his eyes. He was horribly changed. The eyes slewed in our direction, and in them I saw the same look I had seen before, steady, a little sad, but now the sockets that contained them were hollowed out and dark, the skin of the face too, the head motionless and slumped against the chair's padded headrest. The eyes were like living things fallen into amber, the truest things remaining to a false and mutinous body. The skin of the neck, too, was changed, shrink-wrapped around the muscles and bones of the upper shoulders. It was the same with the forearms, exposed from the shirtsleeves down. Stephen's left hand gripped the cart's controls in an ungainly, fisted way. The forearms and the thighs looked dropped into position haphazardly, the top half of the body skewing left compared to the bottom, as if the body were being seen half in water, half out. I looked down at the gray particulate sidewalk to reset my view and looked up again, smiling.

Hahn made the introductions. She told her husband he'd met me once before, briefly. He said he recognized me. He'd heard a lot about me. The voice was slow, slurred, atonal—the word *mongoloid* stole into my mind before I could banish it. The sentences issued from Stephen's mouth with great difficulty.

Yes, he'd heard a lot about me from Linda. His mouth hitched up into a wayward, curtailed, plasticine grin.

"Almost all of it good," he said.

I laughed at the quip—too loudly, perhaps. I suddenly had no idea what to do with my hands. Stephen's lay at the end of the armrests, soft and inert; I didn't dare reach out to shake one of them. I found myself clasping my hands in front of me in a bizarre, vaguely Asian gesture of respect—strange gesture for a dying man.

And he was clearly dying—memento mori in the hollow cheeks, memento mori in the eyes.

At dinner Hahn confirmed it: amyotrophic lateral sclerosis, ALS, or Lou Gehrig's disease—degenerative, terminal. Three years earlier when I'd met Stephen for the first time the first symptoms were there—they knew this now, in retrospect—but they'd tracked any number of other symptoms of other maladies, lesser maladies. It could have simply been the tremor doubling down a bit, intensifying. Old and gray and full of sleep, and a little trembly, right? That's what we were all born to. Hahn mustered a smile, her lips inturned. At the time Steve still spoke normally, he moved normally, he was normal. Until he wasn't anymore.

"I'm just so glad we never had children," Hahn said. "It's bad enough for me to see him change like this."

"I had no idea," I said. "I'm so sorry. I didn't know the extent of it."

"A month ago he was walking on his own power. He could walk up the stairs and into the apartment on his own—it was slow, but he could do it. Now he needs the wheelchair for everything. He's in a wheelchair. It's accelerating. This thing—it's breaking into a run."

"And what comes next?" I said. "I mean about treatment options. Forgive me. I meant in terms of treatment."

"You mean in terms of management," Hahn said. "That's all that's left. The doctors are masters of evasion, false optimism, statements that sound substantive until you think them through—every one of them could run for office—but even they don't give him more than two years. It could be two months, two weeks. We're living like children, in the horrible present."

Hahn laughed suddenly, bitterly, wagging her head at the filigreed teakettle at the center of the table. "Do you know where they went today?" Hahn said. "Renilde and Steve? It wasn't to the marina, I can tell you that. Renilde isn't licensed to captain the boat and Steve's not able anymore—and he knows I know that. He's not even trying with his cover stories anymore. No, they went up to Woodlawn Cemetery. How they made that wheelchair-accessible I don't know, but they went there to visit the grave of Herman Melville, at Steve's insistence. In his retirement he's started reading more, and the heavy stuff, too, Melville, Beckett, all the godless metaphysicians, and so today he goes and leaves a pen at Melville's tomb. That's what he does now. He reads books about endless water, and visits cemeteries."

"God . . ." I said.

"Yup. Yup."

Hahn forked through her plate of chicken tagine, half eaten in a rubble of couscous. What pinot noir remained in her glass looked purplish, the color of a dark bruise, almost black in the dim lighting of the restaurant. We sat at a smooth simple lacquered table near the bar. Wineglasses hung upside down above the bar and caught the light going down in a perspective row, glinting like Christmas ornaments. I watched the bartender, thirtysomething in an old Brooklyn Dodgers jersey, bearded, head shorn, light a row of tea candles along the bar top with sacramental care. The little fires warmed the underside of his face and the faces of the few people hunched forward against the bar at the outset of dinner rush. A few more showed up in the time I watched. The restaurant began to glow orangely, cocoon-like against the darkness outside. The couples through the sunk-in picture window and the metal scrollwork of the patio sat fading in the gloom, disappearing. Beyond them, across St. Mark's Place, squares of warm yellow light began to climb up the apartment houses.

When we parted company that night, I told Hahn I'd probably just head home too. She was bloody exhausted—those were her words—and she had homework to do because of me. A little water lit up her small eyes behind the glasses. Neither of us said anything. She did give me the music flyer, just in case. I hadn't asked for it. I folded the paper and put it in my pocket, left Hahn with an uncharacteristic hug, and didn't take the paper out again, and didn't unfold it and behold its round serious pretty face again, until the spot-lit glowing arch of Washington Square loomed up out of the darkness at my left.

St. Joseph's Church was a white Grecian temple in the middle of Greenwich Village. Dramatically lit, its thick fluted columns stood to either side of bright red double doors, an incurved arch for the prayerful Lord just above them—the building could have been a stylish stock exchange, or a town hall. The gold stubby cross at the apex of the roof appeared to be something of an afterthought. I was ten minutes late.

A side door, also red, stood ajar, leaking thick muddy chords, fierce attacks, out into the cool dark air where I stood hesitating, checking the time on my cell phone, gripping the door handle, ungripping it. I had turned toward the flight of granite steps when the last chords of the piece rang out, unmistakably tonic. I stepped into the hall under cover of thin applause. The U-shaped whitewashed balcony, a line of blazing crystal chandeliers, a high flat blue-and-white pie-latticed ceiling stretched above me, and I was one of ten, maybe fifteen people in the room. Jennifer Daugherty, her thin white arms pressed flat against her sides, bowed stiffly from the waist at the front of this bright-lit expanse. She stood close to the black piano bench beside the hulking black of the concert grand, its lid uptilted like a massive wing, as if the instrument might take flight at any moment, spiraling up to the ceiling and lifting its nervous conductor up with it. Thirty meters separated me from Jennifer, but in the stillness and emptiness of the crowd—a bevy of gray heads in the front pews, a few friends, presumably, in young dresses and jackets, a goateed priest in his Oreo habit—in this sparseness I could easily see the stress lines on Jennifer's face, and she could see them on mine. Her eyes widened a little as they took me in, then seemed to settle back. I couldn't have left now if I'd wanted to.

In her simple black pants and vest, a blue blouse, long earrings dangling down beside the red-brown wavy forelocks broken free of the chignon, Jennifer Daugherty resumed her seat at the piano. I scurried up to the third row, behind the goateed priest, who turned to me and nodded a smile and handed me a program. I gathered it was Liszt we'd just heard. A delicate Bach partita followed, sprightly, precise, the voices twining and untwining. The interpretation was obviously indebted to Glenn

Gould, not one of my favorites, but the playing was good, very good. The playing was exceptional—who was I kidding? All I'd ever done was dabble in the piano, achieving proficiency at most, learning just enough to know how little I knew compared to a real player like Jennifer, a real musician. Sing, O Muse, and tell of the long-necked, round-faced, auburn-haired girl who nodded her head in time to the allegro section! Her body began to relax into its intricate tasks, first with the Bach piece, then a Schoenberg, no less intricate for its loss of melody. A piece by Scriabin followed the Schoenberg, then a long, minimal-ist piece by John Adams, "The Radicals," with its chords like chants, with eerie passages coming to abrupt, silent halts. (The piece was "a musical record and a critique," according to the program, of the medieval Christian attempts to impose God's kingdom on earth: "Thy kingdom come, thy will be done / On earth as it is in heaven.") The tempos were slowing now, the pieces getting longer, more contemplative, as if the concert had run from the shore into the foam and the breakers and waded out into deep, dark water, drifting, slowly swelling—the end-less sea.

Out of these depths came the songs I remember best from that night, the songs Hahn had mentioned to me and the ones Jen would later play for me again and again at my request, even teaching me certain sections of them—the Rückert-Lieder by Gustav Mahler. One of the finely dressed young women in the front row had gotten up beside the piano and now began to sing a series of searching, dreamy arias to Jennifer's deft accompa-niment: "I Breathed a Gentle Fragrance," "Look Not on My Songs," "At Midnight," and finally "I Am Lost to the World." This last song began deep in the bass clef, the same muddy depths where the concert itself had begun. Slowly the music climbed up to ground level, a starting place, and then back down, and back up again. Into this unsteady progress came the mezzo-soprano's long, sober, beautiful lines, reprising the bass part.

> *I am lost to the world,*
> *with which I've wasted so much time.*
> *It hasn't heard from me in so long*
> *it might as well think I'm dead.*

Slowly, slowly, a lento march—each word, each phrase an age. The singer's thin face strained visibly, her throat tight and striated, to sustain the effortless-seeming notes. This was Mallory, one of Jen's closest friends, though at the time she was only her voice, the vehicle for that low-flying sound that Jen had provided for us, ceding the stage to this voice and these songs because she loved them so much, she felt grateful just to participate in them, and also, she later admitted to me, because she was struggling to get to an hour of memorized music for her program, as her department required, and needed something repetitive, something verse-based and simple. And lovely, and true. *I have died to the world's turmoil,* sang the soprano, *and I rest in a silent realm* ("*stillen Gebiet*"), the note stilling on "*stillen,*" low and perfect.

It was the kind of music that could make you fall in love.

Quickly, then—to the summer months. Thirty days had June, thirty-one July and August. I spent most of them with Jen, in her bed or mine, no covers, no cover at all from that *forno* heat. I couldn't help but think of Florence from the summer before, my trip with Alex. The thoughts came to me in the languorous times before and after with Jen, every *after* a *before* if we waited long enough. Suddenly Alex in her pink frayed hoodie would materialize, and sometimes she wore nothing at all. She was the last woman I'd been with, the woman I'd loved casually, by which I mean easily, effortlessly, like water, and in those moments a certain undercurrent of loss would pull on what was newly found. Jen. Jen with her lithe piano-player fingers, with her stack of music books in a wicker basket by the piano, an electric model, which she played with headphones on as often as not, conscientious of her neighbors through the thin plaster walls. Jen with her HGTV shows—*House Hunters International*, *Property Virgins*, *Love It or List It*. Jen with her Agatha Christie novels, Dorothy Sayers, P. D. James, and also George Eliot, the Brontës, Thomas Hardy, a smattering of books in French and Italian—she claimed to know the languages only as far as dynamic markings and song titles went, but the books were well read, underlined, decorated with a tight looping brand of marginalia.

Jen and her friend Mallory, the mezzo, and another roommate I rarely saw shared a three-bedroom walk-up in Astoria, Queens. When the heat was killing, which was most of the time, the air conditioners made a glistening beaded curtain of falling condensation down the front of the faded building, the gummed dirty sidewalks spattered with water. Pollock drips, Jen's copper freckles—on her cheekbones, the bridge of her nose, everywhere, it turned out. The sex was incandescent—of course it was—and slippery, slick, our bodies greased by the heat. One weekend it was just Jen and me in the apartment— the clothes came off and stayed off, bunched into corners as we wandered in our *Blue Lagoon* innocence. From the bedroom to the kitchen to the little nook where Jen had installed a small green couch cushion beside the piano, the concert perch, she called it. In boxers and bra and panties, respectively, we played and listened and listened and played, taking turns at the piano and the green perch, Jen helping me with the first building sections of "I Am Lost to the World," the notes halting, heavy in my hands.

"Don't think about it so much," she said. "Imagine it's easy, move your hands smoothly over the keys, and the tone will follow."

"I'd like to move my hands smoothly over your keys," I said a little absently, almost out of habit, every phrase an opportunity for innuendo. It was a running joke we'd developed, and yet it worked, too—those early days! Soon enough we'd be back in the bedroom or on the living-room couch with a bathroom towel (that respectful towel) underneath us, or in the bathroom itself, or the cramped grimy shower under weak cold water.

Anything to cool us off, anything to sate us . . . Back at the piano Jen would sway histrionically to Fiona Apple ballads, but the words came out pure, high, in her plaintive, unvibratoed voice, because all this sex made her melancholy, Jen said, smiling her red-lipped, natural smile. Her lips held color in a way I'd never seen before, as if pacing her hair, and at first I didn't believe her when she said she didn't use lipstick, didn't care for it. I chalked it up to some reflex of female modesty, the light deception that says *no lipstick* when what it means is *a little lipstick*. But now we were into our third day together, a long weekend of nonstop seminude time together, and we'd showered together and done what little dressing there was to do together, and the lips still shone pinkish-red, like the cool smooth lining on the inside of an oyster. Or the cartoon idea of an oyster, anyway. With her cartoonishly perfect pink lips Jen sang to me—

> *And you can uuuuuuuuuse my skin*
> *To bury your seeeeecrets in . . .*

"And you'll settle me down?" I said.

"I'll settle you down all right," she said, and back to the couch.

How is it that so much sex isn't tedious? How is it that the body can store so much appetite for so much of the same thing—well, slight variations on the same thing. I'll dispense right now with any misput suggestion that I'm much of a bedroom artist. We talked a lot, Jen and I, laughed a lot during lovemaking, rolled around, groped, joyously struggled, but we weren't breaking records, weren't innovating the *genre*.

And yet we couldn't get enough of each other. Sex felt necessary, essential, like breathing.

During one of our *after* breaks Jen told me about the mint green couch to which the cushion I sat on once belonged. It was in her first off-campus apartment, in Alphabet City, full up like a punk house, except most of the musicians were classical and baroquely averse to mess and sprawl. Too bad for them. The place was overrun with roommates. "The indignities of capitalism, right?" said Jen. I nodded my head, a little smile to match hers, though I knew I was being teased.

"Don't you wish you could take back that C plus now?" she said. "I was a diligent student."

"People in your line of work don't care what you got in Poli Sci 110."

"Not true, not true! Raymond looked at my transcripts that first day and shook his head—he had this very disappointed look in his eyes. The only B plus I ever got in a college class and it comes in the last semester? He must have known I was on a slide. I'm sure it's affected my pay."

This particular Raymond was the musical casting director who'd hired Jen to accompany the vocal tryouts of Broadway actors, aspirants and old pros. Jen liked the job, she said, but considered it a stopgap. It kept her sight-reading sharp, and it was money for music, a rare thing, but it was also a lot of repetitive I-IV-V stuff, a lot of camp. Jen's real ambition was to go on to graduate school in musicology, but her first round of applications in the spring, before I'd really gotten to know her, hadn't panned out. Perhaps the B plus was a genuine sore spot. In my defense, I hadn't actually graded her other two papers, but it was likely that my first hard over-swift evaluation had spoiled the pot for her. Jen seemed to sense I sensed this and took pains to keep the B-plus jokes away from the higher-voltage lines of the grad-school question. When she did talk about the applications she talked about luck of the draw, hypercompetitiveness, a crapshoot. She said she hoped a year of real-world experience in the music industry might help her chances, and that she'd apply to more fallback schools next time. In the meantime there was "Bye Bye Blackbird," "Bewitched, Bothered, and Bewildered," "Mack the Knife," "I Dreamed a Dream," etc.

But back to the mint green cushion. Jen described roommates everywhere, seven roommates in a three-bedroom two-bathroom apartment, and sometimes it was eight roommates, effectively, when the couch-crashing friend of a friend had her boyfriend stay over, the two of them sleeping head to toe on the green living room couch. Jen was the girl's name—she'd forgotten the boyfriend's. The other roommates started referring to her as "bad Jen." Pretty soon she'd taken over a corner of the living room; her toiletries stood brazenly on the crowded bathroom sink alongside those of paying roommates.

"And nobody really knew this girl all that well," Jen said. "I think she'd been in a sorority with one of the roommates, but it was more like a favor you didn't know how to refuse. Bad Jen and her boyfriend were there more and more, and their stuff was there, little piles of clothes and whatnot surrounding the couch and in the corners of the room. Every day looked like moving day. It was getting out of hand. Six girls, two bathrooms, and now we didn't even have a common space we could use? The squatter was amazing if you think about it, her shamelessness—I was sort of in awe of her. How could she just keep smiling at us like that? Hi, how are you, how was your day? If she had a job, we didn't know about it. If her boyfriend had a job, we didn't know about it. The boyfriend's stubble started speckling the sink—you could see where he'd tried to wipe the hairs away with his hand, in a pass or two. It wasn't enough. It was getting totally out of hand. But we couldn't rat her out to the landlord. It wasn't any nobility on our part, we just didn't want to implicate ourselves in hosting a squatter for most of the semester. One day we came home and Jen or her boyfriend had hung a sheet from the ceiling with thumbtacks—it divided off the sofa, it claimed half the room. When we confronted her about it she started crying and said she was just trying to create a little privacy for herself. She said she'd just broken up with her boyfriend and was looking for work but it was impossible in the city, unless you wanted to work crap restaurant jobs, and even then. She promised us she'd leave soon and said she was really grateful for all our help. We were all really good people . . .

"Fast-forward a week. She's still there. The sheet's still up. We haven't actually seen the boyfriend, but the little black hairs are still showing up on the sides of the bathroom sink. We could have had the locks changed, but how to explain that to the landlord? We could have just owned up to the landlord, but we weren't that brave. What we ended up being was incredibly passive-aggressive. If bad Jen got in the shower, one of us would take down the sheet, another would stuff her clothes into shopping bags. The next day the sheet would be up again, the bags unpacked. We'd try again. All of us were involved by the end, even bad Jen's former sorority sister. She'd get in the shower or leave the apartment for some reason and she'd come back and all her stuff would be packed and ready to go. She must have been getting the hint, she'd stopped smiling at us and saying hello and how was your day, but she still found a way to stay there. It was incredible. Finally she left the apartment one evening and we moved the green couch out of the living room and locked it in one of the bedrooms. We were so paranoid and frightened—I think we were scared of her by now—that we distributed the cushions throughout our different closets, like a mob kill. And that did the trick. Her stuff was gone in the morning. We kept expecting her to come back, but she never did. We ended up getting rid of the green couch, but I kept the cushion in my closet for the rest of the time I lived there, like a weird souvenir. It turns out it's a very comfortable concert perch."

"This very cushion?" I said.

"That very cushion. Unspeakable things were probably done on it."

"It does feel a little stiff in places—call it 'character'?"

Jen guffawed, hid her face behind a curtain of wavy auburn hair. If she washed it and left it to air-dry, it kinked and waved like lasagna noodles. From behind this wavy curtain she said, "Oh Lord. I did wash the cover, but maybe not well enough."

"I'd like to do some character-building exercises with you—bad Jen."

She unparted the hair and smiled a wondrous smile— blessings on those fuchsia lips, those straight white teeth, the cheekbones with their copper freckles. "If anyone ever heard us talking like this, you know I'd die, right?"

"I'd be mildly embarrassed myself, but I think I'd survive it."

"Well, just so we're clear—Naughty Professor," said Jen, and she tugged me back to the couch by the band of my boxer shorts.

In my defense, Jen had turned twenty-three that summer— only five years separated us now, and we'd never once touched during the semester. When people asked us how we'd met, we said "in school," vaguely. I said I was just starting into a PhD program, which was of course the biggest lie of all, and Jen said she was working a little before grad school. The story worked just fine, for what that's worth. Maybe little. Would it help to add that we didn't really think about it much—our accidents of meeting were mostly a joke now, a bit of goofy role-play, foreplay. Anyway, it's not really my purpose here to try to defend myself.

This was the summer of Soline.

One of the brag points of wonky business journalists in those days was that only wonky journalists, and the fraudulent insiders themselves, stood a chance of understanding what was then coming to light about the multibillion-dollar energy company. Nonsense. Read Marx in *The German Ideology*, read Luxemburg, Gramsci, Jameson, or just open your eyes—it's already there in front of you. It was there in 2008. It was there with Enron, of course. (From an article in *Forbes*: "If Enron, operating in a deregulated market, was calculus, Soline and its many-fronted micro-frauds was a kind of *multivariable* calculus.") It was there in the history article I read in my senior year of high school, when I was far from a math whiz, but I didn't need to be, did I? The article described the British land enclosures that yanked the common fields out from under the peasant farmers, the first wave of proto-capitalist consolidation, with wave on wave coming in behind it, a new ocean, a new reality. Rather miraculously, I've rediscovered this article in a social-studies reader in the library here, among the primers and tech manuals, the expurgated novels, old water-warped copies of *Scientific American*, the donated refuse of a hundred other collections arranged sparsely on the blue metal shelves. In the article is an old protest poem from the days of King Henry VIII, a piece of light verse that once wrought heavily on me:

> *The law locks up the man or the woman*
> *Who steals the goose from off the common,*
> *But leaves the greater villain loose*
> *Who steals the common from off the goose.*

Five hundred years later, and what's really changed? The instruments of oppression may have digitized, they may blink and scroll and refresh to the millisecond now, but they're still the same shrilling vacuum hoses that suck from the many and give to the few, and more often under the law's protection than its suspicion. Soline was remarkable in how cleverly it stole, how completely it ended up erasing the livelihoods, the retirements of its workers—but in this it was only an outlier, a sinner in degree, a good citizen in kind. This was capitalism being capitalism. Let the notebook-dumping journalists self-flatter about the arcana of deception, let the Wall Street experts talk a technocratic blue streak about "depreciation timelines," line costs, loans as revenue, "mark-to-market" valuations—it was still some asshole who set the detonator, another asshole who okayed it, and the assholes had a choice. That's the point. That's the *real* point. It's what the Group was saying all along, I think, or trying to: There's a choice. It isn't always easy, or easy to spot: Predatory capitalism has never been more invisible, more inevitable-seeming, more adept at impersonating nature. And how can you fight against cyclical "Nature"? How can you fight a degenerative disease that passes itself off as a mere tremor, an "instability in the market," or worse, a kind of weather system, a system no human hand can control since no hand set it in motion to begin with? The unmoved mover, or some such bullshit.

Sam Westergard had his ideas. He was new and he was brash and when he raised his long lanky arms to serve that summer, he looked like a Moses, a Prospero summoning new powers from the air. He was beating me easily now. Somehow, somewhere he'd turned a corner in his play and I was struggling just to keep things competitive. Sometimes I brought Jen along and we all played a lighter brand of tennis, two-on-one, more relaxed. Other times I took my beating—three–six, four–six if I was lucky—and then Sam and I sat in the beech tree shade, stretching down, rehydrating, planning the revolution.

"We occupy the White House lawn," Sam said. "Or we bring the Hoovervilles back. We find some way to disrupt the Soline trial."

"That's theater," I said. "And insane."

"Or we occupy fucking Larry *Bosch's* front lawn. 'Here's where Soline's criminal CEO lives'—have you seen that palace of his up in Westchester?—'here's Bosch's castle, and meanwhile thousands of his subsidiary workers are scrounging to make rent.'"

"You're going to put that on a sign—'subsidiary workers'? You're going to sloganeer that while you're being dragged away for trespassing? It's just theater, Sam. It's impractical."

"Well, at least it's something. And theater can be useful, can't it? Anyway I thought we were just blue-skying here."

"'Blue-skying'? Dear God, you sound like one of them."

"A joke, comrade, a joke! Give me a little credit. Besides, didn't Mao or somebody say something about knowing your enemy?"

"I'm sure he did."

Sam looked at me with a peaked high face, waiting.

"If you're going to do theater," I said, "you do it small, pointed, with a name and a face and a street address you can access without the National Guard showing up."

"I'm on bated breath," Sam said.

"You're on snark is what you're on. I should have never given you that Eagleton to read."

"But I'm so glad you did! He's actually funny! What's wrong with a bit of levity, huh?"

"Nothing," I said. "But will this levity of yours hold up in one-hundred-fifteen-degree heat?"

The question did the work I wanted it to—Sam blinking, quirking his head a little, a little smile of genuine curiosity on his thin, fleshless lips. He had never even attended an ISO meeting, had wrung his recent "conversion" (his word, not mine) out of a handful of books and pamphlets, ten at most, had a tendency to confuse basic concepts (base and superstructure, say), but he was genuine, I felt, articulate, and a good tennis partner. I felt confident I could get him in on some actual action: a woman named Maria Nava and her two children in a little foreclosed bungalow just off Baseline Drive in Phoenix, Arizona—this was the face, this was the address. We had heard through Alex about Maria losing her job and her benefits and her twenty-year retirement with Alta Gas after that company went down with the great pirate ship of Soline, which had acquired it in the last months of its plunder. Of course I'd read about the "preferred-stock retirement plans" that the employees, new and old, had felt pressured into taking, and how the company froze its workers out of those accounts once the stock began to plummet—these were some of the machinations the journalists most reveled in. Yet the particular details didn't interest me much, if I'm honest. I knew a rabbit hole when I saw one, and I refused on principle to be shocked by Soline's last-ditch tactics, as if there was anything novel in the executive class chucking its workers overboard. The fact was that Maria Nava was behind on her mortgage, the bank was making good on its shameless threats, and Soline was in clean, cool deposition rooms, lawyered to the hilt. If a settlement ever did come down, if it exceeded the legal fees, if it fought its way free of escrow and appeals court, if the burgeoning welter of other *ifs* fell eventually just into place—well, but Maria couldn't wait for that.

"I'm in," Sam said.

"You're in? Don't you want to hear the details first, the money piece?"

"Sure," he said, "but I'm in."

"Have you ever been to Phoenix before?"

"Oddly, no. But I know the desert. I was born there. It's in my Mormon blood."

"Weren't you supposed to be born a tepid Protestant, or a good agnostic, with a last name like yours?"

"One of the many wrong turns we Westergards have taken."

"Ah," I said.

I'd never been to Phoenix either.

From the airplane the city looked more like a scorched cave floor than a city, sere browns and darker browns, beige buildings like stalagmites rising from the flat gridded spread of the valley where it gathered at the downtown. A few sputters of green resolved into trees as we sank back to earth, but mostly the city looked dry, and brown, and hot. Put a chunk of the world in a waffle iron, Phoenix comes out. You understand my bias. A child of the East Coast, I conflate beauty with greenery—I reduce it to that. This was Sam's message to me on the car ride from the airport, with Alex driving. From the backseat he lectured loudly over the loud blowing air conditioner. He said I was making the classic, myopic mistake of enshrining fragile life, green life, as the lodestar of the aesthetic. But what about stubborn life, resilient life, brown and hard and drought-resistant life? Did beauty have to be so exclusive? Above the scrim of tract homes and power lines green scrub poked out of the mountainside like weird eyes, saguaro cacti sliding past with their strange stubby arms outstretched, half outstretched, in greeting. Sandstone scree lay all about, dully blushing, scored, sharing the sloping foothills with the cacti and scrub until the mountain broke vertically, shot up into shelves of dark rocky crag. Those canyon lines were what hemmed us in, what rose above us, our tallest buildings—the utter dominance of nature.

"This really turns you on, doesn't it?" I said to Sam. "This is sexual for you."

For a moment the foreground houses and chain stores abated as an open unfenced lot, a tract of land, really, flashed a closer sea of scrub brush, the sharp dry blooms blurring past like a cloud of anemone, wavering strange life. It was the desert reclaiming its own, or maybe the developers were just biding their time.

"I'm saying I can appreciate the landscape," Sam said. "You just look up a little and it's there."

"Eli tells me you're a poet?" Alex said.

"Not really," Sam said. "I write poems sometimes, I've landed in an MFA for poetry, but I don't really think of myself as a poet."

"Sam and I are on the run from our chosen selves," I said. "It's really quite something."

Whatever that was supposed to mean. If it was bait, Alex didn't take it. She was smiling the smile of a Mona Lisa, cryptic, distracted, beautiful. I'd forgotten how beautiful she could be in her tossed-off, anti-beautiful way: the tomboyish hair that she cut herself, the dark straight bangs that boxed in her round olive face, the large eyes, the strong and aquiline nose, a little ebony stud at the line where the nostril began to rise. Ancient people survived in her face, some of the Aztec blood this country and others had worked so hard to wipe out. Alex's family lived in a town outside Tucson. Her mother had been a small, dark, elegant, slightly jet-lagged woman in teal jewelry when she'd come to visit Alex in New York the previous year, calling her Alejandra, taking me in with a standing, wary smile over the croque monsieurs and mimosas that we ate and drank amid the rowdy Sunday brunch crowd—my foolish suggestion. I thought we might have been riding in an Esposito car now, a Honda, simple, responsible.

"There's nothing wrong with being a poet, is there?" Alex said.

"No, there's not," Sam said.

"You could help us liaise with the media," she said. "Or maybe write press releases, who knows? I'm thinking we should go mainstream with this. Maria is the sweetest woman and she has the most beautiful, photogenic children—I actually thought this—and her neighbors love her. Some of them joined us in the occupying yesterday. Some others brought over a vat of carnitas last night. No one's not on our side this time, no one that matters. We should milk this."

The chain stores and white glowing strip malls had dropped away, the empty scrub lots multiplying. The tract developments with their trailing stucco walls and names like The Sunset, Shangri-La, The Desert Rose—these were soon replaced by the blinding ranches, the chain-link fences, the dead, crisped, yellow-brown lawns. We turned off Baseline Drive onto a smaller street, skirting the dirt field where a lone shirtless bedouin of a teen passed a soccer ball between his knees. In the car you could feel the sun pushing through the windows, compressing the air-conditioned air. You could feel the heat cradling the car. When we pulled up to Maria's house and cut the engine, the heat rose around us like a flood. A pair of green tents had been set up in the front yard and quickly abandoned: They looked like weird shrubbery at either side of a red faded door that hid against the ranch's rosy stucco. A small garage, too, connecting to the house's main façade with its picture window, blinds drawn, the gray bleached segmented walkway curving up to the front door, the sparse hanks of stubborn crabgrass betraying the outlines of the individual concrete slabs. Red Spanish tile covered the roof, reddish gravel lay in the small garden planted with ground-hugging fierce shrubs I couldn't begin to name. Poster-board signs and pickets surrounded the tents, studded the entire lawn. A handmade banner stretched most of the way across the low chain-link fence: SOLINE IS ON TRIAL, NOT THIS FAMILY! Another sign shouted for Soline CEO Larry Bosch to pay Maria Nava's mortgage: LET BOSCH PAY BACK WHAT HE STOLE! PEOPLE OVER PROFITS! another sign said. HUMAN NEED NOT CORPORATE GREED! RIGHT IS RIGHT— COME TO THE LEFT! And several others.

"We need to clean this up," I said, "make the signs more pointed, less generic. This looks like an undergrad protest."

"And you sound like a grad student," Alex said. "We'll see what we can do, but check your hypercritical mode at the door, okay? This isn't academia, thank God. I hear you're dating jail-bait, by the way."

Alex with her brown shining eyes watched my reaction and laughed deliciously, the car struck like a bell. "Yeah, we've got some catching up to do. Are we ready? Leave the bags in the trunk, we'll get them after dark. The last thing you want to do is touch metal here in the middle of the day."

Inside the small house a group of twentysomethings, a few thirtysomethings, sat around the wall-unit air conditioner in the back of the living room, five to a couch, four to a love seat, a few hangers-on hanging off the armrests, smoking, talking in lazy, heat-subdued voices. On the couch I recognized several of my comrades from the New York ISO. We all exchanged greetings, hugs. I introduced Sam around. Out of the kitchen stepped Tiffany carrying a glass of water in either hand. She was unchanged from the grading sessions we'd had together with Hahn. I was surprised to see her, and surprised how happy I was to see her. I hadn't known her to be more than rarely involved in ISO activities. How had she heard about this one?

"From Hahn, actually," Tiffany said. "And I've been following the Soline news, getting infuriated. And then from Ms. Persuasive here, who finally made me—"

Tiffany stopped short, taking in Alex, who'd lifted her finger in Plato-pontifical mode—but now we saw she was actually asking for silence. A car idled outside, and it wasn't Maria's, apparently. Alex tilted her finger floorward to where blue and red light now skittered on the warm tile floor, just managing to penetrate the blinds. Then we heard the quick telltale *whoop-whoop* of a police siren. In an instant our quorum broke and reassembled in the front yard, ranging down the curving walk, standing guard in front of occupying tents, beside protest signs—a number of people from ASU's progressive group, apparently, and Tiffany, Andrew, Dawn, Nate, Adam, Sarah, Ali, all from the New York ISO, and Sam, of course, a few others whose names I've forgotten, but a decent-size group, fifteen of us in all. We all shielded our faces against the sun, blinking and blinking in the sudden ferocious glare. Alex made her way to the front of the staggered group, leading Maria by the arm, or anyway leading a small compact woman I assumed was Maria—Sam and I hadn't been formally introduced to her yet. I moved to within a few feet of Alex, feeling Sam's clammy hand at my elbow.

"What's up?" he whispered.

The police cruiser cut its lights, its engine.

"Not sure."

"What happens now? Should we do something?"

"Just sit tight," I said.

The first officer, a Hispanic woman not much bigger than Maria, stood behind an open passenger-side door. Her arms were held out slightly like a weight lifter's, to make room for the belt riding high on her waist and studded with weapons like dark strange barnacles. When her partner finally unfolded himself from the driver's seat, he rose high above the white wide car roof, a giant of a man. You expected this man to open his mouth and speak with the voice of Elohim. Instead, he approached the low chain-link fence with his partner—it came to her chest, his waist—and kept silent.

"*¿Toda está bien, señora?*" the first officer said, addressing Maria. "*¿Es usted la dueña de esta casa?*"

"*Soy, sí,*" Maria said slowly, a little coldly. "I am still the owner of this house, yes. Everything is fine."

The first officer introduced herself and her partner in English, names I instantly forgot—Officer So-and-so, and "up there" Officer So-and-so. No one laughed at the attempted icebreaker.

"Are these friends of yours?" the officer asked Maria, gesturing.

"Yes," Maria said.

The other officer's radio sputtered and squeaked in its epaulette pouch; he seemed to startle a little. He leaked a few formalities out of the side of his mouth. His tall dome of a head, bald, stinging white, shone like porcelain except at the sides where the faintest shadow of hair still appeared. He wore mirrored sports glasses, like his partner, gray cargo shorts, a dopey blue polo shirt that hung oversize off him, Sam-like, with the Phoenix Police Department's shield at its breast.

"They've got your tailor, apparently," I muttered back to Sam. "You sure you're not consulting?"

"Huh?"

"What was that?" the giant officer said, lifting his voice across the yard. "Huh?"

Not a giant's voice, it turned out, but a pretty average basso. In brusquer tones the officer repeated his question.

"Just having a conversation with my friend," I said. "I assume that's allowed?"

Alex turned to me and said quietly, "Shut up."

"Why does your cop cruiser just say 'Police'?" put in Adam Carr from deeper in the yard. "Shouldn't it say 'Phoenix Police Department'? PPD? You could spell it out phonetically."

Alex turned around and told him to shut up too—Adam smirking, unaccountable in his white-boy dreadlocks, a Bob Marley from Boulder, Colorado. We'd never gotten along.

"Wow, that's hilarious," the female officer said.

"Very original," her partner said. He pushed his sunglasses up onto his head and took in Maria with his pinkish small eyes, strangely small for the size of the face—acres of cheeks, vast tracts of forehead and skull.

"Ma'am, are you aware that it's against city ordinance to keep standing camping equipment in your front yard?"

"Sir, are you aware that that sounds like bullshit you just made up on the spot?"

Adam again, ignoring Alex's stare.

The officer kept his eyes on Maria. I couldn't see her face, only that she held it very still. From behind me I heard stiff crunching steps.

"Hey!" the female officer shouted. "Hand out of your pocket!"

It was one of the ASU kids—Jason, I later learned—young-looking in his upswept hair, his construction-cone-orange shorts. He lifted a smartphone slowly. "Phone," he said, "only a phone. I was just wondering if you had that ordinance number? So I could look it up?"

"You think we're lying?" the officer said.

"No, no, not at all, not at all. I just want to look it up."

"'Trust but verify,'" Adam said. "That's your boy Reagan."

Maria said, "Please," turning her straining eyes on us.

"That's okay, ma'am," the tall officer said. "We deal with morons for a living."

"If we move the tents to the backyard," Maria said, "would that be okay?"

"We're not here to write you up, ma'am. We just wanted you to be aware."

"We wanted to make sure you're all right," said the other officer. Then she added, quickly and lowly, "*Si tus amigos le dan cualquier problema, avísanos, bien?*"

I'd caught the gist of the sentence, particularly the dubious emphasis laid on *amigos*. I'm sure Alex had too, a real Spanish speaker. Her back was long and motionless in front of me, rather narrow in a pale green tank top, a faint band of sweat, darker green, tracking the length of her spine. The spine straightened in surprise as Maria reached her arm around her, awkwardly, a stiff unpracticed gesture that told in Maria's body language too.

"They're not causing any trouble," Maria said. "They're my friends. They're helping me."

"We understand that," the officer said, "but if that changes . . ."

"Your concern is touching," Adam said.

"They're trying to take her house away from her," Sam said. His voice was reedy, painfully earnest after Adam's.

"Sam!" Alex said, spinning around, throwing her arms out incredulously. "Adam! Everyone! Since when do we talk to fucking cops? Huh? You think these people are your debating partners? They're cops! They're instruments of the state! So let's save our fucking breath, and a little of our dignity, okay?"

Alex faced forward again, the cops stiffening. We'd all stiffened, I think, and Maria especially. It felt like whole minutes before the giant officer softened, scoffing a little, shaking his large high hairless head back and forth, back and forth.

"I take it you're the Occupy leftovers?" he said. "You poor little hipster shits—you guys are all forty years late to the party." He tapped his partner on the shoulder and started backing toward the cruiser. "Real nice friends you've got there, ma'am. Real classy. If they wear out their welcome, you let us know, all right? We'll check in again."

When the cruiser pulled away from the curb, it cleared its throat of a pent-up siren and a burst of blue light, picking up speed as it turned onto Baseline. Maria turned and I saw that her olive face was flushed, glowing with feeling. I don't imagine I was the only one to read second thoughts into those round sweating features, rosy at the cheeks and tip of the nose, the large eyes sharp with adrenaline—or was it anger? Some of us had gathered around Maria, semicircling her. She raised her voice for all of us to hear.

"Please move the tents," she said. "Thank you. There should be room in the backyard. Please do it now."

Alex was herself again, reasoning with Maria in soft, persistent tones. We didn't know if the ordinance was real, first of all, and even if it was, it didn't matter—what were their rules of etiquette really worth if they couldn't protect her, or the town, from the likes of Soline? If they *wouldn't* protect her. It was a power play, Alex said, and we couldn't give in to it. That and the fact that moving the tents to the backyard, slinking out of sight, defeated the purpose, the publicity of the protest—

"Please do what I ask," said Maria, speaking to Alex but also past her. An impressive finality was in her voice. She put her head down and started for the front door, our loose semicircle drifting open like a buoy line, reluctantly, to let her pass.

• • •

That night I called Jen from the close cocoon warmth of the tent I shared with Sam. The heat hadn't broken, exactly, but it had slumped off a bit, lazing away as the long twilight lazed above the distant mountains beyond mountains you could just manage to see from Maria's backyard. The aerial effect, Sam had called it, a photography term he'd picked up from his sister, apparently—that blue on fading blue, that purple on fainter, ghostlier purple. I hadn't even known Sam *had* a sister, and here we were sharing a tent on the edge of the desert. Sam was gone now, giving me my privacy. The last light of the day had gone with him, and the inside of the tent shone eerily from the lantern hung from a hook off the central arcing pole. The light made the roof look particularly striking, green-white, milky, like an inverted firmament with the small buzzing insects on the other side of the canvas for negative stars, little odd-shaped holes to let the darkness in.

"Eerie?" Jen said. "Eerie how?"

"Like ectoplasm eerie—I don't know. This weird green artificial light and the ceiling writhing just a few feet above you. I've never really liked camping, have I told you that?"

"Even with all your Audubon guides?"

"Trees are different. You can study trees from a porch if you want to, through binoculars."

"But surely tent sex is some of the best sex there is."

"Oh, well . . ."

"Are you alone?"

"Not enough."

"Is that why you're whispering?"

Through the green milky canvas I could see the dark outlines of other tents, people in camping chairs, people sitting on blankets. I could hear the steady susurrus of quiet conversation. We were all trying to be polite, well behaved, and maybe we were a little bit cowed too. Unusually for us, there was no weed, minimal drinking—we were conscious of the noise. We didn't want to upset Maria or give the cops the slightest pretext. A wavering world-beat melody wafted up through the campsite from a portable speaker, and of course there were the obligatory boxy chords from a nearby steel string. Nature sounds too: crickets like high violins, a pair of strange keening night birds for woodwinds. For a moment I thought I heard Alex's voice, mellow and confident at the same time, holding forth about something or other, but then the voice changed, modulating higher and thinner.

"You still there?" Jen said. "Sweetie?"

"I'm here. I wish you were, too."

"Does that mean your ex-girlfriend's ignoring you?"

"Har, har."

"How do you know I'm kidding?"

"You'd better be. It means I miss the hell out of you—bad Jen—in all senses. And it turns out I'm a little more alone than I thought."

"Alone and lonely, eh? Should I ask what you're wearing?"

I unbuttoned my jeans, adjusting myself. "A little less than I was a minute ago."

"Oh, really."

"You remember the thing I was telling you about earlier—the aerial effect?"

"I'd like to see *your* effect go aerial."

"Ha! You upstaged me!"

"Why? What were you going to say?"

"I was going to say I'd like to see your *areola* effect."

"Oh would you, Naughty Professor."

"What do you say we add some pictures to this exhibition?"

"*Les sexts?*"

I went first.

"Oh my," Jen said. "Ooh la la. Okay. I see your aerial effect and I raise you . . . just a second," she whispered.

The interval stretched and something in it possessed me to say, "We're like my parents, you know that?"

I wasn't sure Jen had heard me, if she was still by the phone, but then she said, bemused-sounding, "Paging Dr. Freud?"

"I just meant with all the wordplay."

"Wordplay as foreplay—swordplay?"

"I'll stipulate."

"Oh, I'm sure you will."

I laughed. "Do you know what I mean, though?"

"Sure. The son seeks the mother in the lover, in the partner. Was that Freud or was that someone else?"

"It sounds like pop psychology to me."

"And you're saying Freud *isn't* pop psychology?"

"Oh my God," I said. "Jesus."

"You like that?"

"Where did you get a cheerleader skirt?"

"Freshman year of high school. I was briefly a Cougarette. *Aimez-vous l'image, mon chéri?*"

"I'm on the precipice . . ."

"I thought you'd like that. Boys are a bit predictable, aren't they?"

"Permission to land?"

"Wait, wait for me . . ."

I was all the way out of my jeans now, boxer shorts down

around my ankles, going at myself lying back on my sleeping bag. Steps scraped in the burnt grass outside the tent door—I sat up like a cardiac victim, paddles at my chest.

"Eli?" It was a female voice. "Are you alone?"

"One second," I said. "Sorry, so sorry," I said, and I cut the call.

It was Alex, of course.

"Can I come in?" she said.

"Give me a second. Let me just put a shirt on."

"What's this standing on ceremony," she said, as the zippered front flap of the tent began to fall in.

"Alex, seriously!"

When I finally did open the flap from my side, Alex was smiling, wearing that old raffish face of hers. "I didn't interrupt anything, I hope?"

I made myself as comfortable as I could under the circumstances, leaning back on one elbow like a sultan, the other arm placed strategically. Alex sat lotus style, high and straight, boyish in body and manner, on the blue yoga mat I'd teased Sam for bringing along.

"Just doing a little reading," I said at length, matching Alex's smile.

She offered to come back in a minute if I needed one—not a surprising offer coming from her, but I blushed all the same. And here I'd been girding myself for the next round of wisecracks!

I'd forgotten. Alex knew about humor, she could speak that language, but the thing you had to learn about her—the thing you learned to marvel at, if you were like me—was that humor for her was incidental, a little frivolous, take it or leave it. It didn't grease the wheels of the world for her as it did for me, or for my parents: In the Lentz home ("*Lentz*, like the pre-Easter period, but in the plural," my father liked to say. "All the atone-ment we can get"), in our modest split-level set back from a leafy road, we encountered seriousness only where it was im-possible not to encounter it: war, genocide, sickness, death and its grim accoutrements. And even then it was only death joined to specificity—in the abstract, Dad especially was capable of poking fun at mortality, disease. Speaking lightly of renal fail-ure, say, or anthrax scares, he'd stop and announce, "You realize I'll never die of these now, right? Too ironic. Not even your mother's vengeful Catholic God would do that to me."

"*My* God? I think you need to brush up on your Penta-teuch, pal. That grumpy mass murderer was your invention, was he not?"

And so on, Mom smiling, Dad smiling.

It was all of life, then, and most of death, love, metaphysics, all tethered to a punch line. It's not a bad way to grow up—don't get me wrong—but imagine Marx on the heels of that, imagine Engels, Trotsky, Luxemburg, all that volubility, all that high-stakes High Church seriousness! Imagine the very *idea* of a confrontational politics. Imagine Alex Esposito and her sharp black box of hair, the way it waved with each cut, slowly, like time-lapse photography, sometimes straight, sometimes slant-ing down her forehead like a guillotine—imagine me watch-ing her and marveling at her brazenness, her bravery, her sheer *quiddity* as she pressed the *Socialist Worker* on students hurrying to class through Washington Square Park, her loud and unself-conscious sloganeering, the impassioned way she chaired the ISO meetings I'd started attending, I confess, much more regularly, religiously (yes, Sam, I'll say it) after I developed a crush on Alex in my second year at Randolph. A year later she and I had grown into each other's lives like twisting vine, imperceptible at first, then it was a fact, immutable. We had implicated ourselves in the other's affection. I learned everything from Alex, so much. What I called my Trotskyist street voice—that was me imitating Alex imitating Trotsky, I think, though who really knew. I knew I liked the words she chose, and the way she voiced them. Only rarely did they overflow into the kind of anger I'd heard that afternoon with the police officers. It was as if the light gathering sharply on the bald officer's head had blinded Alex to herself.

"Is everything all right?" I asked her. "Are you okay?"

"I think we're okay, yeah. We've got a good core group. We've got our firing group together. Now we just need to make good on it."

I let out a groaning breath, not entirely intentional.

"What?"

"That's from *The Urban Guerrilla's Handbook*, right? Our 'firing group'? We sound like rank phonies when we talk like that."

"Oh, don't be such an asshole," Alex said, yawning a little. "I didn't want to talk strategy anyway. You can be Holden Caulfield tomorrow."

She slid onto her elbows on the yoga mat until she'd stretched out opposite me, our heads at either side of what must have looked satyr-like in shadow, from outside the tent, this strange two-headed beast reclining silently in a green light.

"So what should we talk about?"

"Tell me a story," she said. "Tell me about this jailbait of yours. Or this Mini-Me of yours."

"You mean Sam? The Mini-Me who's six inches taller than I am and can kick my ass at tennis?"

"Eli and his tennis."

"Game of kings."

"I thought that was chess."

"Tennis originated in the French court hundreds of years ago, and who's more regal than the French?"

"You always were taken with that veneer of sophistication, weren't you? That's all the French are good for these days. That and turgid theoretical prose. Where did you find him? Sam, I mean. Is he serious?"

"You and your seriousness," I said.

I told Alex about Hahn and the Marxism seminar where I'd met Sam, Sam there on a lark, at first, an intellectual tourist, the type of thrill seeker Alex and I had seen flit in and out of ISO circles time and again. Was Sam serious? Who could say? I told Alex about the Occupy marches Sam had taken part in. She rolled her eyes. Well, and more to the point, he'd come along to Arizona, hadn't he? Alex asked how he'd paid for the trip, which seemed to me a violation of unspoken rules. When I didn't answer the question, she asked it again, and I told her about the money from my dissertation grant that I'd helped him out with—better spent that way, I figured, than on my fucking dissertation.

"So for all you know he could still be a tourist," Alex said.

"I don't think so."

"But you don't know."

"Of course I don't know. Who really knows anybody, or for that matter anything—"

Alex's hand went up and her eyes, suddenly heavy, sedated-looking, dropped like blinds. No, she said, she didn't mean epistemologically. She hadn't come here for a philosophy lecture.

Outside, one of the night birds kipped and the other, in *responsorium*, kipped back.

What came next? Besides the waiting, I mean—there was never any shortage of that. How long was it before Sam came to tell me about his run-in with Luís and Aida, Maria's children, before he enlisted me in his plan to circumvent the group's plan, the loose "strategy" Alex referred to? It might have been the third day we were there, or the fourth—where memory fails me I'll order by faith, which, as I understand it, means believing in your own cooked books.

Call it the fourth day. Faithful Sam came to me with the sweaty earnestness of a faith healer, a tent preacher. He'd been alone in the darkened hallway off Maria's kitchen, feeling for the bathroom door when he undershot it and opened onto Luís in his bedroom. The boy snapped around owl-like, the whites of his eyes like saucers. He looked much younger in that moment than his sixteen years. Sam gave me the scene in some detail, a good poet—Luís smooth and surprised, swiveled around, his upper body bent over a large brown packing box of neatly folded clothes. Other boxes stood open like mouths around the room. What was he doing? In his own surprise Sam asked the question out loud, as if the answer weren't obvious. All the walls were barren of the pictures and posters that had hung there for years: you could see the naked outlines, vulnerable-looking, on the off-white plaster, where the posters had shielded the sun and dust. To the left of the bed the closet door was open and a pile of old toys, a child's toys, cars and trucks and foam balls, green army men, spilled out.

"And what did Luís say to you?" I said.

"Nothing," Sam said. "I'd asked a stupid question. He was obviously in there packing up his life for some storage facility, and then what? How much does a three-bedroom apartment go for in Phoenix? Or a two-bedroom, a one-bedroom? Does part-time work at a Verizon store stretch even that far, and what if the house goes into deficiency? What's their day-to-day going to be like?"

"Deficiency?"

"It's when the amount you owe on the house is more than the bank manages to sell it for. You lose your house and gain a toxic load of debt in the process. That could definitely happen in this housing market. Tiffany was telling me about it. Did you know Tiffany has a law degree? Did you know she practiced for a while at some fancy New York firm? Anyway, she knows a little about foreclosure law. She and that new guy Jamaal, who was at ASU Law for a while, were comparing notes—a bit of résumé-trading too, hackles up. Mostly his hackles."

"So he dropped out?"

"Huh?"

"Jamaal. You said he was at ASU Law?"

"Too much debt for too few prospects, I guess. Apparently he failed to see the benefits of being institutionalized and un-derpaid and scared all the time. Not like you and me, eh, com-rade?"

"Well—"

"I wasn't done with the story," Sam said. "So I'm in there with Luís, right? I'm in the room when in walks Aida with a grocery bag of packing leftovers, some old trinkets and things.

She was going to add them to the donation pile unless Luís wanted anything. Then she noticed me in the room and went quiet and tight, like she'd just been called on in class. I could tell I was intruding on a sort of intimacy. Luís spread the bag's contents on the floor and started picking through them. It was the kind of stuff you just collect over the years—a snow globe, a little checkers set, that sort of thing. He held up this weathered stuffed giraffe with a long spotted neck and long painted lashes around the eyes, and I could tell it meant something to her, just from the way he held it, like he was asking a question with it. Aida's eyes darted over to me as if to explain why she didn't want to talk about it. Luís said she should keep it—they were keeping it—and Aida just said okay and sort of stood there in the room like she didn't know how to leave. I got down on my knees and helped Luís put his sister's things back in the grocery bag. I handed it to her and I said—I said this to both of them—"

"I think I see where this is going," I said.

"I said that they should both keep all their things. We were going to find a way to help them keep their house. That's why we'd come here."

"Okay."

"I promised them, Eli."

"Okay, look. You're new to this, you're enthusiastic—that's good. I'm just not sure a sentimental attachment is always the most effective means to—"

"What are we doing here, anyway?" Sam said. "We're just sitting on our asses. What 'means' are we employing?"

"Alex and I were making calls just today—the local media needs its 'color stories,' don't they? The pressure's building on the bank, Sam, you know it is—"

Sam waved this away impatiently. "I need you to do something for me," he said.

"Or otherwise we wait for the confrontation on the day of foreclosure—we get the media there for that—"

"Eli," Sam said. "I need you to do something for me. Will you do something for me?"

He called it "knocking doors"—the phrase courtesy of the Mormon missionary work he'd tried for a few months before ditching the work and the church altogether. We'd always just called it "canvassing," but now a religious shadow, a "mission," a sense of conspiracy hung over the day's efforts. At one point Alex knocked on a door, and a white woman in a yellow bandanna, late sixties perhaps, opened and squinted at us—whether from the sun or suspicion we couldn't tell. (I pull this door from a memory trove of dozens, whole hours of them.) The woman, Jan, listened to what we had to say with smiling attention, nodding at appropriate intervals, her expression going sad and chagrined at all the right moments. When she opened her mouth it was a formal, Nordic accent that edged her words. She ran the flat of her palm up and over the bandanna, as if pressing her brain for excuses.

"I think it's terrible what's happening," she said. "I just don't know what I can do to help."

"Ideally you would come and join us in solidarity with Maria," Alex said. "If not full-time, at least on Monday when the bank wants to evict Maria and her children so it can sell the house without her permission. Several of your neighbors have already committed to be with us that morning. We think the presence of community members will send an important message."

"Oh, well . . ." Jan said, and smoothed back the yellow bandanna. "I'd like to be there, but I work in the mornings."

"The eviction notice is for seven a.m.," Alex said. "Many of your neighbors are planning to come before work. Will you commit to that as well?"

"It's just that I run a half-day childcare group and it begins at seven thirty. Parents sometimes drop the kids off early. I'd like to be there. I'll try to be there . . ."

She was averting her eyes now. It was just the two of us, Alex and I, but I supposed we were intimidating enough. I reminded Jan about the name and number of the local congressman we'd listed in the flyer and also the name and number of the home-loans manager at Bank of America. I said we hoped she'd put in a call to them, at the very least, and express her support for Maria. If enough pressure mounted on these people, who knew what could happen.

"Of course. Yes, thank you, I'll do that. I hope everything goes well for her," Jan said, and with a curt quick smile she shut the door.

Out on the sidewalk Alex said, "I wish you'd stop letting them off the hook like that."

"She was never on the hook."

"You don't know that."

"I thought we weren't going to argue epistemology," I said, putting a joshing arm around Alex's shoulder. We bumped along for a few paces like that, our hips knocking together, my palm clammy—I only now realized how clammy—against the warm bare skin of Alex's upper arm.

Alex wrapped her other arm around my waist and said, "You're petit bourgeois, you know that?"

"There are worse things."

"Are there?"

She pulled away and doubled back to the little inlet of another chain-link gate leading onto another cement walkway—an entire street of these, an entire neighborhood of slight variations on this theme. How much longer could this go on? How much longer did it *need* to go on? I checked my cell phone but couldn't quite make out the numbers in the powerful glare. It was pervasive, this glare, palpable, another element. I squinted into it at Alex—a gray tank top today, the same khaki shorts, her legs long and thin coming out of them, dull brown. Today she wore a faded blue Mets cap that cast a brim of darker blue shadow onto her forehead, her sunglasses hung at the bottom edge of it. I couldn't see her eyebrows, but I gathered they were raised.

"We've been doing this for an awfully long time," I said.

"It was your idea, wasn't it?" she said.

"We're going to die of heatstroke."

"Your idea."

By the end of the afternoon we'd collected a few more commitments, none of them firm enough to anchor much hope to, and none of them to occupy with us full-time. It was just as well. The clutter in Maria's backyard had grown by the hour, an almost bacterial expansion, until the half-used ketchup bottles, empty water bottles, rocking beer cans, plastic-bag tumbleweed coated the grass and all the hot-to-touch tarps and towels too, and we decided to create a committee that dealt only with cleanup, and I was its chair.

Alex took a shower when we got back to Maria's, then came

into the backyard to help me and Adam and a few of the ASU crew collect the latest trash, three large Hefty bags full of it. Adam was becoming a little less unbearable—perhaps. In any case he'd joined me in grumbling about the more or less permanent loitering group around the AC in Maria's living room, the group that made the bulk of the overloud, over-messy camp in the backyard at night, then transferred its spirit and sprawl in the daytime to the indoor couches. I'd joined them there a time or two, but compared to them I was Alex-like, Herculean in my commitment.

"Where's Sam?" Alex asked once we'd come in from the backyard. "Where's Tiffany?"

I answered honestly that I didn't know.

Nate from ISO, one of the biggest disappointments of the occupation, a couch occupier, sat watching a video on the laptop that perched on the couch's arm. Dawn, Ali, a few others crowded in beside him, scrolling silently through their phones. Nate didn't look up as he said, "Sam and Tiffany? They left a while back. That Jamaal guy too. They took his car."

"Did they say where they were going?" Alex asked.

Nate shook his head.

"What the hell are you watching, anyway?"

The video showed a younger Larry Bosch in medium close-up, warm lighting, a generic fireplace backdrop—it looked like a *20/20* interview. Fuller featured, less severe than I was used to seeing him in the glare of recent events—the thin bellow-like folds down his neck that you noticed in current photographs were the ghosts of former jowls, apparently. Here Bosch looked comfortable, a well-fed man. His wife, in a collared red blouse, sat a little stiffly beside him, smiling.

"What is this?" Alex said again.

"I don't know," Nate said. "Call it research."

"It sounds like a puff piece to me. The poor rich people."

Bosch was running with a question about his first company's bankruptcy—his sense of helplessness and failure, his responsibility to the investors, to the employees, the sleepless nights, the personal money he'd tried to plug up the leaks with.

"We had to move into my parents' house," Bosch's wife said. Nancy. "Larry was out of work for almost two years. Our kids were in middle school. We were terrified." Midwestern features, a wide high forehead, the pale yellowish skin communicated something honestly strained about these memories.

Bosch rested a chubby hand on his wife's arm, laughed uncomfortably. "That was a very difficult time for us."

"Jesus," Alex said. "Click out of this, will you?"

"What?" Nate said. "I was curious."

"He recovered quite nicely, didn't he, Mr. Rags to Riches? Just remember that this is the same guy who froze Maria out of her retirement account. He cares so much about his employees that he speculates and defrauds them out of a company—not for the first time, it sounds like."

"I hadn't forgotten, thanks."

"No?"

A stalemating silence developed between them, Nate holding Alex's eyes as she stood above him.

Finally Alex said, "Did Sam and Tiffany say when they were coming back? Or Jamaal?"

Nate leaned over the couch side to check his cell phone, mumbling something.

"What?" Alex said. "Nate?"

"No," he said, straightening again. "That was a no."

• • •

It was almost dark by the time they did get back, Sam and Tiffany and Jamaal clod-stepping and swaying into the backyard, where we'd set up an after-meal drink and chat with Maria. Her round face was pleasantly flushed by now. She wore black pants and a red Verizon polo shirt with a little golden name tag pinned above the logo. The sun had dropped below the scrim of dark scrubby mountains behind the house, behind the city, and for once it had taken the heat with it—a watery convocation of pinks and oranges spread out in the lower atmosphere, the desert sky going down medium, medium rare. We were enjoying ourselves, sitting in a circle of camping chairs among the greasy cheese-strewn taco boxes that Maria had brought home for us. When we'd protested she'd said, "I can't eat them all myself, can I?" Her children sat on either side of her, Luís slumped and thin in red soccer shorts, his chin resting on his sternum like a pensioner's, regarding the phone he thumbed expertly at his lap, Aida more compact, hunched over her phone, an armadillo curl to her small back.

When Sam saw us with the Bud Lights he raised an invisible can and called out, "Excellent idea!"

He was the softest on his feet of the three of them, more boneless than usual in a ratty blue polo, each step undulating up his long body like a wave, up his narrow chest and shoulders and his thin putty neck, chin weak, mouth parted—Little Lockjaw no more. Tiffany wore her inebriation better, quieter, true to form, a subtle slackness in her wide olive face, a subtle glossiness in her eyes. Only Jamaal, already relaxed in a bright pink T-shirt—the loose physique, too, the loose dandelion Afro—only Jamaal looked all the way normal.

"You must be the designated driver," Maria said, walking a beer over to him. "Here, take my seat. I was just heading inside."

We all protested this announcement, but Maria said, "Another early shift tomorrow," singsonging the words, falsely cheery. "No, I shouldn't complain. It's what I wanted. It's what we need."

"You can always complain," said Adam. "It's an inalienable right."

"How set in stone is your work schedule?" Sam asked Maria. "If you needed to cancel a shift, or maybe come in late . . ."

"They like you to give twenty-four hours' notice. Why?"

"But if you got sick," Sam said. "You don't need to give a day's notice if you're sick, right?"

"No, I don't think so. Why?"

"No reason in particular."

Maria hesitated, waiting for Sam to continue. When he didn't, she turned to us and put on an easy enough smile. "Thank you for the work you all did today. Thank you again. God bless you. Good night."

Maria's children followed wordlessly after her into the small stucco ranch house. A soft yellow light stood in the sliding glass door, glowing yellower by the minute against the darkness.

"You guys were out drinking?" Alex said to Sam and Tiffany and Jamaal as they settled into the vacated camping chairs.

"Any leftover tacos by chance?" Sam said.

"No. You were at a bar, is that where you were?"

"We went to celebrate. Sort of."

"Celebrate what, sort of?"

Jamaal and Tiffany looked to Sam as if by prearrangement.

He tipped his long white face back in a long swill of Bud Light. A few lanterns had been brought out and set in the middle of the circle to fend off the darkness, and the sharp thin glow of them cast Sam's Adam's apple in stark relief. *Of Man's first disobedience and the fruit of that forbidden tree . . .* What was he stalling for? I honestly didn't know. My only job had been to keep Alex away from the house for a few hours—beyond that Sam had been vague. He was thinking of trying something, he'd said, but it was too provisional to mention, a shot in the dark.

Adam, in the un-Edenic dreadlocks, laid his hand on Sam's forearm when he lowered the can. "What's up?" he said. "Where did you guys go?"

"Okay, people," Sam said. "Open minds." He turned to Tiffany. "You've got all the jargon down. You tell it."

"It's not that jargony," Tiffany said, "and Jamaal should get a lot of the credit too. It was one of his former law professors who gave us the name of a friend, a legal arbiter at the courthouse downtown. The connection was what got us in the door without an appointment, but it was Sam's stubbornness—his asshole-ishness?"

Sam shrugged.

" 'I am not moving from this chair until you pick up that phone and make something happen,' " Jamaal said, hunching his shoulders nebbishly, overenunciating in a parody of Sam's clipped voice.

"That was what kept us in the guy's office," Tiffany said. "I think we might have burned that bridge in the act of crossing it."

"At least we crossed," Jamaal said.

"The arbiter called Bank of America and explained Maria's situation, the Soline connection, our occupation of the property, all of it. He was on a first-name basis with the loans manager, with Ned. After about ten minutes they'd hammered out a nonbinding oral contract—which basically means two guys talking on the phone. Maria would need to agree to it to make it real. The gist of it is this: She's not getting out of it. No clemency, no forgiveness of back payments—the bank refuses absolutely, what sort of precedent would it set, and so on. The bank will, however, offer a partial debt forgiveness in the form of a waiver of any potential deficiency judgment after the sale of the house. In a deficiency judgment, if the house were to sell for less than Maria's outstanding balance on the mortgage, which is a very, very likely scenario, Maria would still owe that money to the bank, with interest, and typically these rates are highly injurious. It'd make a bad situation much worse, extend it out for years. But what the arbiter has tentatively arranged is for the bank to let Maria walk away from the sale free and clear, no deficiency, no further debts, nothing. A clean start. The arbiter has also offered to walk Maria through the paperwork tomorrow, which is a bit of a miracle on such short notice and bearing in mind that we basically barricaded ourselves in his office, had no power of attorney, and weren't all that grateful for what he did do. By the end of an hour our relations with this guy were only *amicable* in the legal sense of that word. Here's his card, with Ned the loan manager's information on the back. Ned Chamberlain. My advice would be for somebody to go inside and pull Maria out of the shower or wherever she is and give this to her immediately. The home-loans manager said the papers need to be signed tomorrow if they're going to be signed at all. Come Monday it's too late and the eviction notice stands as is. That was made explicit."

Tiffany held out the business card to no one in particular. At length I took it and brought it to my lap without really looking at it. The crickets had come up, the night birds.

"Huh," I said. "Huh."

Alex took the card from my hand and tore it neatly in two, dropping the halves at her feet.

She said, "Who else knew about this? Did you?"

"I didn't," I said. "I had no idea."

"You think this is good news?" Alex said to Sam and Tiffany. Jamaal was beginning to look chastened already. "Where is there a shred of good news in this?"

"She's going to lose her house," Sam said. "She's out of options there. We're all out of options there."

"That was made explicit, was it?" Alex said. "By Lord Fucking Chamberlain?"

Sam stood up from his camping chair, listed a bit, like a sailboat, a sloop in sudden wind. He moved across the circle with unsteady purpose and gathered up the torn business card at Alex's feet.

"This is *real*," he said. "This is a real option. What do we honestly think is going to happen Monday morning? We chain ourselves to the furniture and the cops just capitulate, the bank says never mind? They'll just dig in harder! This isn't some Marxist theory class, it's reality, and there's a real family that has to live in it."

Sam was looming over Alex's chair, not meaning to perhaps, but looming higher with each breath, like an oil derrick.

"You need to sit down," Alex said.

"I'm taking this inside to Maria. This is a real option."

Sam stepped uncertainly toward the house and Alex caught a hank of his shirt and hauled him back, levering herself out of her seat with the action and pulling Sam down into it in a move so swift and efficient it might have been choreographed. Alex crossed the circle toward Sam's empty seat, tossing back over her shoulder that I should talk to my protégé, talk some sense into him.

"Why didn't you tell us about this?" I said. "Something this important you should have told the group beforehand."

"Not to mention Maria," Adam said.

"Not to mention Maria. If I'd known this was what you were planning—"

"You knew about this?" Alex said. "I thought you just said you didn't know."

"I didn't. Not specifically."

"He knew," Sam said. "Oh, he was in on it. His job was to distract you while we made off to try something practical, something real in the real, material world. We didn't know exactly what, and we didn't know if it would work, so we didn't advertise our plans, least of all to Maria. We didn't want to get her hopes up."

"Eli?" Alex said.

I was shaking my head, shaking and shaking it.

"Is that true, Eli?"

"It's true," Sam said, "but it's not the issue. The issue is this card you tore up and the opportunity attached to it. A hundred thousand dollars in debt forgiveness is real—whatever we're playing at here is not."

"We spent four hours canvassing in heatstroke heat, Eli,

and the whole time your Frankenstein is out trying to undercut it all? The whole time it was just a decoy?"

"That's not the issue," Sam said.

Alex said, slowly, "You need to stop telling me what the issue is. We'll decide that as a collective—that's how this works. You think you're swooping in to the rescue like some action hero? Debt Forgiveness Man?" She turned to the group. " 'Debt *forgiveness*'? Is that why we came here? Soline detonates an entire town and we come in in our hazmat suits offering *forgiveness* to the victims? Guess what, Maria, we're aiding and abetting the bank in taking your house now! We're apologists for predatory capitalism, we're 'reformers'—we would have told you sooner but we didn't want to get your hopes up!"

"I live on earth," Sam said. "Maria and her family live on earth, in the real world, and what you're talking about is some ethereal kingdom come—"

"You need to stop fucking telling me what I'm talking about," Alex said. "I know that a lot better than you do."

"You're waiting for the revolution to come and in the meantime a family's about to lose their house and gain a toxic load of debt in its place."

Sam stood up again, wavered again. ASU Jason was there to block his path, then Nate from ISO, then Dawn and Adam.

"These aren't eggs you break to make some grand omelet," Sam said.

"That's true," Nate said.

"That's true," Adam said, "but sit down."

"We'll decide as a group," Dawn said.

At length they all sat down, smoothed their hackles back into place. Another silence came over the group, night-pricked, humming, and in the middle of it you could hear Tiffany's slow, deliberate intake of breath.

"There's one other condition we should have mentioned," she said.

In the end we put it to a vote, a grubby circle of dim-lit buzzing parliamentarians. Sam and the ayes narrowly carried it, but with a rider provision from Alex's noes tacked on: We'd wait till the morning to tell Maria about the offer.

In the tent Sam and I were silent, avoiding each other's eye, each pinned to our opposite corner as if we'd fallen into a centrifuge. You could hear Alex outside going from tent to tent pressing her case for appeal. At one point Sam looked up from his Nietzsche and said, "Tent canvassing," and I managed a little smile. Minutes more passed like this, the crickets out in force now, the kippering night birds, not much else to compete with them since our camp was unusually subdued tonight. Our last.

Finally I said, "I wish you hadn't done that."

"I'm sorry," Sam said. "Really. That was shitty of me."

"Do you even know what I'm talking about?" My meanness again, my Trotskyist bark.

"Well, what I'm talking about is what I said to Alex in front of the group, about our arrangement."

"Oh it is, is it?"

"Yes. I am sorry about that. That was childish of me."

"I suppose that's what I meant too," I said. "Gratefully your other disclosure upstaged it—a little flesh wound in the back, then the grenade."

"I've murdered The Occupation," Sam said, flourishing his

hands dramatically, "capital *The*, capital *Occupation*. Will I ever forgive myself?"

I shook my head, turning away from him, turning back to my reading.

"You voted for it too," Sam said. Then softer, "We're doing the right thing."

I had voted for it too. The other condition Tiffany mentioned was that the occupation disperse immediately—the bank didn't want a scene at eviction, didn't want protesters at the house or at the Bank of America offices. Tiffany had let out this news in little hesitating winces, waiting for the blow that never came. No one was much surprised by then. Shut the blinds, turn the lights off—par for the course.

It would be a sorry way to go out, but Sam and Tiffany and Jamaal were probably right. The risks were too great, and in the end it wasn't our decision to make. It never had been. If Maria wanted to take her chances with our occupation, leave the deficiency waiver on the table, then by all means let her. But she wouldn't. Somehow I knew she wouldn't, and apparently I wasn't alone in that intuition. The camp was quiet now, and weirdly tidy—towels and tarps had been folded and gathered in in preparation for tomorrow's teardown.

Outside, Alex's voice rose loose and relaxed, lark-like. Then it came to the door of our tent.

"Are you boys decent?"

I opened the flap onto her grinning face, the curt bangs and the strong Roman nose and the ebony stud catching the lantern light—she looked like Caesar. She leaned her upper body into the tent holding a half-full dime bag of dry flaky weed—it could have been pencil shavings, or birdseed—and in the other hand she held by its plastic scruff a cluster of Bud Lights.

"I've come to either smoke or drink a peace with your Frankenstein," she said to me.

"I thought Frankenstein was the scientist," Sam said. "Isn't the monster just Monster?"

"Don't get fresh or I might change my mind. Do you want lowercase bud or capital Bud?"

"I'm not much of a weed guy, actually."

"Of course you're not."

"Repressed habits die hard."

Alex turned a goofy, kinking, tight-lipped, high-browed smile at me. "No wonder you two get along." She slipped into the tent and assumed a cross-legged slouch beside me, flopping the slim bag of weed into my lap. "You're welcome to as much or as little of that as you'd like. It's not as bad as it looks. But please go smoke it somewhere else. Maybe on a cliff edge, or in traffic."

"At least one of those beers is mine, isn't it?"

"No, it isn't, Eli." Alex blinked at me.

It couldn't have been more than half an hour later when I heard the first laughter sounds coming out of the tent. They were laughing together, their twinned silhouettes leaning in close like conspirators. Maybe it was a trick of my hearing, a deception of the greenish light or my green, wasted state—I observed them from a distance, a stoned voyeur orbiting the yard with the skunky weed in a small glass bowl—but I doubted it. I called Jen and got her voice mail, only realizing the time difference (it was almost two a.m. in New York) after I'd left a message about how much I missed her and how I wished, although of course I was happy for her and her job, but I wished she were here with me now, things were going well, but then again not really, not if I was honest, etc., the message dropping down through descending levels of lugubriousness to match the descending clauses. I didn't trust myself when I was high—it was true I liked control. In general I distrusted states of consciousness I couldn't re-create out of my own innate tool kit. *A very Boy Scout answer from a very Boy Scout boy,* Alex would say, *had* said—something very nearly like that. Didn't a good book or film or piece of music induce states of consciousness you couldn't get back to on command? Didn't love? Didn't sex? Consciousness, like the reality it pilots, is a contingent thing, and I should learn to embrace that. I should learn to do a lot of things. I should learn, I should learn, I should learn, I should learn . . . What were they talking about in there? What were they laughing about? How were they laughing just a few hours after they'd shouted each other down like drill sergeants? One more loop around the yard's perimeter, stepping stealthily, observing all the time the green tent with the two twinned shadowed bodies shifting against the canvas like the shadows in Plato's cave, the parallax effect, young Marcel and the spires of Martinville aligning, disaligning . . . But I was tired of literature, tired of philosophy, tired of ideas and the whole sham show of it. Tired of action, tired of inaction.

Something buzzed in my pocket, and again. My phone.

"Hello?"

"Hey, sweetie, is everything okay?"

"Oh, Jen . . ."

"I got your message. Is everything all right?"

"I woke you."

"That's okay."

"I'm sorry I woke you."

"That's okay. What's up?"

"Petty politics. It's nothing, really. I'm sorry I bothered you with it. I do wish you were here, though. I wish I could hold you."

"I wish that too."

"You know I love you, right? I guess we've only really said it in a jokey playful way—'Oh, I love you, you're so funny,' that sort of thing. I mean it, though. Absent irony, absent hedging. You're perfect for me, Jen—you're perfect. A lot better than Alex ever was, if you really want to know. Not that I'm comparing you, not that it's a competition—"

"You're not comparing us?"

"Or if it is, you win by a mile, that's what I'm saying. What I'm saying is I love you, Jen, and I miss the hell out of you."

"I love you too, Eli."

"You do?"

"I do."

"You really do? Really truly?"

"Are you a little tipsy, *mon amour?*"

We said good night while I was at the far side of the yard, over by the ASU quarter, and by the time I'd circled back to the green dome tent Alex's shadow had slipped out. The sleeping bag was warm and fragrant with her body when I settled heavily down on it.

"You two sounded like you patched things right up, huh?"

"She already had the votes to overturn it when she came to the tent," Sam explained to me. "That's what accounted for her chipper mood."

"And what accounted for yours?" I said.

"Huh?"

"You'd always be second in her ledger, you know. Not to skip ahead too much, but there it is, comrade—a warning. That one's married to the revolution."

"Huh?" Sam said.

see that a certain zeal is at work in my recounting of everything bad, wayward, careless, mean and destructive that marked our last days at Maria's. It's a masochist's zeal, a self-punishing one, perhaps appropriate, but it does leave a lot out. The night after his shouting match with Alex, and the subsequent makeup session, Sam displaced me from the tent altogether—or maybe I volunteered to move? Who can remember from this distance? It was easy enough to see the writing on the tent wall, anyway. I'd talked to Jen on the phone again, self-pityingly floating the idea that she come out to the occupation. It turned out she'd already booked her ticket. By the time she arrived on Saturday evening, the bank's offer to Maria was dead and buried, and Maria had never even known about it.

On Monday morning the police came. Adam Carr got himself flex-cuffed and taken in for "resisting an officer"—no real surprises there. ASU Jason ended up joining him in the holding cell, which surprised me a little more, and Alex and Sam did too, which surprised me not at all. I can still see Sam flushing out of the tent behind Alex on that last morning, like some ridiculous desert bird, the loose folds of his oversize T-shirt flapping against his thin upper arms.

• • •

One more moment in Phoenix, or really in its shadow, its aftermath.

Jen and I had rented a car and were driving up to northern Arizona in gloomy silence. This was according to the plan we'd made, though of course we hadn't planned on any of the preliminaries: getting kicked off the property so roughly, the rushed awkward goodbyes with Maria and her family, the collection we'd had to take up to bail our comrades out of jail—my comrades, anyway. In the back window of the rental car Jen's giant pack hulked, complete with the yoga mats like scroll ends and the hiking sticks that had hung down from either side of Jen, like holy tallithim, when she'd first arrived on Maria's front porch. She said she'd hoped we might get in some Americana on the back end of the trip. I'd said why not.

Quickly to the Grand Canyon, then—above miles of open, carved-out, calcified sky, like loss embodied, a present absence, and where was the vast spiky mold the land had been imprinted with? Taken up into heaven? I really was sounding more and more like Sam.

"Well?" Jen said.

"Well what?"

"Do you like it? Isn't it impressive?"

"Of course it is."

Sienna on darker sienna, burnt umber, ocher, a riot of reddish browns, a vast layer cake of them, and the aerial effect stretching back and back through the dipping receding endless wedges of canyon. It was one of those sights that no amount of pre-seeing could quite prepare you for—I had to admit it—and I had to swallow yet again some of the flippancy I'd reserved for the West with its hard-hewn landscapes, its ancient absences. *Take a freeway excavation, take a foundation dig. That's a new-born canyon, isn't it? Close enough . . .* My father liked to say that forty years wandering in the wilderness had been plenty—he wasn't a camping man either, and my mother didn't press him. Mostly our experience of the outdoors was the woods around our house, the little footpaths cut through brambles and thorns and undergrowth that we walked for exercise or relaxation, or a bit of Frostiana in my poet phase. If serious Jen in her thick hiking boots and spider-bottomed canes had showed up for a walk in the woods south of Boston, she would have felt distinctly overdressed, I'm sure, but the pitch and difficulty of the going would have matched the Grand Canyon rim trail, if not exceeded it. I don't remember breaking a sweat during the hour or two we walked the trail, most of it paved. Large oak and juniper roots sometimes clawed through the pavement and buckled and broke it, but other than that Jen's hiking sticks weren't needed, were merely decorative, something rhythmic to do with her arms. No matter—two-thirds of American sporting was buying the sporting gear, wasn't it?

"A little barbed," Jen said to this, "but I'll take it. At least it's words. At least you're talking."

"I'm sorry. I am sorry. I think I'm still back in Phoenix a little."

"I can tell."

It was then, at a scenic turnout from the trail, in front of an easel-like topography display that showed the Colorado River eating away at the ancient plateau over ages and ages, it was then that I told Jen about the loan manager's compromise we'd left on the table. The evening sunlight was climbing down the rough terraces of stone, the light thickening to orange, moted, honeyed. Jen was silent for a long time, looking out beside me long enough to watch the light change again—it was granular now, arced, the sun slipping down behind the western shelf of a horizon and tipping its last rays brilliantly into the sky like tee-tering cables. Then the edifice collapsed altogether. I reached for Jen's hand in the sudden chill; she allowed it to be taken, squeezed my hand in turn, but I sensed a certain reflex in the gesture, a certain loyalty.

"Of course I regret it now," I said, "in retrospect. I'm sure everyone does . . . But there it is. Anyway, I wanted to give you a little context for my mood."

Jen asked, "Why didn't you tell her?"

"The group decided against it. It was a collective action. You can't go in there with one set of procedural principles, then switch them on a whim, an individualist whim."

"I see."

"I feel awful about it."

"Would you say you did more harm than good in the final analysis?"

"In the final analysis?"

"Don't do your semantics thing. You know what I mean."

"I think it's a little hard to say at this point."

"That's an academic's answer. That's the kind of hedge you hate."

"Yes," I said. "Yes, I think we probably did more harm than good."

The sun was down now, the canyon fading before us, an absence ebbing away into the general absence, and there was another chill in the air, the evacuated high air. The mood had broken, though, like a fever, and on the coarse starchy hotel bed that night Jen and I made love, gently, full of need but careful of it, too, careful of ordinary need—it was strange and lovely. Coming down from those heights the blueing light of the TV played over our bodies. We settled into each other's arms, my shoulder blades cold against the faux-leather pad of a headboard, but only for a moment. In the upper channels we found an old episode of *Columbo*, one of Jen's mother's favorites, one of Jen's favorites, and we drifted off to sleep to the sound of the bumbling, dissembling, charming detective who always gets his man.

We kept on in the morning, up and around the big broad rim of the canyon that looked like a green shifting weather system on the rental car's GPS. Up through piñon forests, the trees bristling from above, roughly uniform, as if a huge sponge of green paint had been dabbed over the land. Up through climbing mountain roads with the sharp rising banks of pinkish earth on either side like geologic cutaways, rocky fins. The land was bunching up, smoothing out again, accordion-like, uncertain. Finally we crossed into Utah, into Sam's old stomping grounds, and the desert sky lowered like a boom, the power lines running eternally up into the high mesas. A rust-red promontory rose in the distance and soon signs were announcing the little town of Kanab. Gassing up there, driving through the gridded downtown, I half expected to see sober bearded men in formal dress, prophetic distraction, leaning their arms out of pickup trucks or trailing their much younger wives behind them in heavy braids and long calico skirts. In the end I saw only a few people, and mostly they were tired-looking, on the older side, and dressed for the heat. In Zion Park, too—this was our destination, the other stop Jen couldn't not stop for, and I was game now—but in Zion it was more of the same. Normal people keeping their outlandish ideas to themselves, apparently. The most foreign experience we had was overhearing a troop of bronzed chatty Germans with their packs and sticks—they looked like Jen, like us. We were doing real hiking this afternoon. The sun was broad and flat and strong and in its light you had to squint through sunglasses to make out the signs and wonders: ANGELS LANDING, 3 MI. Up ahead a giant saddle of red-rock mountain broke from the assorted pines and rose and rose. We stood at the foot of all this, the start of a gradual, switchbacking, rock-walled trail—slow and steady, etc. I wasn't intimidated, but I asked Jen just to be sure.

"Sure I'm sure," she said. "If those Germans can do it, and they have at least twenty years on us."

"They're genetically modified, bear in mind. *Übermenschen.*"

"Here, take one of my sticks."

"It's the Moses look. I'm Charlton Heston."

"Let's go, my people."

A few minutes later, in good breath still, I said, "I'll let you take one of my sticks tonight, if you know what I mean."

"I was hoping you'd say something like that. It's nice to have you back."

The first mile of the hike was easy, or easy enough. The next mile we had to lean into more, the switchbacks narrowing, steepening. All around us vast striated hunks of rosy stone shot up from the green-dotted canyon floor well below us—it was officially intimidating now, and, yes, very beautiful. In the last half mile or so the switchbacks fell away altogether and a long, thin, steadily rising ribbon of blushing stone trail traced the spine of the mountain up to its top. Here the pin oak and piñon didn't range up the sides of the mountain to cast thin shade over the trail—these trees *clung*, they were smaller and sparer, bonsai-like, clinging impossibly to the steep rocky sides of the mountain, their roots like grappling hooks.

"Jesus Christ," I said, looking over the side. "Don't look over the side."

"I know. I know that."

There was a slight tremolo in Jen's voice—I was relieved to hear it, comforted somehow. She had stowed our walking sticks back in their pack-side holsters, the sticks swinging on certain steep boulder-high rises and clacking behind her like giant castanets. In a few minutes we were holding on to cordons of anchored chains, a feature the park had added, Jen informed me, after too many hikers had slipped to their deaths. The steps were of hard uneven red rock, planing away at odd angles, smoothed slick by weather at points, by too many hikers. I stopped to rest for a moment and realized my hands were shaking. When I'd recovered myself a little, I asked Jen how she knew so much about all this anyway. How had a Western yen cropped up among the piano books and conservatory studies of a central New Jersey childhood?

"It was at Randolph," Jen said. "I went through a Messiaen obsession. Do you know him? *From the Canyons to the Stars* is a musical ode to this place."

"It must be terrifying music."

"It's beautiful. A lot of ondes martenot. I've got some on my phone if you want to listen." She looked up and behind her. "Maybe at the top? We should probably concentrate on this last part, huh?"

A rock-hewn stairway the height and pitch of a roller-coaster climb, maybe three feet wide all the way, the little trees down to shrubs now, weeds, mosses, the kind of life that clings to life, and that barely. Five minutes without talking, without breathing, really—all the faces tipped down in seriousness, deep concentration. At the last steel pole anchoring the last length of chain I allowed myself to look up. Jen was there with her outstretched hand, her smile beautiful, heat-blushed, almost sexually relieved, and all that thin blue air behind her.

I rendered my verdict over a lunch of peanut butter and honey sandwiches, gas station trail mix. "I never want to do this again—ever—but I'm glad we've done it. Half of it anyway. And I like the view better than the soundtrack to the view," I said, removing the earbud that piped in Messiaen's high, windy sounds. "Maybe when we get back down to terra firma, huh?"

We were eye level with the high brontosaurus humps that cast everything else in ridiculous relief: the pygmy river below, the pinpricks of large spreading trees, the scrub brush on the river's banks much smaller and vaguer than model train foliage, a kind of mere greeny smudge.

"I don't even want to take pictures," Jen said. "Pictures wouldn't do this justice. I just want to try to remember."

She brought the back of my hand, calm now, to her dry, warm lips. "This is good," she said. "This is a good, good thing."

"I'm glad we did it."

"Do you know what I mean, though? When you wouldn't change anything? On the phone a few nights ago you said you loved me. I think you were a bit buzzed when you said it—"

"I meant it. I mean it."

"I mean it too," Jen said, tipping back her hat brim, lifting the shadow off her white freckled face, smiling. Her mouth was warm and sharp with the taste of peanut butter. It was a long kiss, too long under normal circumstances and in public, but in the hard thin light at the top of Angels Landing, in the gusts of wind that made you brace the stone underneath you, though you were a hundred feet from any edge—in all this a certain inhibition dropped away and an honesty born out of exhaustion came up to take its place, an honesty of the body. We kissed for a very long time. You felt this was a person you could crawl inside of and rest in. This was a person in whom you could find shelter, warmth, affection, understanding, counsel, gentle reproof, love, all good things in good supply.

No one was paying much attention to us anyway. The middle-aged Germans had circled up closer to the edge, passing around clear bags of flax, it looked like, and behind us a regular stream of hikers crested the summit with a rush of relief to blind them almost completely to the amorous couple sitting cross-legged and centered at the summit's rough table, whispering and kissing by turns. Really it was only the little birds that watched us, hopscotching toward our set-aside meals, fearless, darting for crumbs. Yet whispering felt right. It was a fragile thing we'd found, a sudden thing, a kind of secret we'd discovered between the two of us and we were nervous to let it loose in the rough bracing air. Jen said she'd had some recent good news at work to match the good things that were happening in her life with me. When Raymond had learned of her grad school ambitions, he'd taken it upon himself to disabuse her of them. It was a gentle, joshing process, conducted over the course of several weeks of strategic compliments, strategic jokes (*I heard that key change you added—really beautiful playing. Imagine how much better you'd play with eighty, ninety thousand dollars in extra student debt . . .*), all of which culminated in a sit-down lunch a few days ago at a Greek café within view of the Guggenheim, just the two of them. Raymond told her it hadn't been as easy as she might think in New York City to find a gifted sight reader, a gifted musician, who would show up dependably, coax the best out of each of the auditions, and put up with the industry-standard slave wages they paid her. Not to mention the transcribing and arranging she'd volunteered to do in her after-hours.

Here Jen interrupted her story. "Raymond talks as if that kind of thing is drudgery, but it's just because *he's* tired of doing it. I love it. You think the natural medium for composition is the instrument itself, and it is, but it also isn't. Until a piece moves from the keys to the staves it's just this fleeting, private, unstable thing."

"So he's got you composing for him?"

"Not for him exactly. He works with a network of composers and songwriters, some of whom pride themselves on being 'intuitive' musicians. That's code for theory illiterate. Sometimes he'll just give me a songwriter's practice files and it's my job to try to make something out of them. Then last week he sent me a raw score, something he was co-writing, 'toying with,' he said. It's a reworking of *Kiss Me, Kate*, and it's a mess. It's just placeholders, vague ideas. My job was again to punch up what was there, make it more rigorous, more complete—"

"Are you getting paid for any of this, Jen? Did Raymond really call them 'slave wages'? If he's only paying you with compliments, he's underpaying you."

"Easy, Engels, easy. I'm getting there."

"But the upshot is you're not applying to grad schools again? You're quitting?"

"Eli, let me finish the story. We're still at the fancy Greek place, square plates, several forks—you see where this is going, right? Raymond loves the work I've done on the score. Everybody who's gotten back my work, whether it's transcribing or 'organizing,' quote-unquote, everybody says great things, you know? I'm really good at this, Eli, and Raymond recognizes that. He gave me a substantial raise, and I see what you're thinking—you'll just have to trust me that it's substantial. But he gave me a raise and a week's vacation—hence this trip, this view—and he also said he's going to get me a co-writing credit on the score if he can scare up the funding to produce it."

"Why is any of this exclusive of graduate school? I thought that's what you wanted."

"It's what I thought I wanted. But I didn't know what I wanted. I was frightened. I'm a classical musician in the twenty-first century, I'm always worried about where the next rent check's coming from. But this could be a good thing, you know? Eli? I thought you'd be happier for me."

"I am, sweetie," I said, "I am. Of course I am. Come here."

Everyone was dropping out of graduate school. It was a sinking ship, with the true believers stuck in steerage. I limped along for my sixth year at Randolph, picking up courses through Hahn's generosity, her forbearance, really. I wasn't much more diligent in my acquittal of duties than I had been before, showing up to meetings with papers half graded, or very, very loosely graded, intending to go back to the batch once I'd survived the norming sessions and do the students the justice they deserved. It didn't always happen. I tried to imagine in each student a Jennifer Daugherty banking on her grade in Poli Sci 110 like she banked on a scholarship disbursement, or a meal—it didn't always help. Hahn and I still met occasionally for dinner, usually at the Moroccan café near her apartment, which really was excellent. It was as if a certain region of my palate had been waiting and waiting for the taste of tagine, like the soul's lost half that Plato describes, and now it had found it and needed to binge. Hahn usually paid, despite my halfhearted objections. "Don't embarrass yourself," she said once. "If you had the money you wouldn't be TAing for me, would you?" She also knew not to ask about my dissertation or the grant money I'd frittered away in its name. I knew not to ask about Stephen, her dying husband. I had seen him a time or two more—he wasn't squirreled away, Hahn wasn't embarrassed of him—but the effect of the brief encounters was chilling, if I'm honest, a constraint on the rest of the night. Steve spoke through an electrolarynx now. The thing had attacked his very vocal cords—ravenous, ravenous appetite, devouring him wholly, cutting him off from the world of friends and acquaintances, who could only smile so long in the presence of his world-weary jokes, his self-deprecations, crudified now by the stiff toneless voice entrusted to deliver them, as if his mind had been switched out for a hard drive. I said none of this, of course, not to Hahn, much less to Stephen, not to anyone. Yet they both sensed it coming off me—they must have—like a scent. Steve leveled his weak whey face at me one day and said through the electrolarynx, "The trouble with living death is that the party goes on without you, doesn't it?" And Hahn, pushing me to the door, said, "Please, honey. I'll be back in an hour."

What was happening with Sam and Alex and the rest of the Phoenix crowd? Not much that I observed. I knew Jamaal and his willowy Afro and his bright, loud loose-fitting clothes had come east from Arizona. I saw him around at a few ISO meetings—he stuck out pleasantly from the somber gray-clad masses of Manhattan. I knew he was in Queens now, with Sam and Alex and a few others from the occupation. Sam had invited me out to their rented house in a couple of tepid text exchanges, or in the post-tennis banter that began to feel forced, sparse, windy—and pretty soon months had gone by without us seeing or communicating with each other. We'd never really talked about what we'd done together in Phoenix, only about the heat and the fucked-up politics of the place. They didn't even celebrate Martin Luther King Day, Sam informed me.

One day in the middle of my seventh year at Randolph—and believe me that that number could sometimes catch me up breathless—but one day I left Hahn's office after yet another norming session and set a course walking due south. It was late afternoon and I was on my way to meet Jen and her parents for dinner at an old, dark-wood-paneled place I hadn't heard of, but apparently it was swank and soaked through with history, a holdover from Melville's Manhattan. *There now is your insular city of the Manhattoes*, the poet of the sea had written, *belted round by wharves as Indian isles by coral reefs—commerce surrounds it with her surf.* I'd been rereading *Moby-Dick*, some of Beckett too, tacking on to Steve's obsessions, or maybe just avoiding my dissertation. What this meant in practical terms was that I now carried thick books in my shoulder bag that thumped against my side like an unwieldy externalized heartbeat. The books were giant, world-swallowing, absurd, but of course their very absurdity made them necessary, and their necessity made them absurd (this is from Beckett's *Watt*, I believe). In any case, I found comfort in this course of reading, a comfort I tried to draw on now as I headed south toward the commerce-racked Wall Street of my destination. Silly to say, I know, but lower

Manhattan often put me in a gloomy, End Times mood, as if it weren't just the edge of the island I slid toward but the edge of the world, a fifteenth-century seaman, superstitious, scared of sea dragons and usurers, evidently. That my fiancée and her quiet hippie parents waited for me at the end of my journey made it a little less treacherous, but only a little.

Away from the noise and harry of the avenues, I was cutting through Washington Square Park when I heard a familiar voice. It was high, insistent, straining against the wind, shouting out rhythmic, rising lines about billion-dollar cables going into the ground to help the rich get richer faster, about the rising compensation for the top one-tenth of one percent—we weren't the ninety-nine percent anymore, we were the ninety-nine-point-*nine* percent, the vast democratic many against an oligarchic few, and the oligarchs were winning! And why? The rest of us didn't care enough, we weren't mad enough, we weren't *organized* enough! Alex waved a rolled-up copy of the *Socialist Worker* at passing head-bowing students. They leaned forward under their heavy backpacks like Sherpas, or stared at their phones all the more intently. Alex looked like she might just whap the shy passersby with her newspaper, like an owner to a dog that shits the rug. Her hair was jet-black, India-ink-black, much darker than usual—she must have dyed it—and against that sharp-cut contrast her olive skin looked flour-white. It was as if Sam had rubbed off on her too. I should mention it was March, the sun was dead and buried beneath a thick slate sky, the streets constantly dark and wet. Everyone's skin seemed to luminesce a bit more, glowing dully or brightly pale as the case might be—we were a city of deep-sea invertebrates. It was still a little startling to see Alex's pallor, though, seeing her unseen as she shook her head after another slip of undergraduates. She looked geisha-like, a little thinner, too, around the jawline and the long pale neck that descended into a gray wool scarf, a long peacoat. The small stud was gone from her nose, I noticed, only a blemish-like dot where the piercing used to be. I was almost on top of her before she saw me.

"You," she said.

"You," I said. "You're still alive!"

"I'm still alive."

"Where have you been? How are you? I hear you and Sam moved in together?"

"Something like that," Alex said. "We're all keeping a low profile for now."

"What does that mean?"

She didn't answer me.

I said I hadn't expected to see her out paper-driving and sloganeering. I was under the impression she had more or less quit the ISO. It was almost a year since I'd seen her at meetings.

"Those meetings are a joke," Alex said. "They're just masturbatory grad students and undercover cops. And this stuff"—she gestured wand-like to the square with a rolled-up newspaper, as if she'd be content to make it all disappear—"this is mostly a decoy. We're not going to find anyone for the Group here."

"Come again?"

"We're not going to find anybody for the Group we haven't already found."

"*The* Group?" I said. "I thought Jamaal was joking. The Phoenix Group? You guys have a name now?"

"Mostly just the Group," Alex said, "and Sam wanted a name. I don't particularly care one way or the other. It's just—"

She cut herself off, stiffening the shoulders she'd lifted

lazily. Her look had changed; her eyes stared past me, wide, walleyed. I turned to see a tall man in a bloated dark parka, dark sunglasses, and a pulled-down beanie sprinting toward us with long swift windmilling strides. Something flashed in his hand, metallic, shearing light—he was right on top of me, swerving at me, and I still hadn't put together who he was—and now the shiny something punched hard and flat against the open V of my jacket, right against my shirted sternum, shocking me. The blow pushed me back several steps, took the wind out of me less with the force of it than the shock.

"Move!" the man said in Sam's voice, but deeper, gruffer, and he took back his arm and pushed past me, sprinting on. I felt the hard weighted thing slide down the front of my shirt inside my coat, lodging at my waistband, as a late teen in a blue ski jacket broke out from behind a crowd of other students. He was red-faced, yelling after Sam. "Stop him! Stop him!"

The student rushed past us before I could get a good look at him, but he went with the reckless, splay-footed stride of a non-runner, a non-athlete. This was Sam's salvation, apparently. Alex was pulling me away. She had the paper-drive samples tucked under one arm, her other hooked through mine and pulling me in tight. We moved briskly but not too briskly.

"What the hell was that about?" I said.

"Don't look back there," she said. "Come on."

We exited the park and sought refuge in a dark Irishy sports bar a block south of NYU—mounted TVs showing *SportsCenter*, a scrum of freestanding tables beside the bar, a wall-hugging row of high-backed vinyl booths, unaccountably sticky, each with a dim green hanging pool lamp over a thick slab of dark-wood table. It was against one of these that I slapped the weighted rectangular packet I'd removed from my waistband. An encased iPhone. It looked new, newish. Alex plucked it off the table.

"Turn it off," she said. "They've got these tracking things now. Oh, wait, oh wow, this genius didn't even set a passlock."

"What the fuck are you doing, Alex?"

"Restoring to . . . factory settings . . . now . . . and now . . . done."

The screen that had dimly etched the lines of Alex's face went dark and the face with it. She put the phone in her pocket and laced her fingers together on the tabletop.

"You know what I meant," I said. "What are you guys doing?"

"Yes," she said, "I know what you meant."

Again her eyes shot away from me and I followed them to the door of the bar—it closed slowly and heavily, restoring the gloom as a middle-aged man in a ponytail shuffled over to the barstools. A minute later Alex's eyes did the same wary tracking and this time the door admitted Sam in blue jeans, a thin gray sweatshirt, the top half of long johns, it looked like, and a rather bulging backpack that slung off him like a reverse kangaroo pouch. He'd lost the sunglasses, the pulled-down beanie, and in their place he wore a crooked, triumphal smile. He slid into the booth beside Alex and kissed her on the temple.

"I get your adrenaline up?"

"You're such an amateur," she said, fighting a smile of her own.

"Proudly, proudly." He turned to me. "Old buddy old pal, how have you been? Jamaal told us about your engagement—congrats, mazel tov, many happy returns. Oh, and thanks for the help back there. I didn't hurt you, did I?"

"What are you guys doing?" I said again. "You're common thieves now?"

"Common thieves," Alex scoffed. "Do you hear this guy? At least we have a cause to expropriate *for*, Eli. What do you have—mood swings? Judge not lest ye be judged, am I right?"

"Good God. Sam really has worn off on you, hasn't he?"

My old friend looked taken aback at this, pulling his head back, literally, on his neck, turtle-like. The progress of the last several months seemed to have pushed the tide of his hairline noticeably farther up his forehead, hollowing out the pool of his cowlick bald patch that much more, the place where his cowlick used to be. When he looked up from the table I could see his jaw sharpening, the small fibrous muscles twitching through a swallow.

"We haven't seen each other in a while," Sam said. "Some things have obviously changed, but it's good to see you. Congratulations on your engagement."

"Thank you."

"What else is new? How's the dissertation coming? Sensitive question?"

"Sam," I said, "Alex, I need to know why you're stealing phones from hapless undergraduates."

"They'll be fine," Alex said. "Send an e-mail to Mom and Dad and a new phone's in the mail same day. These trust-fund kids . . ." Alex's face went bright with remembering and she turned to Sam, taking his hand with a thoughtless easy intimacy. "Your Doogie Howser today didn't even set a password lock on his phone."

"You already wiped it?"

"We can post it tonight."

Sam reached under the booth and from the squeal of zippers produced three more phones. He dealt them neatly onto the table in front of him, one beside the next beside the next, bracketing them with his forearms.

"A good day then," he said to Alex, though really he was looking at me. "One of them's locked, but let Jamaal work his magic and who knows . . ."

"Wow," said Alex. "Impressive trawl."

Sam hadn't removed his eyes from me when he said, "We can get up to four hundred for a phone in good condition. Jamaal jimmies with the ones we pick up locked. Tiffany posts to an online marketplace from a safe IP address—she knows computers too, apparently."

"Tiffany's in on this?"

"You haven't seen her around campus much either, have you?"

"Adam's in too. ASU Jason came out last summer after he graduated," Alex added.

"Why are you telling me all this?" I said. "What happened to mooching off family and friends, getting *our* parents to put money in the mail same day?"

"That's not adequate anymore," Sam said. "And for me expropriation is the only way I can contribute. My folks haven't exactly been openhanded since my first arrest."

"Your *first* arrest?"

Sam looked to Alex, raising his shoulders and eyebrows in subtle tandem.

"The reason we're telling you this," Alex said, "is because we miss you. We really do want you on board. What are you accomplishing with all those motions and sober discussions at ISO meetings, all that impotent talk? We've got actual plans in the Group," she said, tossing the stack of *Socialist Workers* to fan out on the table. "A lot more than hocking dead trees at NYU students, that's for sure."

"Like what?" I said.

"Are you in?" Alex said. "You could still keep on at Randolph if you really wanted to, though I don't see why you'd want to at this point."

Sam put in, "We've collected a decent little group out there—they're all serious, good people. You'd like them."

"Vanguards," I said. "You guys sound like you're putting together a party of amateur vanguards."

"Which of those words is a dirty word?" Sam's face approached another thought, then backed away from it. "You know what? We're being way too sober about this. Let's get some beers in us, catch up a bit—we are at a bar, aren't we? First round's on me?"

Sam raised his arm to flag a server as I reached my own across the table, slowly, with all the energy drained from it, with old battery acid sludging up my veins. I picked up one of the stolen phones, pressed the power button at the top and brought up a screensaver photo of two twentysomething men, lovers by the look of their smiles, their two smooth faces pressed together at the cheeks, their eyes tipping up for the camera.

"The happy couple," I said, pushing the phone back to Sam, who fumbled quickly to turn it off again.

"Looks like we're leaving," he said.

"You'll be sorely missed."

"You're a real prick sometimes, you know that?" Alex said to me.

I'd started into a slow clap, just loud enough. "Excellent work, guys. Really noble, important work. Hey guys?"

At the door they didn't turn around.

• • •

I stayed on at the random sports bar for a beer or three or four—it was only polite to the server who'd arrived with his ordinary face to take my order. Probably a trust-fund face in disguise, in poor face.

Adrenaline must have propped me up, like a laboratory monster, to get me the rest of the way to the dinner with Jen's parents that night—they were just sitting down when I arrived—but now when I think of the meal I remember almost nothing from it. Jim Daugherty survives as a pair of beige broad cheeks looming up from across the table, Evelyn Daugherty, paler-complected, gray-haired, a wavering smile at her lips . . . I remember the smile beginning to crack a little as I turned aside the questions about my dissertation, with bluff practiced quips, about the academic job market I was assumed to be preparing for, about the wedding Jen and I were assumed to be planning—

"What *can* you tell us, Eli?" Evelyn said at one point, or something like that. "You're awfully slippery tonight."

"I'm against positivism," I think I said. "Just say no to the positive, no?"

On the train ride home Jen said to me—and this I remember distinctly, her voice a sort of jump-start to the stalling apparatus—"Are they such outlandish questions to ask? Are they really so prying?"

I heard the threat of water in her voice, a bed of hard stony gravel underneath it. "What?"

"It's like you're giving a deposition: 'We can neither confirm nor deny that we've set a date. Those discussions are ongoing and private.'"

"Is that really what I sounded like?"

"They were making polite fucking conversation, Eli! They're trying to get to know their future son-in-law!"

"I've had a really shitty day, Jen. I don't want to talk about it right now—"

"Oh *you've* had a shitty day?"

"No, look, I'm sorry. That's not what I meant. Jen?"

She'd already turned her face away as a couple in their rain-sheened winter coats sat down beside us. Was it raining outside? I might have seen a tearful rivulet, too, in the L train's dark reflecting window. I tried to talk to the back of Jen's silent, unyielding head, leaning in close to that forest of scented hair. She never turned around.

When we got back to the apartment it was Mallory's presence that now intervened—politesse like a gag order. Jen didn't want to talk in the privacy of our bedroom. What if Mallory heard us? Didn't mortified voices cut through walls?

Or maybe she'd just finished talking for the night.

For the next several hours, with the lights in the room dropping off one by one, all I heard was the buzz of intensifying rain through the open window. It was Jen's long habit to leave the window at least a little ajar, rain or shine, night or day, winter, spring, summer, fall—much more important that the air should "circulate," the thinking went, than that the heating or AC bills should stay low. I'd made the mistake of challenging this custom early on, a Daugherty ritual, apparently, a *trait*, deep-sunk in the family gene pool. She'd just always done it that way, she said. She couldn't imagine getting to sleep in a shut-in room. And I should be grateful she wasn't her father, known to put up a full window fan in full winter. Things could always be worse.

I sat at the foot of Jen's bed—our bed—fully clothed, while

Jen's sleeping form hardly disturbed the smooth covers. I hadn't been banished here, exactly; it was more like a self-exile, a self-quarantine. I needed to understand my own mind. How often had Jen hinted at a date herself, or tried to joke her way into the conversation, and how often had I diverted it to other topics, diverting her with a quip or two about bourgeois respectability, the race for a bread maker, a new dish set. Of course none of that actually accounted for my hesitation—I knew that much about myself. Nor was it the mulish, dumb-male commitment paralysis. On nights like this I felt closer to the truth as I narrowed my inward vision to that sludge of old battery acid climbing up my veins, rising like a dark hardening *stuff* through the tubes and byways to stuff up my heart. A hemlock of self-loathing, a sense of waste, in both senses of that word. I knew Jen could do better than me.

A rill of cold air sank in from the windowsill, pebbling my skin at the thought. In spite of precedent I covered up Jen's exposed arched feet; she'd kicked off the covers again a moment later. On a typical night, I imagined that the bottom hem of the covers and sheets must have looked like a tangled trapezoid, slanting up sharply from left to right—left was my side of the bed, right was Jen's.

A sudden panic seized me— *If I should ever lose her* . . .

I moved to the little alcove of Jen's side-sleeping body, reached my hand out to her shoulder.

"Please don't," the voice said, quiet and crystalline.

"I thought you were asleep."

"No."

"Oh . . ."

She rolled away from me, facing the other side of the bed.

I said, "What were you doing if you weren't sleeping?"

"I was thinking."

"What about?"

I said, "Sweetie? Talk to me. Please."

"Do you have any idea how much you embarrassed me tonight? Showing up like that, obviously drunk, slurring your words, and then what you actually did say—or didn't! All your evasiveness, like you'd been forced to submit to a police investigation."

I rested my hand again, almost imperceptibly, on Jen's shoulder.

"Please, Eli."

"I want to explain myself. I want to feel close to you . . . It's like—I don't know—you want your life to be worthy of the person you love. You want an equal exchange, an equal merger of lives going into something like this, and I'm just not there right now. I'm not even close. I have these days where it all becomes painfully apparent to me, how much time I've wasted, how little I have to show for what I've done. Today was one of those days. It's not an excuse, I know, and I am sorry. Genuinely. I'll write a note to your parents tomorrow."

"Don't. That'll just bring more attention to it."

"Tell me what to do then. Tell me what to do."

"Why did you even propose to me, Eli? Why did you let me say yes?"

"A girl like Jennifer Daugherty you've got to lock down."

"No. No quips. If you can't say it straight—"

"This is a lifelong relationship. I wanted you to know that. And it is—*it is*. You do know that, don't you? You have to. Jen?"

At length she reached up and took my hand. I got under the covers as she gathered it to her breast, the steep rise and fall of her back against my shirted chest. We'd be okay, I told her. I promised we'd be okay, pulling her in close to me, being pulled, my arm held to Jen's waist with a sudden animal force, a boa constriction to force our love out into the open air where we could catch and keep it, trap it alive.

"Do you promise?" Jen was whispering. "Do you promise me?"

"I promise," I said. "I promise we'll be okay."

One other point to pick up from the dinner that night, with Jen's mother asking the questions—Evelyn, who'd also wanted to know about my dissertation and my plans for the academic job market, and who'd balked when I turned her questions aside so glibly, something I regret now. The truth is I'd given up on academia altogether. I'd started looking for other jobs, halfheartedly at first, in the short term, with my grad school funding running down. I knew an eighth year at Randolph was basically out of the question, and when Hahn confirmed this to me I took it more or less in stride. I did get a little chippy with her, which is something else I regret.

"I thought you knew the end was nigh," Hahn said to me, at lunch this time. "I figured you must have known."

"No, I didn't," I lied.

"Well, are you even close to finishing?"

"You know I'm not."

Hahn explained that if I could somehow finish my dissertation over the summer the department might just see its way clear to a final extension of funding while I went out on the academic market. But just that phrase in Hahn's mouth—the academic market!

I was all the more determined to seek my money elsewhere—

skipping ahead to the stopgap economy, then, to the indignities of a job search in the late-capitalist city. I'd applied already to the Strand and McNally Jackson, and later I tried Greenlight Bookstore, BookCourt, WORD, Housing Works Bookstore, Barnes & Noble (four of them in two boroughs), Kaplan Test Prep Center, Central Park Tutors, Huntington Learning Center, Brooklyn Roasting Company, the Queens Kickshaw, Ninth Street Espresso, Applebee's (three of them in three boroughs), TGI Friday's (two in two), Mike the Glazier, Sasha's Framing and Supplies, Gotham Carpet Cleaners, Starbucks—a month, a month and a half of my life, not to mention the job applications I'm probably forgetting. I did get a quick call back from a slow-voiced Starbucks manager, but I let the message languish. I was waiting on too many others, I told myself, but really I could see how it would go: the studious distance on the faces of the mock-busy clerks, their neutral smiles as I described my long-ago experience in retail, leaving behind my applications just in case. Thanks, sure, they'd see what they could do . . .

Apparently tip jobs were out, too. You needed to know somebody, Mallory said. She knew that much from experience. One night over takeout Indian I asked her about her job as a paralegal at a midtown law office, the job that had helped her afford the nicer place she and Jen now rented together, the two-bedroom in Greenpoint, Brooklyn, the sometimes fortress of politesse. If we'd gone straight three-ways on the rent, I'd have come up empty-pockets in no time. Not that Jen had asked me to three-ways the rent, and not that I'd made my discomfort explicit—another long story, ages long, I suppose, stretching back at least as far as Abraham and Isaac and all the other patri-archs. How that foolishness clings to a man!

I was asking Mal about her paralegal job. What exactly

did it entail? What did it pay? Did she like her boss—bosses? What?

"Oh, no, I'm not laughing at you," she said, "I'm laughing at me. The pay's pretty bad when you think of all the work you take home, all the extra hours you put in. Your boss is pretty much anyone in the office with a law degree, which means you work for a wide and impressive variety of assholes. I'd say the best preparation for paralegal work is a major in vocal performance and a crushing amount of student debt. Or maybe a gambling problem? That could work too."

Impish and thin-faced, her brown-green eyes spaced just a breath too wide apart, or maybe it was the way her long nose spread out very suddenly into the broader delta of her brows— but there was something slightly alien in Mallory's look, over-evolved, knowing. Mal Mallory. She was bad cop to Jen's good on most nights, and on most nights that took some doing. They goaded each other to heights of greater and greater outrageousness.

"You *like* when they treat you bad," Jen said. "Don't you?"

We sat at the high table on high wooden stools in Jen and Mallory's kitchen alcove. I didn't place myself on the possessive deed after three months of living there—I wouldn't after four months, five, not even after another round of lowlier applications finally turned up a job at Tommy's Pizza and Subs in Astoria and I started paying something, meager somethings toward the rent. I knew I was an impostor no matter how much Jen tried to reassure me to the contrary.

"Well, maybe I like it a little," Mal said. "I do like a few spanks from those paddles they've all kept from their prelaw fraternities."

"Sororities too."

"Of course. They hit the hardest. More to prove."

"On your bare ass, I hope."

"Where else? Undies at my ankles, bent over one of those big, hard, ergonomic chairs—"

"Wow," I said, "you're really going for this, aren't you?"

"You're uncomfortable? He's uncomfortable again," Mal said to Jen, with her sideways smile, the knowing look that at once acknowledged and excluded me from the long-held rhythms of their friendship. I didn't begrudge them these moments—I understood them, took a certain comfort in them. Why shouldn't they feel comfortable enough to look around me at times, through me?

Our tri-sided dinners became little islands, little points of reprieve for all of us soon enough. In the evenings I was now coming home with the smell of flour and marinara sauce like some aural tattoo on the inside of my nostrils. This is still the abiding impression of my time at Tommy's: burnt flour, the insidious, crystalline spread of it, an unstoppable osmosis. It mixed almost festively with the red sauce on my pine green apron, speckled and spattered—Pollock comes to mind too, and again, except that here the artistry consists of mindlessly circling sauce onto eight-inch disks of personal pan pizza dough. Better that, I figured, than working the firing range at the front of the kitchen. It wasn't just that the range sat in plain view of impatient customers, or that the stinging bits of boiling cheese and meaty grease jumped up and bit your soft inner wrists, the feel of fire ants—it was also Marco, it was *mostly* Marco, the beak-nosed ponytailed manager who ran the register and policed the grill like an Iron Guardist. From behind, the short gathered rump of his ponytail looked like a cowering rodent through the gap in his pine green hat. Then snapping around, he'd bark at you about the order on your left, the order on your left was burning, it was drying out, and the one on your right, you'd forgotten the cheese, and the one in front of you you were taking off already? Hold it, hold it, here, *wait*, and he'd motion for Rodney with the tattoos like smudges on his thin black arms to take over at the register. He'd shoulder me aside, literally, with a line of customers looking on, scoop up the of-fending brown sizzling mass of meat and vegetables and cheese, flip it, redice it in expert time, the spatulas blurring, drop one of the spatulas to grab a squeeze bottle of water to prime the grill, drop more cheese, prime again, and scoop up the salvaged sandwich into its waiting roll, just so.

"Impressive," I said once.

"It's not that impressive, Stopgap. Mix the ingredients to-gether, heat them up, put them in a fucking roll, and fast. It's not rocket science. You don't even need a PhD to do it."

"Good thing, too, since I don't have a PhD."

"Shut up, Stopgap."

By the time I got home from a shift and showered and dressed, and went out for pickup perhaps, I could feel a little of my humanity beginning to return, like the skin of my fin-gers that eventually smoothed and re-plumped when I'd been on dish duty. (I still carried the sharp smell of burnt flour in my nostrils, though, always, always, as if I'd been snorting the stuff.) After dinner Jen usually retired to the piano and I took up my spot on the brown suede couch under the gooseneck reading lamp. I read Beckett or Melville or one of Jen's mystery novels, whatever I wanted now, reading to the sounds of Jen's evolving score for *June vs. Hurricane*. After the modest Off-Broadway success of the *Kiss Me, Kate* reboot, Raymond had secured enough funding for an original musical comedy that he and Jen had now collaborated on for a year: Raymond was the words man, Jen the music. It had taken no small effort on my part, but finally I'd convinced Jen to unplug the headphones and let the apartment listen in. She was in the final stages, she said, fine-tuning, which was the only reason she'd agreed. And we shouldn't get used to it: In the blank-page phase of composition she'd rather sit stark naked on the piano bench than unplug her headphones. In that case, I said, I wouldn't mind.

One night Jen was playing and playing again through a spare but rising, plaintive recitative section. I asked if recitative was the right word for it in a musical.

"Good question," Jen said. "Let's say yes? Why not? Wagner called his operas 'musical dramas.' He didn't mind mixing terminologies."

"Shall I get you a Wagner bust for your electric piano?"

"Have him scowling maybe."

"My frowning baby's frowning muse."

She showed the real thing at this, or a hammy simulacrum of it: the pursed mouth, the diving brows . . .

In truth her composing face looked less like a frown than an all-face furrowing, an intense gathering in of the features as if by some inward centrifugal force. She didn't like me watching her as she worked, but I'd done enough surreptitious observation to get to know and love this muscular squinch. I think she may have needed glasses, too.

Jen returned to the music, waiting music, spare but rising, quietly yearning. In Raymond's draft of the libretto (why not?) the main character, June, wanders a Jersey Shore boardwalk as the light fades. (Raymond, like Jen, was a New Jersey native, and this was another point of bonding between them.) The music rose only to drop down again, wavering, foraying down into the muddier depths of the piano as something brooded, something took shape. It was Hurricane Sandy. On this particular evening Jen had Raymond's lyrics up on the stand, sometimes singing them under her breath. *What can I do when there is nothing to do? What can I say when there is nothing to say?* A little moody for a romcom, I said from behind her. I'd moved over from the couch—hovering, yes, but then the words weren't her words. I hadn't realized that the title of the musical referred to a literal hurricane, but there it was looming up in the stage directions: [*storm sounds rise, winds, rain . . . whatever the budget can manage!*]. I made a comment about this too and drew a swiveled rebuke from Jen—her pressed-lip smile, an abridgment of a smile.

"How's Beckett coming? Or Melville? Or who is it you're reading for your dissertation these days? How's that coming along?"

It wasn't. I'd abandoned my dissertation once and for all, as I've told you, and I'd been meaning to make this clear to Jen for weeks now, months. For now I said, "I know I'm being annoying—I just thought it was lighter fare, a sort of coming-out comedy."

"It's light and it isn't," said Jen. "I don't know. Raymond's changed things around a bit."

"June's still in high school, though, still struggling to tell her parents and her boyfriend?"

"On leave from college now. Her father's sick."

"Her father's sick?"

"Colon cancer."

"Jesus."

"Well, people get sick."

"Does she still come out to them?"

"It's harder now. There's more at stake. They're strict evangelicals."

"Strict evangelicals on the Jersey Shore?"

"Please, Eli. I'm trying to do this."

"It's too much," I said. "Sexual repression, religious fanaticism, colon cancer, a devastating hurricane ... Are you guys sure about all this?"

"Sure, *we're* sure about it," Jen said, suddenly fierce and reaching for her headphones on the stand.

It was around that same time that I started meeting up with Sam again, too.

It's a kind of admission to say it, to recall it, and almost as unflattering to me as the ham-handed incursions I've showed myself making into Jen's evolving musical. (It wasn't really hers to evolve, I soon saw.) But the truth is I enjoyed seeing my old friend again. He'd somehow found out where I worked and was now coming into Tommy's on Tuesdays and Fridays, our ancient tennis days, buying Gatorades from the little counter refrigerator and sitting at a table with *Flesh as Collateral*, say, or *Us vs. Us: Corporate Schismatic Strategies and How to Combat Them*, or some such awfulness that he'd diligently read and take notes on as he waited for my shift to end. For my part, I'd started bringing a duffel bag to work.

Into the back comes Marco one slow afternoon, the shop cavernous in its post-post-lunch-rush silence. I was washing the counters, the dishes done. Rodney was on his phone in the break room, really an alcove with a mini fridge and a stool. When I heard Marco's step, I turned around and tried not to grimace. He was smiling nose-first, as he always seemed to do, his close narrow lips curling up and around the crooked totem so that it looked like the nose had leveraged the smile, winched it up by pulleys. His eyes were small and dark brown. With his hat off, the pulled-back slick of his hair looked flat and dully grooved, like a record.

"Your boyfriend's here, Stopgap. Looking hornier than usual, I must say."

"That's good. Very good. That'll do nicely in the harassment suit."

His smile widened.

"Speaking of which," I said, "why 'Stopgap'? Have I ever said anything about this job being temporary?"

"Your face says it, Stopgap, your slow-ass work says it, the way you talk—everything about you says it."

"I see."

Marco mocked the phrase back at me Britishly, then lifted his chin at the wall clock and told me I could finish up the counters and head out at the top of the hour. Some thirty minutes early.

"Let no one say you're not a broad-minded, magnanimous man," I called after him.

"See you tomorrow, Stopgap."

At the top of the hour I went to the back room to change into my tennis gear and retrieve the personal effects Marco made us store in a bank of blue lockers the size of several shoe boxes stuck together. An old-school gesture. He didn't want us out front with our phones, zombie-eyed and head-hung as customers came in. I found the rule equal parts repressive and endearing, a bit old school myself, obviously, but now I found it merely tempting, especially in my present mood, since managerial Marco, efficient Marco, stupid Marco had somehow left his locker's padlock unfastened in its catch. The little arm of the lock hung free just above the joining place. Was this hubris or accident on his part? Was it a cosmic Dare? Inside the locker I saw a wallet and a Samsung phone—I took both of them, leaving only a pair of keys behind.

Outside, I followed Sam toward the subway, shaking. Summer lay heavily on the city, the damp heat and the sick-sweet garbage smells rising, the sheets of light coming off the mirrored buildings. At an intersection a crosstown breeze brought a moment's relief—the sun went behind clouds, the glass storefronts revealing their wares again. For a moment people seemed to speak softly on the sidewalks, soothingly, for my benefit, but my hands still shook. I told Sam I was quitting my job at Tommy's.

"Oh yeah?" he said. "What happens after you quit? You got something else lined up?"

I pulled out the cell phone and the wallet to present to him—a puppyish gesture. I'm embarrassed of it now.

"What's this?" Sam said.

I told him.

"Are you kidding me?"

"What?"

"How fucking stupid are you?"

"From your glass house you throw stones," I said.

Sam started back the way we'd come. "Come on, we're going back."

"What the fuck are you talking about?"

"We're going back, moron! Come on! Do you know how traceable you are? Hurry!"

We walked double-time back to Tommy's, where Marco

was manning the register with a bored, slack expression that wavered into a smirk when he saw me. I'd just be a minute, I'd forgotten something in the back room.

"Couldn't keep away, eh?" he called after me. "You like us that much, Stopgap? Awww, Stopgap . . ."

Morose Rodney was still on his cell phone in the back, still on break. He looked up as I passed into the little room with the lockers. "Forgot something," I said, half choking on the word as I saw with an all-body clench that I'd shut up the padlock, or someone had. I pulled down on the lock and nothing happened. I yanked down—quietly, quietly, but I yanked—and nothing happened. I rotated the first of three crenellated number strips and pulled down at steady intervals. Nothing. Hot breathlessness filled my body. I could hardly hold the lock for shaking. How long had I been in here? Shaking, I tried the leftmost strip again, forcing myself to go slow, stopping at each crenellated break in the silver number line, rotating, stopping and pulling, rotating—

Pure liquid feeling broke open in me as the catch fell suddenly open.

"You okay?" Rodney said from behind me.

I whirled around—"Shit!"—feigning shock, tearing wallet and phone from my pocket and throwing them clanging into the locker, falling against it. My shock was genuine enough, come to think of it—only the laugh I faked.

"You scared the shit out of me!" I said.

Rodney stood in the doorway. He made no response, only slid his eyes left toward the sound of approaching footsteps.

"Where'd your boyfriend go?" Marco said. "I'd hate to think we offended him."

I grabbed my duffel bag and started for the door. I said I'd accidentally taken my phone charger with me the first time and decided to come back to drop it off. Bad battery on the phone, probably needed a replacement—

"Your locker's open," Marco said, nodding.

Idiotically I followed his eyes to where the blue metal door gaped open and dark as a mouth.

"Wait, isn't that my locker? What the fuck is my locker doing open?"

He looked from me to Rodney, moving quickly to his property, checking his phone, rifling through his wallet.

"I saw him throw something in there."

"It was an accident."

"I don't see any cell-phone chargers," Marco said.

"It was an accident. You can stop looking. I didn't take anything from your fucking wallet, Marco."

"And I should take *your* word for it?" Marco said, suddenly turning on me, chesting into me. "The fucking thief?"

"Am I? What kind of thief brings the stuff back, asshole?" I tried to sound angry, affronted, but my body backed sheepishly toward the door.

"Don't you dare move. Rodney, keep him there. Who do I even call for this? Do you call 9-1-1? Jesus God—Rodney, keep him there, keep him while I find a fucking number for the cops."

"Oh, that's perfect: 'Yes, hi, 9-1-1? I wish to report that nothing at all has happened. Nothing was taken from me. I'm just a paranoid bigoted piece of shit.'"

Rodney grabbed halfheartedly at my forearm, but I broke past him into the open store.

"You don't think the cops care about attempted robbery?"

I was backing through the dining room, hip-checking tables, ready to run if Marco pursued me out of the back.

"I've got your name, I've got your address," he shouted, "I've got your work address, you fucking thief! Where you *used* to work—"

I crashed out of the store and fell into a jangled run-walk, a jittery dance that could have fooled no one. Sam stepped out from under his prearranged awning, his face like a moon reflecting mine, white and taut. "Good Christ, are we running?" he said. "Should we just run?"

By the time we got out to the courts in Sunnyside and into our warm-ups, we'd mostly calmed down. We tried out a few lame jokes to prove to ourselves we could joke about it. Our *second* warm-ups. I remember how fast the court played that afternoon, notwithstanding all the cracks and weed patches that made me pine secretly for gentrified Hoboken. I felt loose-limbed and live-armed with the racket, unusually loose, unusually alive. Free and uncalculating. Did I litter up the stat sheet? I must have. Did I lose? Of course. But I remember I also hit several clean winners past Sam charging hard at the net—he was experimenting with serve-volley tennis of late. I felt invigorated, rattling with angles and possibilities, the air wet but clean in my lungs. Sam looked like a wrestler at the end of his sweat-suited training run, a large oval of dark gray dropping down from his neck and spreading through the middle of a Randolph Athletics T-shirt almost to the navel. I hadn't realized those shirts were for sale: I recognized its kind from the Randolph locker rooms, recalled its stiff itchy embrace. You handed the gym people your student ID as collateral, they handed you a graying T-shirt made from burlap.

"Not exactly for sale," Sam said, "but I wanted a little souvenir of my time there. They could keep my student ID. What did I care?"

"So when you steal it's a souvenir and when I steal it's, what, suicide?"

"That was a suicidal move you pulled back there, yes."

Onto the grass now, drinking our Gatorades and stretching. The grass felt stiff and crabby under my thighs, sparse, like patchy stubble on the underlying dirt that turned to mud with the sweat seeping into it, but at least we were cool in the shade of a courtside oak. Sam was getting abstract now, moving from the particular to the general, like a good Marxist. I watched his face as he spoke: Little colonies of silvery sweat beads still perched on his narrow upper lip, on the high jutting cheekbones, rosy with sunburn, and all along the long jutting jaw. His eyes were more recessed in their sockets than they'd once been—he too had lost weight—and his tall slick forehead stood in the shadow of a black Federer hat, a new addition. He looked like a skeleton with skin stretched over it. (We were all that, of course, but lately Sam reminded you of it more.)

"Anyway, I assume you've heard about old Larry?" Sam said to me.

"Larry?"

"Old Lar—the disgraced Soline CEO, just got off scot-free in the trial, to no one's great surprise? We're on a first-name basis now."

"Of course, yes, sorry."

Larry Bosch, man of the hour again. At the start of a forced but rich, a very rich retirement, he was readying his forty- or fifty-odd million in cashed-out, apparently un-touchable stock to take with him to the gated obscurity of Westchester County, or maybe over to the Hamptons or the Vineyard, down to Florida. No one quite knew his final hiding place—reports differed—but the general shape of it we'd seen enough to lift our shoulders, most of us, with something less than shock. The captain of industry sails off into the sunset in his looted ship, leaving behind crowded raftfuls of lawyers on huge retainers to continue muddying the waters. The plausible denials must be kept plausible for the appeals process, a few of the lower-downs appeased in their country-club prisons—*le capitalisme americain*. I'd seen and read plenty about it in the news—you couldn't not—yet the heart that hung under the head registering all those nouns and verbs was already gamy, contracting, already packed tight with its own troubles. Life was then pizza dough and stinging flour and gray scalding dishwater, as I've said, and now it was also a fiancée whose first foretaste of professional failure had pushed her so deep into herself that for all my attempts at comfort I must have looked like a sea lion awkwardly battering an oyster. (The show was rumored to be losing backers, and initial rehears-als had gone disastrously. Raymond had moved things to a smaller venue, pushed back the theoretical opening, etc.) Nor could I get Jen to dissociate herself at all from a production that she herself had called a hijacking—she was merely tak-ing orders now, "shaping" again, doing damage control. The depression she'd sunk to also belied, frankly, what she'd once told *me* by way of comfort, roles reversed. All jobs suck a little, on Broadway or in the academy or on a grill line—most of the time you're doing someone else's bidding, biding your time, and the important thing is to keep your perspective. But now?

Some blogger for *New York* magazine writes a glorified gossip piece ("*June vs. Hurricane*—And the Hurricane Appears to Be Winning"), and Jen prints it out and pins it to a corkboard hung above the desk in our bedroom, double-underlining the worst parts.

Failure! Failure everywhere! More than enough failure to go around! In between long pulls on his fruit-punch Gatorade, the gulps like live squirming worms moving down Sam's throat—out of this vivid grotesquerie Sam produced even greater ones from a seemingly endless store of facts and figures about the Soline result. Eight cents on the dollar, he said. That's what the thousands of Soline victims could expect from the compromised settlement more than two years after the fact, two years after most of them had lost their savings or their retirements or their homes or all three: The prosecutors would get their generous cuts, the victims would get the leftovers.

"I know. It's depressing," I said.

"It's *accepted*," Sam said. "It's basically unchallenged—Lazarus under the table waiting patiently for the scraps to drop, only now there's no afterlife to make it up to him in. Do you know what eight cents on the dollar actually means for these people? One source I saw estimated that each family will get less than three thousand dollars apiece, whenever they do finally get it. That's eight fucking cents on the fucking dollar."

"Jesus," I said.

"It's a joke. It's disgraceful."

"Well, what is to be done? That old, depressing question."

Sam stood up. "Are you coming back to the House today?"

• • •

I still had a little caked dirt clinging stubbornly to the backs of my thighs when we arrived at the Phoenix House. The other times I'd visited, Alex had been out, but now here she came down the front wooden stairs like a fifties housewife in her blue-checkered dress, supple and smiling. She looked a lot better than Sam did, anyway. Her color had returned, and a healthy bit of flesh. I was tempted to greet her as the Italians do—*You've gained weight!*

Or not really. And the Italians don't actually prize plump edges anymore, do they? It's the imaginary idea of Italy, the ancient idealized *idea* of a thing that clings to the mind.

"Comrade!"

This was Alex's greeting to me, a happy one. I gave it back in kind, with a pair of impromptu European air-kisses—and all was forgiven.

From the outside the Phoenix House looked unremarkable, a faded yellow semidetached at the end of a street full of faded semidetacheds, just another homely tooth in the long gappy smile of the block. Only on the inside did the House distinguish itself as the sort of punk pad–cum–commune it aspired to be: Trotsky beside Lenin beside Baraka on the sagging weathered built-ins, a few novels and flimsy chapbooks to ward off the suggestion of narrowness, a mess of washed-out Persian rugs on the hardwood floors, tacked-up festoons of Christmas lights on the walls, and beneath them several unframed photos and handmade signs: Polaroids of the Group members, the obligatory red fist, a Sharpied encouragement to FUCK THE POLICE! There was also an apparently working record player overhanging the salvaged end table that stood next to a quadrant of dirtied, deeply used couches . . . It was the signature decor, the feng shui of another, older time, only now it belonged to our time, too, by sheer insistence. Past and present together. Not dead, not even past.

I thought of Florence again—helplessly. At any moment it seemed the present world could drop away and sunstruck tangerine-colored Firenze could float up to take its place: the patched stucco walls, narrow cobblestone streets, the chilled frescoed chapels, the green-and-white canvas restaurant awnings that rippled from across the piazzas like sails. Only a week in country, but it was more than enough time for Alex and me to put on a little Italianate flesh of our own: We ate meals of pasta and pizza and risotto, minestrone, mozzarella di bufala, or sometimes straight gelato, affogatos galore, espressos at all hours and in all weathers, great quantities of cheap wine, stinging grappas tossed back in one go, Hemingway-style—all that wonderful peasant food. *Il cibo poveri!*

We loved the taste of the language too, though we understood so little of it, spoke even less. We went to our guidebook for relevant words and phrases that we practiced like vaudevillians in the privacy of our little *pensione* room. *Il cibo poveri!*— the local lilt leaping up and jumping down each word, each syllable a seesaw, with the pinched swirling hand flourish too, of course, that we inevitably let slip into our real interactions with real Italians. You asked directions of a kind-looking man in uncomfortable-looking shoes, the classic nose—must be a native—but at the end of your question about *un ottimo caffè* your hand floated up and circled as you looked helplessly on, too late, like a Tourette's sufferer.

"I can't believe you did that," Alex said the first time it happened.

"You think he noticed?"

"Of course he noticed!" She threw her head back, laughing,

the beautiful white horseshoe of her upper teeth exposed. We laughed together. I don't believe we ever did find that *ottimo caffè*—we made do with another guidebook-recommended gelateria instead, more ice cream for dinner.

But I return, a little reluctantly, to the Phoenix House.

I'd sunk down into a low gray couch opposite Sam and Alex, Sam stretching out his pale thin legs, stork-like, his tennis shorts riding high on his thighs. I noticed the downy white hair there, and Alex's hand coming casually to rest. I thought of the undersides of my own legs. Should I put a towel down? Or was there a bathroom I could freshen up in?

Alex craned her head behind her past the kitchen, half open above a yellow laminate island, the matching counters with the stands of opaque vodka bottles, cereal boxes, a coffeemaker, more photos on the fridge.

"Give it a minute?" Alex said. "Or maybe more than a minute? I think there's a bit of a happening in there."

She didn't elaborate further, only lifted down the record player's arm onto Sam Cooke's haunting, beautiful song "A Change Is Gonna Come." The famous keening voice rose up out of timpani and big-band strings—

"Nice call on the music," I said. "Your namesake, Sam."

Sam was looking at Alex. "He could use the bathroom upstairs, couldn't he?"

"Downstairs is community space, upstairs is for House members," Alex said, as if speaking only to Sam.

"I know that."

"Okay, then."

"He's an honorary House member, isn't he? He's basically here on a trial basis."

"Is that true?" Alex said, turning to me.

"I just don't want to dirty up your couches."

"They've seen worse."

Alex looked into Sam's long face again. She turned back to me slowly. "Here's what you do. Go take a shower upstairs. Make sure the little window's open or you'll die of mold ingestion. Dinner's in an hour, maybe two. Everyone'll be here. Okay?"

Sam Cooke was singing out from the depths of his gloomier bridge—

> *Then I gooooooo-ooooo to my brother*
> *And I say, "Brother, help me pleeeeeaaase . . ."*

The nearer Sam, meanwhile, looked satisfied, nodding, not quite meeting my eye.

I climbed the stairs with my duffel bag and came down several minutes later to find the music changed, and everything else in the House too. Several people buzzed in the kitchen, talking loudly and knowingly about things I could just miss the meaning of, or just miss the larger meanings behind the smaller ones, I suppose I mean. Jamaal in a bright pink T-shirt that said THIS IS WHAT A FEMINIST LOOKS LIKE said, "Anyhow, how touching, right? How hopeful! Democracy! Bipartisanship! Reaching across the aisle! Eli!" He side-armed me into a hug when he saw me standing there, holding up his other hand ashine from a bowl of tossed salad on the counter. I eventually gathered that Jamaal's sarcasm—I'd heard it dripping from the first—referred to a private-jet-setting consortium of American billionaires, mostly New York–based but with a few outliers in Chicago, Houston, Silicon Valley. Democrats and Republicans, Yankees and Southerners, men (and they were all men) who spanned radically different industries and "cultures," but they'd all come together to promote competitiveness, free trade, unfettered innovation—or really ballbusting tactics to compete with the ballbusters abroad, exploitation, and death to all regulators. Touching and democratic indeed. I kept hearing the name "O'Bannon" bandied about, particularly in Jamaal's mouth, and with a kind of odd pride, as if O'Bannon were a horse Jamaal had put money on.

"The man is a flat-out evil genius," Jamaal said. "You know he's being investigated, right?" Sam and Alex at either end of a wooden cutting board nodded; Tiffany rifling around in the condiments shelf of the open refrigerator sent up a blasé "Figures." "Yup," echoed Greg—Greg from the old norming sessions, bow-tie Greg, at the stove, sautéing onions. Jamaal must have noticed the look of confusion on my face because he lifted a pontificating finger as if to explain his point, then he shook the hand out. "In short, he's funneled money to every Tom, Dick, and Harry in his fucked-up nepotistic Irish family, but since they're all on the payroll, and since they all have some inscrutable Orwellian title like IT Product Design Overage Underage Manager, as wide a brief as they need to cover their asses, basically—oh, and they've all got their own shell companies! That's the thing! They've shell-companied the fuck out of this steaming pile of till-stealing until the investigators can hardly move. The latest is they tried to subpoena one of O'Bannon's son's hard drives but O'Bannon claimed the computer wasn't theirs to give away—it belongs to the shell company, a separate legal entity, no provable paper trail connecting the two. It's a fucking free-for-all."

"Bravo," said Tiffany wearily.

"But he's still in New York?"

This was Sam from the opposite counter, still slicing off coins of what looked like cucumber.

"I'm pretty sure," said Jamaal.

"You're *pretty* sure, pretty boy?"

"Well, what about your boy? What's the latest on him?"

"Oh he's here. He's still around. His greed keeps him close."

Somewhat absently, a little hard to hear (I'd been drafted to set the table in the other room), Sam took up the conversational line and described Larry Bosch in the late nineties, early two thousands, several years after he'd filed for and recovered from bankruptcy. Now at the cutting edge of a union-busting movement, he'd secretly hired a PR firm to slime the union bosses at the Jersey-based petrochemical company where he worked in the front office. Portraying the bosses as two-bit Castros but just as greedy—how they lined their pockets with members' dues, drove Lexuses, sold their charges downriver for discreet bonuses, etc., etc.

"He was basically calling them class traitors," Sam said, "and the thing is these fucking guys sort of were—huge salaries, lavish vacations and conferences that the workers they represented couldn't possibly afford. They basically handed their own prosecution to the executive class on a silver platter. You wonder what the Madison Avenue guys got paid for."

The conversation had spilled over into the communal meal of French bread and salad and some kind of baked vegetable medley—a ratatouille?—that tasted powerfully of the Pam some two-bit chef had slathered the cooking dish with. I didn't much mind. A general bonhomie more than made up for it. We caught up, reminisced, gossiped. (I shouldn't suggest that all the House talk, or even the bulk of it, revolved around questions of social justice or strategy or one-percenter excess.) At the end of the meal I'd relaxed enough to try out a quip about Maoist self-criticism sessions—when would ours begin? I was ready. All this felt too pleasant and freeform to be trusted. When would we draw blood?

"I bet you'd like that, wouldn't you," Alex said. "A little Stalinist circle jerk?"

"I was kidding, I was kidding!"

"So was I," she said. "You can relax, Eli. You're welcome here."

I got back to the apartment in Greenpoint very late that night, begging a ride from Sam. Jen was awake upstairs. She asked where I'd been and I told her everything. Or almost everything. I didn't mention the job I'd unofficially quit (or the doctoral program I'd quit months earlier). I didn't mention the wallet and the phone I'd tried to steal from my boss, the jerry-rigged atonement I'd tried to make at Sam's insistence, all the shouting that followed. I talked about Sam instead, the visit to the Phoenix House, the reunion with the old cohort, some of whom I hadn't seen in almost two years, and how much the same they seemed and yet different, some of them scarily different. In the blue-black dark of Jen's bedroom—this was still how I thought of it—I lit up the air with my talk, calm and clinical but also a little wondrous, too, like an anthropologist's talk. Each member of the House contributed not to an individual quota but a general goal, and not just toward rent and food (these were cheap when you considered how many people were crammed into a two-bedroom two-bathroom house) but also toward an action fund. I couldn't get anyone to pin down exactly what action they were building toward; they didn't know themselves, they said—

things were fluid, evolving. Sam was still stealing and selling phones with the help of Jamaal and Tiffany, who also had side jobs. ASU Jason worked graveyard shifts at a 7-Eleven, Alex did a little bartending, Adam and Greg had rich and trusting parents. All the House members cadged what they could from friends and family, honed hard-luck stories, lied shamelessly. And all for a cause no one knew anything about—what it was, what its goals were, who would lead it. I never even found out who was in the downstairs bathroom or what they were doing in there for seven hours, closer to eight. I'd been granted a little access but no real access. I'd gotten information but no answers.

"I know the feeling," Jen said, not bothering to hide whatever it was that seeped up into her voice.

I thought to keep going, pretend to the normalcy I'd pretended to more and more lately—normalcy at three a.m., on a work night, in another shared anecdote, since we shared everything with each other, didn't we? I started to tell Jen about the Bank of America ad Sam had pulled up on YouTube to show me. This was much later in the evening, much deeper in our cups. Picture Maria's round face resolving out of the PBR fog and smiling gamely over small white script that read "actual Bank of America customer"—a well-lit room in soft focus behind her, a soundtrack of feel-good acoustic music underneath. She described how she couldn't have gotten back on her feet without the help and understanding of her Bank of America mortgage broker and the debt-forgiveness plan they'd drawn up together. Cut to a brief slow-motion of Maria and her children playing in a green backyard, gamboling around like cartoon sheep.

"That's not their backyard, is it?" I asked Sam.

"Of course not. You think they let them keep the house?"

"I just didn't think a bank could do that sort of thing,"

Maria was saying as the music went tonic, the screen fading to white as the words stood out in simple black script: "Caring. It's what we do." The bank's logo faded last, of course, outlasting everything, tattooing itself on the eye.

"If not the house, what are they talking about?" I asked. "You think she's talking about that deficiency-agreement stuff?"

"Who knows what the small print actually covers," Sam said.

"I guess that's good, though, right? That the bank was still open to something? I guess something's better than nothing."

"Well, she has her reward," Sam said coldly. "God bless, and fuck off."

Jen looked at me hollowly now, peering out from behind dark lusterless eyes set into her darkened face. She didn't acknowledge the story I'd just told about Maria, or half told—the abortive power of her gaze. I laid a gentle hand on her shoulder and felt the strong plane of muscle slip under my touch, a noticeable recoil. Persistent, I moved around behind her on the bed and leaned my weight into a massage that she eventually responded to, leaning back or falling back into my working hands. I slid down the straps of her nightgown and reached for the lotion we still kept on the bedside table. From soft strokes at Jen's warm, smooth back I moved to the sides of her torso, the sides of her small breasts, pushing the nightgown down to her waist and rubbing to the gentle catch of her hip bones, the hem of her underwear.

Jen's voice cut above the white noise of the fan in the window. "They announced the cancellation today."

"What?"

"The cancellation was announced today."

"Of the show? Of your show? What happened?"

"Yes, the show. The money's gone."

"All of it?"

"Why, do you want to chip in?"

"Oh, sweetie, I'm sorry. I'm so sorry . . ."

"Are you?" Jen said.

"What?"

"Are you really sorry?"

I could tell she was looking right at me, and I felt convicted in that darkness and silence. It was true I'd looked forward to the end of *June vs. Hurricane*—I'd looked forward to the mercy kill, I suppose—but I'd never breathed a word of this aloud to Jen. Cautiously, perhaps cravenly, all I'd dared do was mirror her mooning expressions back at her in a weak pantomime of sympathy. When she'd asked my opinion of a rehearsal, or a blunt e-mail from an investor, I'd focused on tone, narrowly, dodging and weaving around content, getting in and getting out with practiced feints, less a boxer than a politician. I told careful half-truths when pressed, general truths. How could the theater establishment expect daring productions, bristling productions, if this was how they greeted them? As if you couldn't experiment in a one-tier experimental theater on West Fiftieth Street . . . No wonder Off Broadway was looking more and more like its lumbering overweight parent, predictable, complacent, risk-averse, tired. It might be that failure in a climate like this constituted a kind of distinction, a badge of honor, a *better* failure, if I could adapt Beckett . . . But I couldn't. I shouldn't have. I'd overplayed my hand.

In the dark bedroom Jen recalled to me the choicest of these comments. Hadn't I meant them?

I said I had—more or less.

"Then why are you sorry?" she said. "You said it would be

a good thing if it failed, didn't you? And you said it was over-stuffed."

"I said it was 'bristling.'"

"A euphemism. An obvious euphemism."

Jen slid out from under my hands, replacing the straps of her nightgown. I heard the white voice of the fan murmuring out from the window again, getting louder.

"Jen, what are you doing?"

"I'm just trying to understand why you'd be sorry that the show's called off. You said you'd be glad when it was all over."

"I was only agreeing with you!"

"Good. Okay, good. And what I was saying," Jen said, "what you were agreeing with was that a piece of work I'd put my name to, that I'd worked on for over a year, was a fucking train wreck. It was a fucking train wreck and I just wanted it to be killed—I wanted everyone to go home. Is that what you were agreeing with?"

"What do you want me to say, Jen?"

"Say what you mean for once. Tell the truth."

"I agreed with you."

"You agree that it was a fucking train wreck of a show?"

"Sure."

"Say it then. Say it."

"I agree that it was a fucking train wreck of a show."

"Wonderful," she said. "Thank you. My dear fiancé."

She got up and crossed the room to the small chair in the corner, conjuring a cream blanket from out of the darkness, snapping it up unfurled from the chair, a kind of magician's trick, as if all the moves had been planned out beforehand.

"This is ridiculous," I said.

"Is it?"

"You're being ridiculous."

At the door Jen said, "Good night, dear fiancé, sweet fiancé."

"Please don't go out there, Jen. Sweetie, please come back to bed. You want Mal to know we've been fighting again? This is awkward for her."

"So considerate all of a sudden."

"I don't understand what's happening right now. I feel like I walked into an ambush."

"You don't think Mal already knows we're in a fight? You weren't here for dinner—you think she missed that? Where was my considerate fiancé for dinner? Where was he all night? Why didn't he call? Why doesn't he ever call anymore? Mal's not stupid, Eli. Neither am I."

"You don't have to go out there," I said.

"I really do."

"No, I mean I'll go. It's your fucking bedroom."

"How considerate," Jen said, handing over the blanket as we passed in the doorway, our bodies not touching.

I once heard an ex-Weatherman say, a penitent, that he and his friends had been downright cultish to go about sacrificing their lives and livelihoods, their relationships, on the altar of some low-level war against the United States, as they thought of their work then. How blinkered they must have been, how beady-eyed to imagine that their cause would inspire others to join it, that with their rallies and their bombs they had set something real in motion, and so on. And this from the same man who'd once said, famously, *If I die in a beautiful cause, so be it* . . . From one extreme to the other—a familiar enough tactic, a retrospective tactic. The past is a foreign country and I was a stranger there, a stranger to myself, and so on. This is one of the avenues of interpretation now open to me, I realize, an escape route. Yet the afternoon I'm thinking of now—skipping ahead once again—has me sitting contentedly and a little bored in Sam's rusted brown Buick. I have no desire to get out, not really. And I can easily recognize myself on that afternoon. I can get from the me who sits here writing now, remembering, to the me who sat there jogging his leg in the front seat, waiting for something to happen.

Eventually I got out of the car to feed the meter. A quarter only got you ten minutes here, but I supposed we'd been lucky to find a parking spot at all. Lower Manhattan, late September. The air studiously neutral, at last emptied of the humid frenetic energy that had made of the city a kind of particulate snow globe in the last few weeks. There was even a slight cool breeze issuing down this uniconic stretch of Wall Street, so narrow and dark with shade that the breeze might have been a low whistle through a pair of pursed lips. The city moved vertically here, two-dimensionally, with the buildings dragging cornices and pretentious friezes up their long gray lengths, and lower down chunky iron lanterns jutting out like uncovered limbs— again my doomy imagination in these nether realms of the city.

Two middle-aged men in shirts and ties, black shoes and pants, gelled hair, moved past me under the temporary construction pavilion that hugged the building to our left across its entire length and gave the Buick that much more protection. One of the men gave me a quick incurious look. When he and his colleague were farther down the street I heard a rapping sound behind me and turned, Sam cranking down the window.

"What the hell are you doing?"

"Stretching, I guess. Breathing."

"Just go feed the meter, okay, and get back here. The more time you stand there, the more people see you, the more likely one of them is to remember you. Put an hour in, forget the time limits. This is taking longer than usual. And Eli?"

"Yeah?"

"Hurry? For fuck's sake?"

"Okay," I said, "okay—"

For a moment I had to stifle a laugh. There was an uprush of pleasure in me (or was it pride? relief?) to think that Sam might be more nervous than I was. People would remember me doing what exactly—standing by a car? And for what reason? And who would ask them to remember? This was the easy part, the least risky element in a hugely risky, evolving plan, a plan that evolved more risk with each after-dinner strategy session at the Phoenix House. Other big-shot businessmen, other deposed kings of industry kept their names in the conversation (Jamaal still talked a lot about O'Bannon, for example), but Bosch and his unpunished crimes, his local address, made him the frontrunner for retribution. One night in an excess of beery courage Greg gathered his pale pinched features under the overhang of his brow and said we should just kill Larry Bosch, shouldn't we? Make an example of him? The collective intake of breath around the table gave way to nervous laughter, with Greg leading the charge, assuring us he was just kidding, just fucking around—we all knew that, right? Not murder, then, but it didn't have to be. Political theater could be high stakes enough. If we couldn't hold our nerve standing outside a car under a plywood construction awning, or use a credit card instead of quarters to secure a parking spot (Sam worried a card would be traceable), then what hope did we have of abducting a millionaire dozens of times over, probably a bodyguarded millionaire, and then holding him—what?—for ransom? For a publicity stunt? For the hell of it? The plan was still evolving, we told ourselves.

At the green box of a parking meter I slid in the last of my quarters, coming up well short of an hour. We'd been here since two o'clock, it was almost five now, and I'd emptied a bulging pocketful of change into this mute dumb machine. Up ahead on the sidewalk, just past the construction awning, an old-fashioned hot-dog vendor stood under a plain blue umbrella.

He was short and compact in a clean white apron, wearing a black Yankees cap and a mustache, working what looked like a large chrome icebox with a grill attached to it. I started toward him, my eyes casually lowered. I remembered the sunglasses parked atop my Mets cap, put them on. At the stand itself I kept my head bowed, pretending to deliberate over the row of prismatic water bottles, sodas, Gatorades, iced teas, the bottles catching the light as the sun leaned into view at the far end of the street. The man's grill was clean and tidy, with little mounds of white onions caramelizing in one corner. Old Marco from the sub shop, unmissed Marco—I hadn't seen him in two months though I'd come home to Jen and Mallory with many fabricated stories about his micromanagerial zeal, his Napoleon complex—old Marco would have been impressed. To Jen and Mallory I'd started paying a slightly larger share of the rent, by the way, from my parents' largesse. (I claimed the money came from the extra hours I was working at Tommy's.) I'd had a birthday recently, complete with a surprise visit from my parents, a trip to the U.S. Open with Jen, then a chance at a private dinner to lay on my parents a true enough sob story about job-market difficulties, rising rents, falling grad school stipend levels, etc. I came away from that night with a ten-thousand-dollar check—a loan, my parents stressed, though they'd been thinking about something like this for a while. I think they worried I wouldn't accept the money if it were presented as a gift—I think of this queasily now, guiltily.

"Two hot dogs with onions, please," I told the vendor without lifting my eyes to him. I watched the spatula expertly slide under one of the caramelizing mounds, then another, then drop the confetti-like brownish onions along the length of the buns.

"Actually, add these in too," I said, taking two Gatorade

bottles down from the row and passing along a twenty-dollar bill. "How about three dollars in quarters and you keep the change?"

"Thanks, boss," the man said, fingering the coins from his small metal safety box.

I thanked him for the food and the quarters and started back for the parking machine.

"You guys don't stand a chance, you know," he called after me.

In my surprise I turned around and took the man in directly, his wide dark face and the high-peaked cap, the darker mustache like a sea creature under his nose, thick and bristled, slightly shining.

"Come again?"

"You guys don't have a chance. Face it." He gestured at my hat.

"Oh, the Mets!"

"You were lucky to get out of the division series. I take Atlanta in four."

"Well, we'll see, we'll see," I said, and turned away. I'd all but soaked through the thin waxed paper cradling the hot dogs by the time I got back to the car, my sweat glands stoked at an instant and not to be calmed anytime soon.

Sam did nothing to hide his anger. "Did you give him your driver's license? Your Social Security number? A DNA swab?"

"You could see all that, huh?" I handed over the hot dog and the fruit-punch Gatorade. "You're welcome, by the way."

"You learn how to use your mirrors when you do this enough. And how not to be flagrantly stupid."

"I figured we needed more change, okay? We need to eat too, don't we? You're *welcome*."

"Sure thing, comrade," Sam said through a mouthful of hot dog, the bite bobbing in his cheek like a mound of chewing tobacco, unmannerly and crude. It would have seemed out of character for Sam, except that lately Sam seemed to be permanently out of character. For now he kept his blue-gray flat eyes trained on the high-mounted small rearview mirror. He wore the same black Roger Federer hat—blackish gray—with the sweat stains wavering along the brim and the faded edges as if the hat had been dipped in salt water. Of course it hadn't been dipped in any water—that was the problem. Personal cleanliness, like notions of private ownership and space, tended to fall off at the Phoenix House, as if that cliché of communal living had to be cultivated and brought up into pungent bloom. Add to that the House members who smoked—Tiffany, usually opening a window in the second bedroom, but not always. Greg too, I gathered—a sympathetic smoker. My own sympathetic responses moved quickly to squinting and headaches in the presence of cigarette smoke. I was crashing on the sunken gray couch at the House every now and then, but most nights I still returned, gratefully, to the clean cool neutral-smelling uncluttered apartment in Greenpoint.

Sam's eyes flinched at the rearview, suddenly straining.

"What is it?"

"Don't turn around. Use the side mirror."

"Is he in there?"

A trio of suits, a quartet, young men by the looks of them, paused on the sidewalk in front of an ornately arched entryway not far beyond the hot-dog stand. The men in their fine-cut clothes and the entryway with its inlaid squares of stone carving, a lip of twisted stone running along the inside of the arch to look like mooring rope, the thick morbid lanterns, the large flags—all this announced the grand ambitions and haute airs of the offices inside. And the ambitions and airs of the men who worked there (they were almost all men—in two-plus hours we'd seen only a handful of women emerge from the bank of glass doors). Haute airs, haute heirs—one of the synapses I'd glued together over the course of this long, tedious afternoon. Somewhere in Ortega y Gasset I'd learned that *patrician* was the Roman term for the man who could afford to make a will and leave an inheritance. The rest were proletarians, the vast remainder.

Another man had joined the group on the sidewalk and now, decisively, all five of them started away toward Water Street.

"That wasn't him, was it?" I said.

"Assholes in suits," Sam said, "but not our asshole. What's taking him so long today?"

"I kind of have to use the bathroom too—don't hate me. How long does he usually stay in there?"

"This is my point, comrade. You know I love you, but I'm not sure these junkets play to your strengths. You have to be able to sit—still—for a long time."

"You don't have a bladder? Alex doesn't have a bladder?"

"You leave my girlfriend's bladder out of this," said Sam, suddenly enjoying himself. "You've lost all privileges there."

"Jesus."

"What?"

"You tell me," I said.

"I think that's him."

"Who? Bosch?"

"Don't fucking turn around," said Sam.

In the spotted side mirror I watched a small, gaunt man, the top of his pate shining powerfully, step to the same curb the suited quintet had just occupied. In a loose coat, tieless, he lifted a phone to his ear and looked tired, shifting his weight from leg to leg as he talked, listing over to one side or the other of his body's y-axis. Two other men stood nearby, taller than Bosch, better dressed. None of them looked any bigger than an inch in the conjuring medium of my side mirror—a simple bringing together of thumb and forefinger could have snuffed them all out.

We followed Bosch's town car at a length of three or four cars, sometimes more, never less. Sam knew the route well. Up Water Street and onto the FDR with the infinitesimal low river like a diamond slick running off to our right, the Brooklyn Bridge's giant legs in the rearview and the Manhattan Bridge's looming up ahead quick and gray. Then the long flat climb to the top of the island, the Art Deco monuments on the Brooklyn side, the low row houses of Queens, ferries on the water, the black whirring freeway rails. At the entrance to 278 Sam split off and let the town car continue on its way. We doubled back into Queens and started for the House.

"You're assuming he doesn't have pressing business in Yonkers," I said. "Or maybe White Plains?"

Sam didn't acknowledge the joke. "Anyway, you know the rest," he said.

"He never stops off in midtown for any business?"

"Not that I've seen. He's persona non grata at Soline headquarters—they've had to purge him, or appear to have purged him. No, it's just Wall Street to home now, Wall Street to home . . . He was in there a lot longer than usual today. I don't know what that means—if anything."

"Do you know how much Bosch pays on his house in property taxes alone?" I said.

"Half a million."

"Oh, come on! You guessed too high! You're supposed to guess something semi-reasonable—remember, we're just talking about property taxes."

"Fifteen dollars."

"Three hundred grand, wise ass. On property taxes alone."

"You got that from the *Architectural Digest* piece?"

"The real estate website—there are all sorts of stats on there, more photos too. Rooms the size of ballrooms. I think there might actually be a ballroom in there. They've got a perfect blue lake that backs up to their land and a little stream that runs through it with a little bridge over it like something out of a fucking Jane Austen novel. Who knows how blue the lake actually is—these photos are like soft-core porn with all the lighting and the touch-ups. The colors are like the Platonic ideals of colors, the Platonic ideal of a blue lake or a red Persian throw rug in front of a fireplace the size of a Studebaker. Do you know how many bathrooms he's got in that place?"

"Thirty," Sam said.

"Fuck you."

"Zero," Sam said. "No bathrooms at all. Just a porta potty out front that they have to share with the construction workers."

"Seven! Seven bathrooms! What the hell does an empty-nest couple need with seven bathrooms?"

"Seven's a biblical number, as I'm sure you know. Maybe he's a spiritual man."

"I think we can assume Larry Bosch is a deeply spiritual man," I said. "Anyway, now what?"

"Now we do it again."

"You mean tomorrow?"

"Maybe."

"What does 'maybe' mean?"

"It means maybe."

"Well, what are you thinking?"

"I'm thinking he's trying to move his money, do something to shelter it, protect it. Three hundred grand is a lot to pay for property taxes, but in the scheme of things, in the scheme of Westchester County and all that criminal wealth, a ten-million-dollar house is middle-of-the-road. I think he's plenty liquid and getting ready to be more liquid."

"You meant you and me when you said 'we' a second ago, right? About doing another junket?"

"You'll have to arm-wrestle Alex for it. We'd be taking her car. And I think she kind of likes this stuff. Makes her feel adventurous, she says. She says it ironically, but you can kind of tell."

"Then there's her famous bladder control . . ."

Sam smiled vaguely ahead at the windshield, cryptically, a shadow of sadness passing over his face. "She says it makes her feel a little like Bonnie to my Clyde."

"Is that right?" I said.

We called these outings "junkets," by the way, since "stakeouts" sounded too Hollywood, and too blunt a reminder of what it was we were actually planning, contemplating, kicking around. How serious were we about an abduction? I wouldn't have been the one to ask. I'm sure some bad ideas do hatch in haste, and out in the open, with a group's enthusiasm or insanity running ahead of itself and in loose hurling concert. Our bad idea was different—secretive, tentative, jolting into a new stage of evolution without the Group being notified of it, with only a few insiders putting their heads together in the shadows. This was the problem with Sam now, too. When he looked through a windshield and smiled a vague little half-turned cryptic smile, or when he disappeared for days on end and no one could tell you why or where to, you realized you'd lost the bead on this friend of yours. This strange, ever-thinning friend, this angular insect of a man with his mandible jaw—who was he? Was he a paranoid now, a sudden introvert? Had I somehow lost his trust? Was he testing me? He ran hot and cold sometimes in the space of a single sentence, and the cold could stop your heart, as if you'd swum out with him into the warm shallows of his old enthusiasm, his old joie de vivre, only to feel the bottom drop out at the continental shelf's edge: Suddenly you're in bottomless, dark, updrafting, freezing water.

By contrast, Alex at this same time became more solicitous of me, teasing, probing, more intimate than she'd been at any time since our relationship—more intimate than she'd been at times *during* our relationship. We still prepared our potluck ramshackle dinners *en famille*, and if it was Alex's turn to spring for the protein or the booze, or if it was mine, we walked together to the greened sooted copper stretch of Roosevelt Avenue where a bodega, a Korean market, and a liquor store all huddled within a block of one another in the latticed shade of the elevated 7 train. A simple shopping trip could take us hours, slowed by the sense that something was being rediscovered, something unearthed in our long walk-and-talks, like the knowledge from a past life that Socrates apparently drew out of his pupils as they walked beside a river. By the time we got home, Alex and I often met with the recriminating stares of hungry House members, some of them asking outright what had taken us so long.

When I asked my own questions of Alex, she usually turned them aside, Sam-like, turning us back to less pressing subjects, gentler subjects. She recalled the time we'd spent together on top of a green mountain in Vermont, at an academic conference overrun with academics—somehow we hadn't prepared ourselves for that. A floating enclave of Morningside Heights, it set down on top of a rural campus and sent Alex and me scurrying off into the woods. Did I remember that? Into the woods to live at least a little deliberately, to suck out the marrow of a misconceived week! By the third day of the conference Alex and I had thrown away our name tags and all the scheduling material. We skipped a panel she was supposed to be on (how did I not see that she was crashing out of academe?), spending the day instead on the dappled dirt paths Robert Frost used to walk during his summers on this same mountain. Copper plaques stood at elbow-resting height in the sunlit clearings along the trails. Some of the chiseled verses you could just make out ("Something there is that doesn't love a wall"), but many others were too effaced, worn out by weather and time, burnished a dull gold in the sun. The bare plaques were like open invitations to add our own verses. You got to contribute at least one, if you believed Whitman. One late afternoon with the sun through the trees turning grainy and thick, honeyed, the golden hour, Alex and I spread a blanket over the low ferns just off the trail and made love.

It surprised me a little to hear Alex recalling all this now, but it probably shouldn't have. My instinct in her presence was always to excise, to gloss over the year of romantic love that had interrupted and rather complicated our friendship, but this was never Alex's way. Today on the shopping run it had been my turn to cover the meat and the booze—I sprang for lean ground turkey and two cases of Blue Moon, pricey beer—and now I felt Alex's hand graze mine as we meandered back to the House. We were wearing matching Mets caps, as it happened, large sunglasses, with late shadows like masks over our faces. I could make out Alex's mouth going lopsided again, happy air through her nose.

"And how about my almost-date with Lyme disease?" she said. "You remember that, don't you?"

On the last morning of the conference she'd come to me in our little cabin/dorm room, her hair wet from the shower, in her towel, raising her left arm to reveal a small unplump tick that had rooted at the edge of the armpit's concavity. Alex's eyes and lips were flat and, I thought, faintly accusing—I remembered that the first trips into the woods had been my idea, that I'd dismissed Alex's concerns over ticks as citified, paranoid.

"It wasn't an accusing look!" Alex said. "That was all in your head!"

"I am a bit of a worrier sometimes, aren't I?"

"A *bit*? You were apoplectic! So now *I've* got to worry that this little fucker in my armpit might be transmitting an incurable disease and I've also got to stop my boyfriend from throwing himself in front of a speeding pickup as some sort of honor suicide. 'Oh Jesus! Oh Jesus! I'm so sorry, I'm so stupid—fuck! Fuck!'"

"I don't remember being *quite* like that."

"Exactly like that," Alex said. "Heaping ashes on your head, rending your garments—it was biblical."

"You really are starting to sound like Sam," I said.

"I say Puritanical, he says biblical. We happen to be in

agreement about you, comrade. You've got a guilt complex, you're an emoter, a loose cannon. What's the opposite of a stoic? That's you."

"Are you being serious right now? Does Sam really say that about me? The both of you?"

Alex must have seen the change in my face, or anyway she looked at me with a changed expression, the puckering eyebrows pulling down beneath her sunglasses.

"Eli, learn to take a joke."

"Does Sam say that about me, yes or no?"

"You can ask him yourself," she said. "He's back tonight. Get right up in his face—I'm sure he'll like it as much as I do."

"I'm sorry," I said, "but Jesus, Alex . . ."

I continued with the bit in my mouth for the rest of the way home, softening my words a little but mostly just slowing them down, drawing out the silences around them like so much difficult taffy. I was persistent, though—I wanted answers. Where had Sam been for the last week, anyway? What had he been doing? And why was it that Alex seemed to know about it and no one else did?

"Alex?"

She kept her face pointed steadfastly east, a rictus smile on her lips. At the turn onto our street a homeless man in a nest of grimy blankets held out his sign perfunctorily—Alex reached into the grocery bag I carried, pulled out a Blue Moon, and handed it off to the man without a word.

Back at the House, Sam had already arrived home, just in time for dinner. He looked at ease setting the table, catching up on the latest with Greg and Tiffany, Asshole Adam (who wasn't so asshole-ish anymore), ASU Jason (now two-plus years out of ASU). I realized I needed new names for these people, new versions. I'd tried especially hard to reconcile the Greg Baxter I'd known through Hahn's norming sessions, pedantic, begrudging, bow-tied Greg Baxter, with the Greg who'd apparently come aboard the House through Tiffany's persuasions. I'd had to adjust what I thought I knew about Tiffany, too. More than once I'd watched her and Alex interlocking hands as they climbed upstairs for the night, Sam following behind a little sheepishly, uncertainly—a cocked eyebrow to me once, on the couch, conspiratorial, a lucky libertine's smiling acknowledgment, but he didn't pull it off. I sensed he was surprised and unsure of his role now. Did this account in part for his distances lately, his sudden silences? His absences?

During dinner I saw that I wasn't the only one being kept in the dark on Sam's recent whereabouts, and not the only one chafing under this ignorance either. Jamaal got up at one point for a second crack at the fajita bar, floating into the kitchen on the helium power of his Afro, bigger and looser than ever, like a flowing electrostatic field around his head. He'd complained of the sweat soaking his hair like a sponge throughout the hot hot summer, but here we were in October now, the home stretch, or so we hoped.

In the kitchen Jamaal reached into a cupboard only to jerk the hand back as if stung. "Fuck! These roaches!"

He detoured on his way back to the table to lift the record player's arm off Sam Cooke, copacetic and soft.

"Just a minute, Sam," Jamaal said. He turned to us. "Black Sam, I mean, Sam with the soul."

"How do you know I don't have soul?" said our Sam. "You've never heard me sing."

"How do you know I'm talking about that kind of soul?"

"I have as much soul as you," Sam said, looking suddenly very pleased with himself, "and full as much heart."

Then his face sank a little when nobody got the apparent reference.

Jamaal sat down opposite Sam but addressed the whole group, leveling a long forefinger like the barrel of a gun. "First order of business: We need to do something about these motherfucking roaches. Next person up for grocery run, get some real traps, not these cheap-ass motels where the fuckers can rest up and watch free cable. Second order of business—" He jutted another finger out under the first, the hand like a two-pronged pitchfork pointing at Sam's chest, a Black Mass of the peace sign. "Second order of business is where the fuck were you and why can't we get a straight answer about it out of anybody? I mean, you must have known," he said to Alex, "but it's like the goddamn Manhattan Project the way you guard it." And turning to Tiffany, "And you too—what's with all the Stalinist secrecy around here? Do we have to join this triad of yours to get answers? Do we have to fuck our way to the top?"

"Wow," Alex said. "What a charming reactionary you make."

Tiffany said, "Nobody told me anything."

"I went to visit my sister is all," Sam said. "She just had a kid, a little girl. I wanted to meet her. Do I need to run my travel itineraries past everyone in the House?"

"Honestly I didn't even know to ask. I didn't realize I'd been excluded from a secret." Tiffany again. "I must have missed that memo."

"It was a secret because you all *made* it a secret," Jamaal said. " 'Where'd Sam get to?' It's a simple question, with a simple fucking answer."

"Okay, okay," Greg said, holding up a papal hand, apparently casting himself in the role of sainted moderate. He pointed out that we were supposed to be in the middle of planning something pretty big, weren't we? If only for that reason we should probably do a better job of keeping each other abreast of things—"updated," he corrected himself.

"Well, actually, on that front," Sam said. "On that front we might need to slow down for a while."

"Says who?" said Jamaal, and the lines quickly redrew themselves. "Who's deciding all this anyway, and behind what closed doors?"

When Jamaal finally shouted that it was Phoenix all over again, only roles reversed—another cabal had been formed—Alex handled the accusation calmly. "Not a cabal, no," she said, "but a leadership group? Well, if the shoe fits . . . Weren't Lenin and Trotsky, Luxemburg, Guevara—weren't these people all part of *led* factions? We wouldn't know about their movements otherwise—"

"So which one are you?" Jamaal interrupted. "Which one is Sam? You're Lenin, he's Trotsky, is that it? You're Bonnie, he's Clyde?"

Sam did another of his startled turtle-jerks backward on his neck, cutting a hateful look at me—Alex slower to respond, comprehending.

"Why *shouldn't* he tell us?" Jamaal said. "We're either an open organization or we're a bullshit hierarchy, in which case Eli's down here with us, in the shadows of the Great Leaders. Solidarity of the also-rans."

Alex spoke very quietly now. "Here's what I know. Sam takes off for a week and everything basically stops. When he and I hang fire, you all hang fire. No one decided this, no one announced it, but it appears that, yes, a natural hierarchy has emerged."

"That's good to know," Jamaal said, scraping back his chair on the way to the staircase, where he turned and gave a deep, faux-subservient bow.

When he'd slammed a door upstairs, I noticed a new hand-made sign hanging on the wall where Jamaal had stood. It was a black-and-white printout of an old-timey police officer—think James Cagney in his later period—complete with brimmed shining hat, the bared teeth between bulldog jowls, the dark glowering eyes. I recognized Alex's handwriting above and below the image: WHAT SHOULD YOU DO IF A PIG AP-PROACHES YOU???

- DO NOT LET THE PIG SEARCH YOUR PERSON OR BAG OR VEHICLE—OR ANYTHING—UNDER ANY CIRCUMSTANCES!

- DO NOT VOLUNTEER ANY INFORMATION ABOUT YOURSELF OR ANY OTHER HOUSE MEMBER!

- MAKE THE PIG STATE CLEARLY THE REASON FOR HIS APPROACH . . .

A little word balloon grew out of the "HIS" in this last direc-tive: "Or 'HER'? Hmmmmmm?"

Pretty soon the conversation had relaxed again, spreading out delta-like as we all moved to the couches. I noticed Alex slipping back into her casual-intimate mode with me, with Sam and Tiffany looking neutrally on. I didn't know how to feel about this. I felt Alex's smiling judgment settle over me like a fallout, gentle and familiar. I'd never understood her, had I? I was a Puritan, an athlete of repression, etc. And maybe that shoe fit as well. I certainly did perk up a minute later—mentally, bodily—when Alex came up from behind me on the couch and ran her hands down the front of my chest. I covered them with my own hands, instinctively. Alex's face soft and close, her cheek to my cheek. She whispered in my ear, side-kissed my temple. The other House members lazing nearby looked discreetly away, I noticed, all except Tiffany—Tiffany with a cautious, warming-up smile. She'd seen this before, perhaps.

And Sam? Sam's eye I carefully avoided, though later I could hear his distinct, heavy tread following behind us up the stairs.

"*Et voilà*, as you'd say, with your stupid French envy," Alex said to me as we crossed into the bedroom.

A little odd to consider, in a House so skimpy on boundaries, but I'd never actually set foot in this room. It surprised me. Out of the roil of things in my body, the muted roar in my head, I chose to focus on the stylish, spare decor, the room glowing like a darkroom from the red-shaded table lamp. Above the table, a red-framed circular mirror floated the reflection of a large, goateed, beret-wearing man on the opposite wall, a marked intensity in his gaze. If I was meant to recognize this face, I didn't. It looked a little like a Lichtenstein print presiding over the constellation of smaller frames, carefully arranged to look uncareful: a gold-winged dragon, like something off a Roman crest; a trio of men and a raffish underfed-looking woman in Bolshevik long coats and peaked hats . . . As for the bed, as for the sleeping situation, this too rather startled in its contrast with the haphazard threadbare sprawl of the rest of the

House. What lurid imaginings I'd allowed myself about Alex and Tiffany and Sam usually involved an unwieldy sultan's bed, as wide as it was long. But here a tidy queen with a white headboard, a simple flower pattern on the comforter, tucked into the far corner of the room, and in the other a narrow bunk bed was made up with clean, cool bedding the color of Easter eggs—pale blue, pale green. Sam took a seat in a black wooden chair beside the table, and Alex and Tiffany sat together on the bottom bunk, taking me in a little coolly now.

Finally Sam gestured to the iPod dock on a bookshelf behind me and said, "Why don't you choose a little music for us, Eli. Anything will do. And turn it up."

In the iPod's artist list I came almost immediately to Fiona Apple, perhaps Jen's all-time favorite pop artist. I hesitated, then chose one of Jen's favorite songs—"I Know." Let it serve as a reminder. The flat porous speakers began pouring out the buzzing piano line and the canny unsentimental voice—

So beeeeeee it, I'm your crowbar—
If that's what I am so far . . .

"You guys know I have a girlfriend, right?" I said. "A fiancée."

Leaning back on the bed, Alex raked her hand across Tiffany's hair like a chime. She laughed. "You really thought you were being seduced, huh? I give you the bedroom eyes and you obey, hey?"

"Here we go," Sam said, "okay." He carried his chair and another nearby to the bedside, motioning for me to sit next to him. We were close around the lower bunk, leaning our heads in like the conspirators the rest of the House probably still suspected us of being, speaking under cover of Fiona Apple's rainy love songs.

"I can trust everyone in this circle," Sam said. "I do trust everyone in this circle. All right?"

"Me too," Alex said.

"Me too," Tiffany said.

Now they were looking at me. "Sure, yes," I said. "Sorry, I do too."

"Okay, good," Sam said. "I'm not sure about anyone else, though. Or not sure enough. Are you guys?"

We started working through the others one by one—what we knew about them, how they'd come to us, how much exposure we felt they could bear. A slow, methodical probe, a little too slow, perhaps, since after several minutes Sam started getting noticeably twitchy.

Alex laughed at him.

"What?"

"You want to show Private Lentz your new toy, don't you?" she said.

"I think we've made a good start, don't you?"

"Very."

"We can come back to this, of course. We will."

"Of course."

Alex toed out from under the bed the worn navy blue backpack Sam used for his cell-phone trawling. Once again it dipped tellingly when Sam held it upright. Fiona Apple was still going on the player, jazz brushes on a snare like rain against a window. It wasn't a squeal of zippers this time, just a slow, careful reaching into the bottom of the bag's main compartment, Sam's arm half gone, as if he were birthing a calf. When the gun came out it was wrapped in a white linen kitchen towel. Sam displayed it on his lap, the pointed ends of the towel like the blooms of an opening flower. The gun looked that much blacker and blockier—it looked fake, shining a little too brightly along the barrel and stock, or handle, or whatever you called it, a fine waffling down the side of the grip. Only when Sam offered it across to me on tray-like hands, like a deadly hors d'oeuvre, did I feel its authenticating heft. It was real all right. I didn't touch the trigger—I didn't dare to.

"It isn't loaded," Sam said. "And it won't be. But we need it."

"We need it?" I said.

"We need it."

"And this is what you were really doing last week?"

"I really was at my sister's in Pennsylvania. They live out in the sticks, hunting country, not far from a truck route, and they're paranoid. They've got three or four of these things. I doubt they'll miss one for a while. Anyway . . ."

He went off into other talk, shop talk—about the gun, its make, how to use it, how his brother-in-law had taken him out shotgun hunting and told him always to aim low, always lower than you think. And how different could one of these be? He was looking at the pistol resting heavily like a talisman in my palm. We were all looking at it, falling to silence now. It was mesmerizing.

One other thing we discussed that night around the lower bunk: my sleeping situation. I was made to understand that I would now be a visitor to the apartment in Greenpoint, a mere checker-in, a keeper-up of appearances. This was one of the conditions of my remaining in the leadership group, or at the House at all—I had to commit. I had to be all in. I can't pretend that at the time I really struggled with the decision.

Within a few days Adam and Jason had quit the House and only Greg and, to everyone's surprise, Jamaal remained. Sam and Alex set Greg to more cell-phone trawling, with Jamaal and Tiffany continuing to help with the wiping and posting—cell phones, iPods, tablets, laptops, whatever Greg could lay hands on. The Group needed the money more than ever, Sam said, but he and Alex needed to concentrate their energies on planning. Not the old plan, we said, but the new plan, which needed to remain secret until it shaped up more. It was grunt work for Greg particularly, and also a loyalty test. Why the long-faced former bow-tie wearer insisted on passing it, his bushy brows unbent, I still don't know.

As for me, I made good on an offer to pick up the rent slack Adam and Jason had left. There went November, December, January. By the end of February I'd drawn down my checking account to eight hundred dollars, all the tough-minded generosity of my parents gone to seed my double life. I'd stopped paying more than token sums to Jen and Mallory, claiming my hours at Tommy's had been slashed. I was afraid I might get fired, I said, but then again who cared, right? Good riddance! Maybe getting fired would jolt me out of my complacency and depression, send me back to my dissertation, or to a better job, or something, anything!

It was after one of these performances, all variations on a theme, the sputtering fugue state of my life with Jen, that Mallory patted me on the shoulder and said, " 'Good riddance!' Right!"

The obvious sarcasm in her voice brought me up short. It was just after work hours, late evening, with a dandruff of snow falling out of the blue-black darkness through the window. I realized I'd forgotten to ask where Jen was.

A moment later Mal emerged from her bedroom still in her heavy peacoat, moisture glistening on the coarse sleeves. She emanated the cold she'd brought from outside, sitting beside me on the piano bench. Up close I could see that the chill-deepened circles of red at her cheeks and nose tip, around the curve of her ears—she looked suddenly like a Raggedy Ann doll—were not pure but mottled, points of white and red in minute alteration, like a Seurat painting. Her wide-set eyes were long and brown and the wedge of forehead skin between them, the thin incurving brows, the top of the long nose sent your attention swinging out into the ski-jump air in front of her face. Mal was looking at the score I'd stopped playing out of shyness.

" 'Lost to the world,' huh? I'd say that's appropriate. Play this part again," she said, underlining the section with a long rosy fingertip, the nail unpainted.

I did as I was told.

"Now sing along to it."

Hesitantly, very quietly—

"Louder."

I did as I was told.

"Yup," she said, "yup. That's what I heard. This passage here," and she sang it herself with soft, brilliant clarity, a low-to-high figure, effortless. "Do you hear the difference? It's not a trombone slide. Mahler's not crooner material. Move up crisply to the next note but hit it soft—transition with dynamics, not your hammy glissando. You try," she said.

I tried.

"Better. That's a little better. You have a decent voice, you know that? You've got a decent mid-tenor. You could do something with it if you took some initiative."

"Thank you?"

"It's a compliment."

"Thank you."

"You want some more advice? I know you didn't ask for any, but do you want some more?"

I could hear in her voice that it wasn't really a question. I might have been squinting, bracing myself.

"You're really fucking up with Jen, you know that, don't you?"

"I know," I said, "I know it. It's all this stuff at work, and some other stuff—"

"Shut up, stop it. Just stop. I know you're lying."

"What? I'm not lying."

"Last month Jen went by your work to surprise you. She was going to take you out on a date—remember dates? It's this thing where two people who love each other, who are still technically engaged, go out and spend time alone together? Anyway, she talked to your friend Marco, got the whole story. He said you're lucky he hasn't pressed charges yet. What are you doing, Eli?"

I took this in for a minute. "When last month?"

"I don't know. Pretty early."

"Early? So she's been sitting on this for six weeks—more than six weeks?"

"Look, I don't know what your deal is, I don't particularly want to know, but I can tell you that you're fucking up royally. Do you know where Jen is right now?"

"I was going to ask."

"If you tell her I told you this I'll kill you. I'll never talk to you again."

"Where is she?"

"She's out with a guy she met through work. Some random guy auditioning late in the day, doesn't make the cut, but sticks around to ask your fiancée out for coffee."

"She's seeing him tonight?"

"This isn't the first time either. I'm telling you this because I like you—I'm not sure why. You're a ghost lately, but you're a friendly ghost—how's that? Anyway, that's my advice."

"I'm not sure I caught the actual advice."

"Stop fucking up."

This was the intelligence I'd received from Jen's closest friend. For several days I carried it around with me like a secret scar—a secret of a secret. It was a button I could push to make my heart go tight, instantly pinched and smarting. It was a kind of penance to push it; I pushed it often. I thought of it that way, too, that Sam-like way—evacuated religion, a giving in to the forms, the temptations of dogma, as I think Derrida puts it somewhere. Sam had influenced all of us, of course. He was the common virus we'd all caught.

I didn't like myself for being jealous, regretful, mournful, whatever I was. I didn't like to think that Mal's information had activated feelings in me that had lain dormant for months, that competition could do what love and loyalty could not, that pitifully ordinary machismo sat so near the seat of my motivations. And I think this is why I did nothing for several days, then a week, then two, staying away from the apartment more and more. On nights when I did stay over Jen came home late, sometimes very late, never disclosing the details of her night—and I was careful never to ask her to. We acted like casual friends more than lovers now, unfailingly polite, a little distant, closed off to each other brick by brick—though it was true we sometimes still made love, sometimes held each other as we had before. This was my resolution: I would do nothing different. With Mal's insider information, with this pen-tip hole in the ceiling that gave on to Jen's double life, I would still play the hand I'd been dealt; I would honor the ignorance that should have been mine. Each day I put on Mal's secret to me like a hair shirt. I pushed the button again and again.

But plot caught up to me. Plot, as they say, is character—which means I might do better to say simply that character caught up to me. I sat in the melting weather on a flight of stone steps stained white with the memory of winter salt, like a recessed sea. The sky over the narrow mid-rise buildings was gray, uncertain, wispy—you could see the atmosphere slipping the lower clouds under the higher ones like sheets of paper. This was Tribeca, not far from Canal Street and Chinatown, where the commercial rents were cheaper, apparently. You had to go downtown before you could go up, Jen liked to tell people about her work—downtown to the light-filled hot creaking hardwood loft they used for auditions, uptown to whatever Off-Broadway venue the lucky few would start rehearsals in. Jen always talked about luck, never talent, as if talent were simply assumed and assumed to be copious, vast, sprawling, hanging out undirected most of the time in the gutters of modern capitalism. Luck mattered more, or unluck—of course they did. How lucky had some striver been to show up for an outside chance and leave with the phone number of a woman like Jen? How lucky had I been?

Well, but here she came. I could hear the freight elevator being drawn back into the raspy lungs of the building as Jen made her way out of the black steel door and down the steps, Raymond following. I was a ways off, but I recognized Raymond's slight frame with the square shoulders, the bleached boyish hair that swirled upward like a cap of soft-serve ice cream. Jen wore her shorter, lighter peacoat with the white Amelia Earhart scarf loosely coiled around her neck, one end of it hanging off the back of her shoulder like a casual hand. Her hair was up in a loose ponytail—she was proud of her cheekbones, I'd learned, justly proud, and easily annoyed with the auburn strands that broke free of her ears and fell into her face. At the tail end of winter the hair had returned to its natural red-orange, much starker than the strawberry blonde it lightened to in the summer months. I liked it better this way—sui generis. Here was a woman you could pick out of a crowd.

If Jen had turned left, in my direction, I was prepared to stand up from the stoop all smiles, surprising her. We would go out for dinner. I would press out the dregs of my bank account to pay the tab at a noodle bar, or whatever she wanted. In a way I wanted this to happen—in one version of these memories, this *is* what happens: Jen and I hang our faces over steaming white porcelain bowls of ramen, talking little but sitting close, side by side, as if the steam could heal us. In one version it does heal us.

But now Jen and Raymond turn right toward Lafayette Street and the uptown trains, and I have to follow.

From the far corner of a 6 train car I watched the two of them reflected in the glare-warped window, my hat brim pulled to my eyebrows, my love with her face tipped delicately down at her cell phone, looking up and smiling at occasional comments from Raymond. She left him at the Union Square stop with a squeeze of the hand, getting off into the throng of rush-hour bodies that I swam in gratefully, anonymously, until Jen cut out of the current that pushed us toward the L train connection. Upstairs in the streets I nearly bumped into her—she'd stepped into the leeward draft of a newsstand just past the railinged maw of the subway stairs. It was another text, I assumed, her thumbs dizzying the screen, that saved me. I took cover under a Best Buy awning across the street, pretending to check my own phone as the glass double doors ejected shopper after laden shopper like tottering clay pigeons into the open air.

The white tents of the green market lined the perimeter of the square, gray-green in the waning light, wet-looking, tentative. People moved in twos and threes, coats open, inspecting the wares piled bounteously, colorfully on the folding wooden tables. The hemming-in buildings looked down on the scene with mute dull faces, blank-window eyes. It was a few weeks since thousands of protesters and activists, some of them our old ISO comrades, filled this square in a show of outrage over the latest in a pile of black bodies that New York's finest had heaped into the mortuaries: a stop-and-frisk gone bad, or worse than usual, a twenty-year-old breaking for his Bronx apartment entrance, reaching for his keys, five bullets in the back. Initially the police made much of the fact that a dime bag of weed was found on the body. Our group chose not to participate in the march—too much exposure, and what was the point? Marches and protests were the release valves a militarized state let the people pull. That was our position then, anyway.

When I looked through a break in the traffic at the spot where Jen had been a moment before—empty air. I found her on a bench in the center of the tent market, recognizing her from behind, that spout of orange-red ponytail. Just then she put her phone to her ear; she stood up, turning all the way around once, twice, smiling, raking her happy gaze past me like a lighthouse beam. Finally she found him. He'd snuck up in plain sight behind a woman with a double-wide stroller and a green puffer vest—Macduff in the moving grove. A kidder. I hated him instantly.

This particular kidder, this interloper (I couldn't help thinking of him in that way) had longish dark hair that swept messily over his ears and low over his forehead, curtain-parted—Al Pacino circa *Serpico*, slightly. He might have looked a little like me, if I'm honest, but of course I couldn't be honest. I couldn't be expected to be, could I? Objectivity is too heavy a cross to lay on the jilted.

The next several times they met up it was more of the same. They'd find each other at Union Square and set off for a meal or a drink somewhere within a few blocks. They were forming routines, traditions, memories, the kind of things you'd tell your kids about when they slid one after the other into your neat and ordered lives: *Your father used to sneak up on me every time we met here, and the thing is I knew it was coming, I knew to expect it, but he always found a way* . . . I remember the day Jen got off the 6 train early, at Astor Place instead of Union Square, and by the time I'd poked my head aboveground they were kissing. The repeating arches of the Cooper Union building stretched off behind them, dull pink in the late-winter light, or early-spring light—I couldn't have told you the difference just then. Young Macduff with his carefully messy hair had joined his stupid face to Jen's, his stupid fingers lifting the hair around her temples out of place. Jen's hands were on his hips, lightly, a little awkwardly, I thought—I hoped. I followed them onto St. Mark's Place, passing the high cluttered brownstones with the fire escapes like strange zippers down their fronts, ready to open up the buildings in zigzags and spill their privacies gruesomely into the street. I couldn't have noticed this at the time—memory labors to fill in the scene. What I noticed was that Jen's new boyfriend had taken her hand. More gradually I became aware of the near darkness, the last light clinging with stubborn fingers to the luminous strips of crosswalk paint, the serpentine coil of graffiti down the side of a corner mailbox, the luster of the stone in the white-stoned apartments. When we passed Hahn's building, blue-white in the gloom, I saw that her living-room light was on, the yellow glow in a window set half below street level. How the mighty were fallen—though I didn't have time to think about Hahn now, either, or dying Stephen.

I had just watched Jen lead Macduff down the stairs to the nondescript entrance into Cafe Mogador.

Cafe Mogador! It took the air out of my lungs to see it—Jen, with this interloper, casually entering what she knew was my favorite restaurant, the one Hahn had first taken me to, the one I'd introduced Jen to, and my parents, and all my friends, the few remaining to me, anyway. I couldn't quite believe I'd seen it. I set up at a spot on the patio with my back to the restaurant's large picture window, not quite daring to look inside. For a long time I watched the mysterious switchboard of the opposite buildings activate, permutate, the lights blinking on and off, shifting, sending mysterious signals. Halfway through a bottle of pinot I couldn't pay for I started to mourn each window light as it went out, each quick soundless fade. I felt no corresponding joy or relief at the windows newly lit. Nightlife was beginning, carving itself out of the ageless dark. At my next backward glance I picked the two of them out of the far corner of the restaurant, the lighted patchwork insubstantial and glossy on one side of the glass and on the other, at a shrunken candlelit table, Jen and Macduff leaning over their plates, stretching their necks like sunflowers. When they kissed again, I stood abruptly and a little unsteadily, rattling the untouched plate of tagines at my place. I passed down the steps and through the tinkling front door and into the close field of tables, past friends and colleagues, couples laughing and talking unawares, into one such couple with a wayward lurching step, the loud scrape of a bald man's chair—I apologized quickly, slurring my words, but it was too late. Jen had looked up with the noise.

In no time she was at the bar side, intercepting me. "What the hell are you doing here?"

Her eyes gleamed in the candlelight fiercely, her face distorted by the shadows, and she said again, "What are you doing here, Eli? You need to leave. You need to leave now."

"What are *you* doing here?" I said, but weakly. Jen and the rest of the room looked shrunken down in the wrong end of binoculars.

"Go home, Eli. Eli? I'm not talking to you like this."

"Our home?"

"I'm done talking. I'm going back."

"You're sure you don't want me to join you two? I'm a famous wit."

"Famous shit," she muttered as she turned away—or something like that. I couldn't quite hear her.

Really, I can't be sure she said anything at all—she was turning away from me, in a loud restaurant—but here again "memory" fills in the gaps: Let it be one last punning exchange between us, however sharp. I turned to the bartender at the bar, the big-bearded Dodgers fan I'd seen when I was here with Hahn. He nodded familiarly and with kindness in his eyes. I ordered a shot and drank it down and brought the glass smarting loudly to the bar, like an Old West chump.

"Add that to my tab, will you?" I said, and turned and headed back out to the patio and out into the night.

At breakfast the next morning, at the Phoenix House, Alex asked, "And where have you been lately?"

Tiffany was at the table too, looking listlessly into the face of her instant coffee, a toaster waffle untouched on the plate beside it.

I told them everything—or almost everything. I left out Macduff. I left out my private junkets following Jen through lower Manhattan. Alex asked about the money I'd stopped contributing to the House.

"All gone," I admitted. "All of it. I didn't even have the money for the train fare out here—jumped the turnstile like a punk."

"That's great. That's great to hear. Take more stupid risks like that," Alex said.

"You sound like Sam," I said. "We all do. Where is Little Lockjaw anyway? Sleeping in?"

Alex told Tiffany to go upstairs and get me some "train money." Alone in the room with her now, smiling fatuously, I told my ex how much I admired her talent for mixing business with pleasure. A column of gray moted light leaned in from the little window above the kitchen sink, spotlighting the small table, warming the tips of Alex's hair that slanted artfully down around her cheeks, like the flaring jawbone guards on a Roman soldier's helmet. Apparently Tiffany could cut hair, too.

"Take the money," Alex said, "and use it to get more money. You need to contribute to the House if you're going to live here."

"On the double, captain! Yes, captain!"

"So this is the Jen situation talking?" Alex said. "That's your moodiness lately?"

Tiffany returned to the kitchen with a timeworn, almost velvety twenty-dollar bill.

"I thought you were wrapping that up," Alex said. "I thought that was the deal."

"Yup," I said. "Yup. Yup."

With House money in my pocket I wandered around for the rest of the day, eating by-the-slice pizza, ducking into used-book shops. I jumped a pair of turnstiles to get over to Greenpoint that evening, using the rest of the cash to buy a supermarket bouquet of drying-out irises, a hint of brown at the delicate tongues, the purple of the petals a fading memory of purple— the best I could do.

I put the flowers in a vase on the high kitchen table and waited for Jen. I went to the piano, playing through the first fragile sections of "I Am Lost to the World," singing along where I could, recalling Mal's advice. I wasn't sure where Mal was at this latish hour. When she did come home I was already in bed, reading in the placid yellow light of the bedside table, like one half of a long-married couple. I remember perking up, puppyishly, until I heard that it was Mal moving around in her room on the other side of the apartment.

Then it was later, the room was dark, and I was vaguely aware of Jen getting under the covers beside me.

"Oh," I said, rousing. "There you are."

"I didn't expect to see you here."

"Did you see the flowers?" I said. "I got you flowers."

Apparently she hadn't seen them.

"Can I ask where you were tonight?" I said.

"I don't think you can, no."

"No?"

"I don't think you should, Eli. Not anymore."

"No?"

I saw now that she was lying not under the covers but on top of them, fully clothed, her dark hair spread over the pillow as if it were floating there—Ophelia-like, lake-borne. She looked straight up at the ceiling.

"What am I doing in your bed, then?" I asked. "Why do I still have a key to the apartment?"

"I don't know," she said. "Why do you?" Then she said, "Do you remember my roommate with the boyfriend who crashed on the couch with her? The green couch that the green cushion comes from?"

"I remember."

"What was he still doing there? What was either of them doing there?"

"You're just trying to hurt me now," I said. "If you really felt that way you'd have said something—you're not twenty anymore. You're just trying to hurt me."

"Maybe," she whispered.

She took a long breath—and something in it wanted out, I sensed. I sensed the magnitude of this moment rising up around me, suddenly, another of the tiny white open-topped rooms that made up the rat maze of Experience, Memory, Sea

Change. You stood inside the little room and above it at the same time, watching yourself scrabble desperately around.

"I brought you flowers, Jen. I came with my hat in my fucking hand."

"Thank you for the flowers," she said.

"But what—my presence isn't required anymore? I should just drop them off and leave? Out the servants' entrance?"

"If you're going to be ridiculous you should just leave."

"Why am I being ridiculous?"

"And I'm not doing the talking here, Eli. I'm not the one who needs to explain things."

"What should I be explaining?"

"Please leave, Eli. I'd like you to leave."

"You mean the PhD stuff? The Tommy's stuff?"

"I don't want to have this conversation anymore. Please just leave."

"Look, I'm sorry. I am sorry. I shouldn't have lied to you about that stuff, but it's just—I don't know . . . You have a calling, Jen. Do you know that? You've been lucky. Sometimes I think you don't realize how lucky you've been."

"Sure. A calling to play I-IV-V over and over again for strangers. To have my first and probably last collaboration just absolutely tank."

"Speed bumps," I said. "I promise you—speed bumps. You're brilliant, Jen, and you're beautiful and you're driven and you have something to drive *toward*, something to get you out of bed in the mornings—and that makes you lucky."

"And you don't have that? Is that really what you're saying?"

"I think I do now, but it takes me away from you sometimes."

"That's bullshit."

"Why is that bullshit?"

"Because it's bullshit! Who proposes to someone and just disappears? Who does that?"

"Sweetie." I reached across the comforter for her hand. "Sweetie, please."

She allowed it to be taken. "I'm going to miss you a lot," she said.

"What?"

"I'm going to miss you, Eli."

"Don't say that."

"It's true," she said.

At some point you start to lose, and lose, and lose again. You become practiced at it, connoisseurial. What's the line again? *The art of losing isn't hard to master*? Yet it's mastery without any of the feelings of mastery—there's no pride in it, no point to it, nothing pointed at all. It's a numbness that comes to you, a muted, white-noise, wandering-through-the-airport-at-midnight kind of feeling. Your skin begins to harden like a mold, and underneath it, moldering, wasting away, Pompeian, is your personality, your little lode of certainties and plans, and your backup plans, too, every one of them, the last handholds on autonomy. You begin to grope, you flail at things. You surprise yourself with the force of your sudden demands. If Bonnie and Clyde are going out on another of their nighttime junkets, you sure as shit are going along. You're not asking. You're tired of sitting around and waiting for the pearls of wise direction to fall from their lips. You're more than a bystander.

"What the hell are you talking about?" Sam said. "It's just a grocery run."

"You're taking the car on a grocery run?"

"Who said we're taking the car?" Alex said.

I slapped my cupped hand over the spidery bulge in Sam's jean pocket—a metallic chirring.

"We're out of everything," said Alex. "It'll be more than we can carry. How's the money search coming, speaking of expenses?"

"You're out of bullshit?" I said. "You're going on a bullshit run?"

Sam laughed a little, shrugging his shoulders. "Do you need to use the bathroom before we go?"

Only a few miles north on I-87 and the high-rises of the city start to sink behind you. The row houses thin out and disconnect, the land spreads out, becomes land. Green within green rises around the highway, mounding into the lower air, hemming in the view. A thick apron of grass rolls up to the tree line like a dais. You see neon golf links flash through the gaps, country clubs, small flickering lakes. Past Yonkers, past Bronxville, past Tuckahoe, Hastings-on-Hudson, Dobbs Ferry, Irvington, past White Plains off to the east, past Elmsford and Tarrytown and Sleepy Hollow—all these soothing names on the square green exit signs, their letters faintly glowing as the sky's fader drops, a gray sky going grayer with the promise of night and rain. The towns themselves tick by invisibly, always out of reach, out of sight behind a screen of trees. Only when you turn off the small highway to seek an address—it is a hamlet within a hamlet—do the white clapboard stores crop up awkwardly, belying the wealth of the people who shop there, or have their shopping done there. Stoplights droop from wires hung like holiday festoons, the telephone lines disappearing into the trees. A gravel shoulder skirts the road, replacing sidewalks. The light fixes milky and nacreous to the low-hanging sky—late light, summer light, though at the bottom of this well of woods it's hard to tell.

Now the mansions begin to arrive, slowly, at long stately intervals. They break through the trees with the bore of a driveway mouth, a place for a mailbox, a fleeting glimpse at a mini Versailles, a mini Buckingham, a faux Parthenon—"old wine in nouveau riche bags," Sam remarks, glancing at me in the rearview. "These people are not imaginative."

Alex rests her tapering hand on Sam's long thigh and I see that the fingers of the hand, the arched fingertips, shake a little.

"Still light out," she says to him.

"It's okay."

"Is it?"

"It's okay."

"Since when is it okay?"

We drive on. The road narrows and turns, dropping down into a gully with the dark ferns and saplings and low branches scratching the side of Sam's Buick. The light is weak except by contrast with the dark teeming trees spinning by, a strobe effect, chiaroscuro, and suddenly the road and the tree scrim swing around close to an open, lighted space beyond it.

"We're at the lake," Alex says. "We're already at the lake."

Through the whirring dark branches the lake comes to life, stop-start, like the action in a flipbook. It shimmers and turns with the road like a great gray disk.

"We need to slow down," Alex says. "We need to pull over somewhere and wait till it's darker."

"We've come at this time before."

"Not at this time of year, though, Sam. Sam, please."

Sam lets off the gas a bit but motions with a careless sweep of his hand to the overgrown roadside spinning like a slot machine, no shoulder at all. Another turn sends us reeling against the door panels like parts in a centrifuge. Finally, with the road straightening, a break in the trees gives on to a little inlet of gravel, a makeshift small parking lot—the slow pop and groan of rocks under our tires. Cutting the engine and the lights, we adjust our eyes to the blue-gray evening. A stand of maple and oak crisscrosses in front of Bosch's Lake, as Sam and Alex call it, though they've seen other mansions spaced generously along the water's edge. From here we can't actually see Bosch's property, that sprawling Austen-scape, but it can't be far. A narrow dirt trail with tree roots like protruding veins feeds into the parking lot at the right side, feeding back out of it and into the woods at the left side, curving away toward the lake. Trees rise all around us, shielding us from the road. Traffic is sparse— only a few cars hum by as the Buick's engine ticks down and the sounds of birds and the night's first crickets fill the car. Alex's hand has relaxed on Sam's ropy thigh, I notice, but now the leg itself bucks and tenses.

"That's him," Sam whispers. "Fuck, I think that's him."

"What?" Alex says. "Where?"

"That's fucking him."

An old man with his pale bald head uncovered, a brown mackinaw hanging open down past his knees, just now emerges from the trail mouth at the right of the lot. He glances up at our car—the same short gaunt face, the freeze-wrapped former jowls, the little eyes. He turns back toward the trail, whistles pure and high. A compact yet long-haired tawny dog trots out of the gloom, unleashed, his old belly swinging low and close to the ground. At the trail mouth the dog pauses to sniff and piss on a cluster of ferns. A hot-dog collie, if a collie at all.

"Yup," I say, "that's him all right. I pictured the dog being taller."

"Look down," Alex says. "Don't look at him. Look down."

Bosch is crossing at the front of the gravel lot, heading for the trail connect. He trails his coated arm behind him and snaps his fingers, whistling again. It occurs to me that the mackinaw is overkill in this warmish weather, an old man's habit. Not ten feet from our hood he gives the car a once-over, notices us, pauses, another up-and-down glance, then he turns down the lakeward trail. When the dog catches up to him, Bosch bends a little stiffly to rake his fingers in the collie's fur.

"He recognized us," Sam says. "We were just sitting here looking suspicious and he saw us."

"Let's go," Alex says. "Let's get out of here."

"How do you know he recognized us?" I say. "Why would he recognize us?"

In the front seat Sam is silent, still, the white tonsure of his bald spot showing above the headrest. He stretches out his arms on the steering wheel; his right leg starts going, bouncing fast and tight like a jackrabbit's.

Alex puts a hand out to calm him. "We really should go," she says.

"He saw us," Sam says. "He looked right at us. He recognized us."

Alex leans across the gearshift and turns the key in the ignition, the old bathroom fan of the Buick's motor belatedly catching and sputtering to life. Sam is doubled over in the front seat like he might be sick. A hollow *pock* sounds behind me as the brown trunk fills the rear window. Sam is out of the car, the air livid with the open door's *ding-ding-ding-ding-ding-ding-ding—*

"Sam?" Alex says. "What are you doing?"

In a moment she is up and out of the car too, opening her arms as if to shepherd him back inside, or block his way. She notices something. Her eyes go wide, pleading. She says airlessly, "What the fuck are you doing?"

Sam has the gun. He tucks the black blocky thing behind his shirt into his waistband. He folds Alex's arms like umbrella spokes to her side, holding them there and saying, "Relax. Wait here. You too," he says, suddenly turning at the weight of my hand on his shoulder.

"Sam," I say.

"It's fine," he says, "just wait here," and he starts toward the trail at a wolfish trot.

For a moment I obey him, I stay put, Alex and I both, stuck to the spot, and then suddenly we're running, suddenly we're sprinting down the trail. Up ahead in the latticed dimness Sam has picked up his pace, not turning around. "Sir?" he calls after Bosch. "Hey, sir!" The man in the too-large mackinaw turns his head at Sam's approach—I see him darkly, distantly, rolling up his shoulders in an instinctual flinch. The voice that comes out of him is defiant. "No press. No press!" Something menaces in Sam's movements, his footsteps breaking, rattling in the dirt. "What do you want?" the man says, almost quietly now—not a yell, not a plea. The yell of pain comes from Sam as the collie sweeps in from off the trail and latches on to his ankle. You can hear the dog growling, grunting as it rips and pulls. A single pistol shot, a loud *pop*, makes the dog lie down.

Now Bosch makes a sound—"God," it might be, or maybe "Gus," a dog's name. Bosch is running away from Sam, with Sam running after him—we are all running now—with Sam shouting after him to stop, wait, stop, *wait*, and now the old man has pitched forward, jerking forward and to the side as if bitten by the sound, then another, then a third loud pop. The last move is decisive but very slow, or perhaps it just seems that way from this distance, this catechized remove. Sam stands above Bosch as the old man rotates slowly on the ground, Sam tracking him with his gun, following his movements, as if stirring something in the air.

The report stops me cold—Alex too. After a few seconds she inches up beside me on the trail, staring straight ahead. Her look is small, white, mindless.

"He shot him," she says.

"Who? Who shot him?"

"Jesus Christ he shot him."

I must have looked mindless too. No light on upstairs, I'm sure of it. All of a sudden I was all feeling, the sum of automatic commands, but I couldn't seem to catch my breath. I was taking in great brimming mouthfuls of air, great gulps of the stuff, and it did no good. A sharp pain was in my chest now, an ocean in my ears. The body on the ground hadn't moved in several seconds—the man on the ground. Fish-mouthed, streaming, gasping, I turned again to Alex, searching out the face of this blank-faced woman who used to raise an eyebrow at me, quirk her pink playful mouth in the middle of a conference talk that had gone off the rails, gone ridiculous somehow—the look acknowledging this and diffusing it. I think I was looking for that look now, if I could be said to be doing anything in this mute, popped instant. Sam was standing twenty feet away from us, checking his clothes, I realized later, for blood.

He put the gun back into his waistband and broke into another trot. Alex put out her arm to stop him, the stile of her arm, and this time he let himself be checked.

"The shells," she said.

"What?"

"The shells."

"Shit."

While they collected them, I was moved on a watery conveyor toward the bodies, unconscious of my steps, my pained breathing, the sweat running down my face and into my eyes, the body asserting and erasing itself in rhythm, a sort of tidal flow. Here was a dog tipped over on its side—forelegs sprawled, a modest swell of dark cranberry blood slicking the hair down the neck and upper back. The whitish tongue lolled sideways in the parted mouth below flat, dark, crow-like eyes. I was distantly aware of a conversation about footprints. Alex was off the trail trying to wrestle a low leafy oak branch from its trunk while Sam, lanky Sam, muttering, bent and bent at the waist like an oil derrick as he scoured for the last shell, he couldn't find it, it wasn't there—

"Here," I said. "It's here."

A lucky penny catching the light, a gold doubloon, it hid half under the dog's back leg, in the wispy sandy hair running off it. The shell was warm in my hand, dully shining. Something burnt hung in the air, something wet underneath it. I was less attentive to Bosch, or really more afraid of him, but now here he was too: on his back, one side of the beige mackinaw fallen open to reveal the swell of gut pressing out against the pale blue button-up blooming with black-red spots, black galaxies of blood. His legs twisted awkwardly away from him, in mid-stride. The thin bellows of his neck stretched out under his chin, his face cast back, eyes open and full of shock—a bronze expression, cast. The mark on his forehead sat too high for a Hindu's bindi, but this is what came to me even then. What blood there was pooled darkly in the little well just below the vanished hairline, the skin around it bruising already, and under the eyes. His color was changing.

"For fuck's sake," Alex said, pulling me out of my crouch, throwing me backward toward the car. She had the leaf-rake in her hand. "Follow Sam!"

In the car Sam drove at speed, taking turns that pushed and rattled me like a loose cracked egg from one side to the other of the cavernous backseat. I was leaking something, emitting strange sounds. When I looked up the trees were streaming fitfully by in the window, another chiaroscuro, more dark than light now, a nauseous-making darkening strobe. I closed my eyes and opened them again and the scene hadn't changed.

"Sit up," Alex said from the front seat, turning around. "Put your seat belt on. Be quiet."

I obeyed and obeyed. I was waiting for sirens, roadblocks, helicopters lowering down to block our way—I knew with perfect clarity that someone was coming for us, and then no one did. Perhaps no one had heard the shots in that isolated wealthscape, or if they had they'd mistaken them for hunters, teenagers playing with leftover Fourth of July noisemakers . . . Apparently we'd been lucky. Then, a little above Yonkers, our headlights began to mist over, lighting like amber the first drops of rain, little flecks of it, mote-like, then the long limpid lines. From the elevated highway through upper Manhattan the lights of the city appeared crazed, schizophrenic, trailing down the windows in long prismatic strips and cracks—a smell of rain mixing with the urine (my own, I realized) and everything else the rain kicked up, ammoniac, sweet, sulfuric. In the front seat Sam had the window cracked. I heard him breathing in that watery shearing air.

"You think this rain is getting up into Westchester?" he finally said.

When we got back to the neighborhood Sam parked the car a good mile from the House—we didn't question his judgment on this point, but Alex was saying, almost whispering at first, her voice just rising above the million fingers of water on the car's broad roof, "Nothing planned, nothing fucking planned . . . No message in it, no meaning in it, nothing organized, nothing fucking *planned* . . ." she said, with the litany rocking her up into a hoarse scream. Sam rolled up the window. Alex rocked forward and back in her seat, rocking the car, rattling visibly. I was on a wavelength with her, on the horrible conveyor again going past the horrible features of the dog in its false sleep, Bosch with the cast-back neck turning ashen already, the birdlike sheen in his eyes.

"People know who he was, what he did," Sam was saying. "They'll put it together."

"Oh they do? They will? So that was your plan all along? That was your plan all along? That was your fucking *plan*?"

"He saw us," Sam whispered. "He recognized us."

The bullet hole was high and to the right on the forehead, the little shining well of blood with the dark bruising all around it, starlike, an explosion of nerves.

"You think people are going to remember what some corporate asshole did two years ago? You think people are going to care? Joe Six-pack wearing a hole in his fucking couch?"

The bruising around the wound looked synaptic, a new decaying life, like the bruising on a pear.

"Tell them I did it on my own," Sam said. "The police. Tell them you had nothing to do with it, it was only me, and it was. I didn't mean to, but it was. He wouldn't stop. He saw us—"

"Shut up."

"He recognized us. Tell them you tried to stop me. Go tonight, right now, go right now and tell them—"

"Shut up! Just shut up!" Alex said. "Just shut up and shut up and shut—*up*!" Alex said, lifting off on the last word into another scream, soaring on it.

Sam reached for the driver-side window handle and cranked it down again, gasping in the rainy air.

In the backseat I reached for my eyelid, my left, suddenly. A sudden something, a larval something had hatched and was beating its stiff wings unceasingly under my eye. I'd begun screaming too, matching Alex decibel for decibel.

In other versions of that night Alex and I do go to the police. Who knows what we say there—I haven't worked that out. The catharsis, the resettling of gravity in the seat of the stomach, is simply in turning up, trudging into that harsh-lit room, linoleum floors, maybe a chain-link gate at the intake desk. We are soaked and shaking, but we are there.

"Did you see this?" Tiffany said the next morning.

She put the open laptop in front of Alex at the dim-lit breakfast table, gently, with a kind of reverence. The *Times* had the story, the *Posts*, the TV news stations with their helicopters hovering over the lot where we'd parked, now marked off with police tape. I didn't know what Alex was pretending to see for the first time exactly, but I knew enough. My eyelid twitched and gathered, an involuntary puckering. I felt the pores of my forehead yawn open. I hadn't slept. I hadn't had solid food in nearly twenty-four hours, and I had no appetite.

The computer's pale glow lit Alex's features from underneath, making cavities above her chin and eyebrows, dark raccoon circles of her eyes—she looked stricken but to me utterly staged. She wore a carnival mask.

"What is it? What's up?" Sam said, bringing a cereal bowl over from the counter, hovering at Alex's shoulder.

Tiffany watched them reading the screen; I watched Tiffany watch them. She wore an oversize, Sam-like T-shirt that said "Lifeguard" on the front of it, with a large red cross underneath the word. The shirt made her look younger, more naïve, washed up on the far shore of a teenage sleepover. She frowned a little, a perplexed searching frown that took Sam in as a smile grew around the corners of his lips—a sliding scale.

"Wow," Sam said. "Is this for real? Is it my birthday today?"

"What are you talking about?" I sensed it was my turn.

An early-morning jogger had discovered the body and alerted police—no search party had been organized, no alarm sounded previously. It made you wonder about the state of Bosch's marriage that no call should go out to the police when he failed to return home from his evening walk. Maybe the dog was mostly Bosch's, maybe he had another apartment, a pied-à-terre in the city to work and play in. Who knew how the other half really lived—their intrigues, their secrets, the array of their enemies. All the articles we'd seen so far had been variations on the AP story and basically useless. Tiffany's article too: a few brief facts about the body's discovery, and lower down a brief paragraph of background on Bosch and Soline, Soline's "violations" (sickeningly toothless word), the subsequent bankruptcy and trial, Bosch's ultimate exoneration. The police were investigating all possible leads—a piece of boilerplate—and asked anyone with information to come forward.

In another version of these memories the mad heartbeat in my eyelid, the fluttering wing pushing out of my eyeball carries me off to a private corner of the House, out into the bright glaring streets, anywhere. I make the call myself. I tell the police what I know. Which means what—a plea bargain? Immunity in exchange for testimony? I call a lawyer. I call my parents with their lawyer friends. I take Jamaal aside, I take Tiffany, the local Juris Doctors. Or else I climb up to the third-story roof of the House and contrive to leap headfirst for the sidewalk.

Sam turned to the table now, addressing us with a clownish, overextended smile. "Somebody beat us to it! Where should we send the thank-you card?"

My skin slipped under its hardening layer, like a shudder of water under ice. It was the glee in Sam's Grand Guignol style—

"Jesus," Alex breathed.

"What?"

"A lot of good it does Maria Nava and everybody else," I said. "The eight-cents-on-the-dollar crowd."

"Fuck Maria," Sam said. "I thought we'd established that. As for the others, well, yeah, I guess you're right. It was always going to be hard to get back the money Bosch stole from them, but I guess you're right."

"Since when do you read *The New York Times*?" Alex asked Tiffany.

"I saw it linked."

"Linked where?"

"On Twitter."

"Twitter?" Alex said. "I thought we weren't doing Twitter— any of that corporate-troll bullshit. We're supposed to be limiting our exposure."

"I don't *send* tweets, I just follow a few friends and old ISO people."

"Deactivate the account," Alex said, and turning to Sam and me, "You guys too. Or no, don't deactivate, just stay off it. Keep quiet online. Even this Bosch story—keep the searches to a minimum, don't establish any patterns. I don't like to think what Big Brother can swipe from the ether nowadays. And another thing: No more sticky fingers, no more trawling for cell phones, laptops, whatever. We need to cut all that out for the time being, shrink our exposure to zero."

Alex's look, roving slowly across the table, dared us to disagree. Tiffany held her face perfectly still, I noticed, like a bell jar.

"And the money piece?" I said.

"We'll figure something out. You'll help us figure it out, Eli."

"Shrink it down like a tightly puckered asshole," said Sam, looking at me as he curled shut the fingers of his right hand into a fist, making a sealant *schloop* sound. I can't be sure but I think he might have winked at me then.

He was coming unhinged. I suppose we all were.

"Is this really so funny to you?" Alex said. "We haven't exactly been discreet in our opposition to Soline and Bosch. We could be suspects in this."

"Suspects in what?"

We all turned at the sound of Jamaal's voice, a little groggy coming out of him as he filled up the kitchen doorway. He wore a V-neck undershirt, loose basketball shorts, rubber sandals. Greg was behind him and apparently showered and fully dressed, his wet bangs icicling down toward the bunched bushy brows that seemed to repeat Jamaal's question.

"Come check this out," Sam said excitedly, waving them over to Tiffany's computer. I couldn't tell if the flapping-pennants tone came out of Sam genuinely or not. I think now that it did. And why shouldn't fake enthusiasm at someone else's murderous work shade into real enthusiasm, as if the work really were someone else's? Wasn't that what was happening to me? Each time I flashed on the scene—each time the scene flashed on me, broke in on me—I felt less and less attached to it, less attached to my life, my body, the conveyor belt lifting me off the ground until I floated above the trail, silently, above the bodies laid out underneath me like bones in an archaeologist's dig, the wasted fragments calmly waiting for some magical touch to piece them back together again, wire them upright.

We lay low in the House, all of us, for another two days. No one had had to tell Tiffany or Greg or Jamaal to stay inside—they just followed our lead, crouching when we crouched. Our faces shone with strain, everyone squinting indoors, communicating through private signals what strategies they'd worked up to cope with the minutes like hours, hours like slow carving knives against the skin.

For my part, I thought of Jen. I sought her out in the whited-out, shocked spaces of my mind, trying to re-etch her there. Stray moments obliged me by reappearing, brief scenes, pale figments that I managed to hold, tremblingly, like water in my cupped fragile hands. In the foolishness of my passion I'd deleted all photos of Jen from my phone, all videos, text messages—all the sweet banal e-mails going back to the first tentative weeks of our relationship. Passion's passionate inverse, really. It was the storm I'd carried with me out of the calm, quiet breakup. All keepsakes I'd trashed too—down the garbage chute in Jen's apartment complex went the small cardboard moving box silted with romantic notes, movie tickets, theater tickets, concert tickets, the playbills that featured Jen's name just inside the front cover, the creased trail map we'd used to navigate Angels Landing in Zion Park, the single-sheet program from Jen's senior recital with the baroque embroidering notes in the margins, the doodles I'd made during the Liszt and Gouldian Bach pieces that bored me, the other notes, complete with rapturous underlines, that I'd made during the long John Adams piece and the Mahler lieder that enraptured me (*remarkable tone* . . . *eerie yet beautiful* . . . *beautiful* . . . *BEAUTI-FUL!* . . .).

It was more than the idea of Jen I loved, I'm sure of it now, much more than her talent and her beauty. The deleted e-mails I mourned the most were the ones in which she'd massed all the sweet silly punny texts we'd exchanged over months and that her phone could no longer hold. Intending to file them away in her computerized journal, Jen was typing them out one evening at the high wooden dining-room table. I snuck up behind her, hovering my chin near her shoulder and whispering some hammy accusation about what was *zees*, incriminating notes from her *paramour*?

A little ridiculous to have to clarify this now—I am the source, I realize, the *fons et origo* of this ridiculousness—but at the time Jen and I were still buzzed on our recent engagement and Jen's actual paramour, her Macduff, was more than a year away. On that evening at the table Jen slapped shut the laptop, refusing to show me what it was she'd been copying down. It made me wonder. I teasingly asked about it several times in the following days. She only assured me there was nothing to worry about, they were only good things, but they were private, bound for her journal . . . The next time I caught her compiling the notes I abandoned all subtlety and snatched the computer away from her. I promised a full-body massage if she'd let me read, holding the laptop at stiff arm's length (negotiating from a position of strength). And I didn't mean the half-assed foreplay massage, either, but the real, arduous thing, the kind of massage that would make us both sore. More and more Jen complained of the knots that formed near the graceful wing-bases of bone in her upper back (Neruda: "fever or forgotten wings") and that came from sitting upright at the piano, her arms outstretched, hour after hour, day after day.

I did the lower back too that night, the backs of her arms, glutes, hamstrings, calves, the sensitive soles of her feet. And eventually I did get to see in e-mail form a long run of compiled text messages that read like sloppy unguarded haiku, or the transcript from some blissed-out surrealist trial.

> Hey there bear. Just sitting here and missing you.
> Do you swear?
> Didn't your boy Jesus say you must NOT swear?
> You're my only boy!
> Correct answer
> Ach, gotta go
> Raymond giving you the lipless smile again?
> Talk soon, mon amour

> Mon cher?
> Here!
> I really miss you today
> Early period or late period Cher?
> The one with the tone warbling. My voice is boxy with love of you.
> Hurry home to me then! I'm dead inside in this empty apartment
> Soon!

> Fuck if I can put a single sentence right today
> It's all right, sweetie. Come back to it later

Actually it's all wrong. Aye, there's the rub.
I'd like to rub you a little later on
Deal

Miss my heart
Ditto! A thousand dittoes!

These are reconstructions, of course, earnest best guesses. It soothed and distracted me to write them down in the marble-covered notebook I'd labeled "Notes on Something, Anything Else." Later, I changed this simply to "Notes," a placeholder title for a project that felt at once more and less meaningful, more and less urgent, more and less confused. What was I writing about? What was I writing for? I filled several of these notebooks, eventually, with stories, scenes, recollections, meditations, litanies of regret, things I thought I might be able to make some end-run sense of, but to what end? What good could understanding do me anymore? Here were unbudgeable facts: Life had changed irrevocably, once and for all. Nothing and no one could be brought back from the dead. Not a man with a field of blooming red flowers for a chest. Not a relationship you'd killed.

Yet it soothed me, it did distract me to make my notes, sitting at the kitchen table late into the night or at the red-lit desk upstairs, always writing privately, surreptitiously. I got down all the text exchanges I could remember, some of them specific, miraculously recalled, most loose and representative. I tried to get down some of the late-night conversations, too, all the talks about music and literature and politics we'd had, Jen and I, in those first heady weeks. You're trying to find out if this is a person you can find rest in, and give rest to yourself, that vital shelter. You're trying to find out if this is a person you can make a life with. Very much contra Engels and his anti-monogamy arguments, of course, but who really cared about those anymore? I certainly didn't.

Other details, other realities that cut through the overgrowth of theory—

Jen had a pattern of small orange freckles across the bridge of her nose and onto her cheeks that sometimes looked constellatory, little suns lit up and burned brighter by the light of the sun overhead.

There was something slightly waxy in the skin of her face, not false, not over-tight, just a certain paraffin sheen at the shelves of her cheekbones, the curve of her forehead. It may have been the soap she used, a brand I'd never heard of—Newpeau, something like that. How oddly touching it could be to see the blue-and-white squeeze bottle sitting squat on its cap beside the electric toothbrush—Jen swore by that, too—in the bathroom. You felt you'd penetrated some mystery, or really that some vital door had been opened to you: Here was true intimacy, quotidian, routinized, unembarrassed.

"I used your foaming face wash," I told Jen one day.

"You what?"

"I hope that's okay."

"Why? Your skin is perfect."

"I wanted to feel what it was like—those little scrubbies are like microbes or something? Or what's in there?"

"Who knows. I've been using it since I was thirteen, fourteen. Force of habit."

A decade of the same face soap! More! At the time I figured that boded well and I went about inspecting other signs and talismans in the bathroom Jen shared with Mallory. This was the two-bedroom place in Astoria, where the air conditioner dropped a shimmering bead curtain of condensation down the front of the building. I learned Jen had fierce opinions against antiperspirant—not just sticky and gross but cancerous—and that she took a rather French view of deodorant in general: A little went a long way, she said, even in a New York summer. More than once she came home to my ravenous, rooting embraces and kisses that sought out her breasts, of course, but also the faint musty resin on her inner arm and armpit, the hint of salt there that I licked with bovine earnestness and languor. At first she squirmed under these caresses, giggling, but soon she must have sensed what they did for me, and real passion ensued. It's difficult to describe. The body is equipped with so many delicate buttons and levers, wondrous and variable. But this was more than bodily, certainly more than a mechanical reaction. I think the real excitement lay in the mutual taking down of barriers, guards, insecurities, uncertainties, hesitations, fears.

It was around this time that Jen told me about the handsome young priest she used to masturbate to, the thought of him sitting there perversely aroused in the latticed darkness of the confessional. These had been the last days of her observance—eighteen years old, a new freshman at Randolph, and like most of us she'd borne the accidents of birth through her childhood and into young adulthood, the dying sparks of them anyway, the last scuds of momentum. Within a year she'd made peace with her agnosticism ("Taking off God was like taking off my clothes at night," she said. "It felt natural and honest"), but for now she was still a confessee, a penitent. In the darkened box she said the words she had to say, mentioning the sins of the flesh she and her first college boyfriend had shared in. I knew very little about this boyfriend and never found out much, never asked much. These were the limits of my own inhibitions—and to think that in exchange for this comforting ignorance I took a measure of pride in my sophisticated restraint! (My faults have been obvious enough, I suppose, but here I confess them outright. Let the four corners of this page, and the next and the next, make up my belated confessional.)

Jen knew her confessor by voice and by sight, the thirty-something recent seminarian sent to palliate the Gospel to the college set. Father Otto's sermons floated down from the pulpit like wafted balloons, lightly, religion as self-help and inspiration, but in the confessional booth his manner changed. He asked Jen how many times, how often, and how recently. He asked if and how often she'd initiated the sinful encounters.

"He really asked you that? He called them 'sinful encounters'?"

"Yes."

"So much for softening the Gospel."

"He was a Ratzinger disciple, soft in tone, hard in everything else. You learned that youth was no guarantor of progress. Or not in any predictable way. Sometimes you need whole generations to die out before it's safe to come up for air."

"And what did you tell this guy? What did you say to him?"

"About my boyfriend? I told him everything. It was dozens of times, sometimes two times, three times a day, and I initiated plenty."

"And he was titillated? You could hear it in his voice?"

"Oh no, no, I doubt it. Not like you," Jen said, "Mr. Raring to Go." She cupped her hand around me through the bedsheet and pretended to downshift, dropping her voice. "We'll take care of this in just a minute. Let me finish my story, okay?"

"I know, I wasn't trying to . . . I couldn't help it."

"I wouldn't want you to. But in a minute."

It wasn't until several months later that Jen came back to the image of the young priest sitting straight-backed and tempted on his side of the filigreed partition. Jen and her boyfriend had tumbled out already, not much to say to each other in the postcoital moments, or ever. When she pictured Father Otto sliding his hand under his habit, it was a conscious blasphemy, and this is what titillated. It was all about her, though, it was about her and for her, a gesture of freedom. And this freedom was now in everything she did—how she thought, how she talked and wrote, and how she played, with a new looseness, a new dynamic boldness, a new disregard for the inevitable small mistakes (or big mistakes) that marked the way to real progress.

For her senior recital Jen called on Father Otto to let her use the beautiful white-pewed chapel for her performance. She remembered the low-hung crystal chandelier, like something out of a European great house, and the Art Deco flair of the white-and-black-checkered linoleum at the front of the space, the inverted bowl of a ceiling, the white balcony that circled not far underneath it like the upper tier of a wedding cake. It was a little girl's fantasy of a wedding cake set down in the darker, stranger dream space of a Lewis Carroll story—she could think of no better place to hold a recital. The acoustics, too, were surprisingly good, though this was almost an afterthought. I pictured Jen as the little dark figurine planted plastic-feet-first in the cake's lower tier, a little stiff and nervous-looking in her long black scoop-necked dress, her hair in a brassy chignon, her hands clasped together at her front as she made the littlest bow after her Liszt piece, still early days. The grand piano was behind her with its broad black wing stuck up in the air and threatening to whirl up like a wind-borne maple pod (we called them "helicopters" when I was a kid and stuck the split sticky ends to our noses). The concert grand was something Jen had to master, tamp down, and at the beginning of the concert and from my vantage at the back she looked slight to the task. At the keyboard, though, something changed. She seemed to grow and grow, Alice-like, filling the room with huge confident sound, sitting straight-backed and commanding at the bench, her arms outstretched and moving hypnotically. Watching her play like that again in my mind, I realized how this slight pale frame could hold enough brazenness to approach Father Otto after her private desecrations of him, and after four years of absence.

"It wasn't quite four years," Jen said. "I'd turned up once or twice more for sentimental reasons—Easter, Advent, the high pageantry stuff. I hadn't actually spoken to him, though, and I'd never gone back to confession."

"What did you say to him when you asked about the recital? He was at the concert, wasn't he? Salt-and-pepper hair, cool-guy goatee?"

"You were sitting in the row right behind him. Handsome, wasn't he?"

"Wow," I said. "It's masturbation as thought murder."

"I didn't *kill* him, Eli."

"You killed his relevance. You'd killed his magical authority over you."

"All I said was that I wanted to play beautiful music in a beautiful space and he said of course. He didn't hesitate. Father Otto was a nice enough man with the keys to a beautiful building. It was that simple. No more magic than you brought to it yourself."

It was that simple. We lay in bed naked and simple and

conducted our lives for each other, our pasts, our desires, everything—or almost everything. We didn't go in for total disclosure, honesty as blood sport. We weren't foolish enough to think that the heart's dark corners look good under a klieg light. Some secrets you carry around forever, like scar tissue. Later on, of course, there were secrets I could have unburdened her of if I'd been paying better attention, if I'd been present in mind as well as body, and later there were secrets I could have unburdened her of if I'd been present at all. Jen was right about that too.

These were secrets that wouldn't have needed to be *secrets*, I wrote, *that wouldn't have existed at all* . . . And here I stopped my note-making, checked my pen. I was at the edge of another counterfactual no-man's-land, a field littered with what-ifs. What good did it do to imagine how things would have been if they'd been different than they were? The body was there now, irrevocable, unbudgeable. It wouldn't be reanimated. It wouldn't move again.

In the last of the kitchen cupboards there were half-empty bottles of cumin, chili powder, coriander, onion powder, nutmeg, and cinnamon stacked in a maladroit pyramid. There were two cans of Campbell's bean and bacon soup in another cupboard, a folded packet of taco seasoning at the terminus of a red powdery trail through the sawdust and filing-small cockroach droppings. There was an old roach motel in another cupboard, dry and ineffectual. And that was it. Nothing to speak of in the refrigerator or freezer—greasy condiment bottles, frozen peas hard as rock salt, a box of stale Cheerios on top of the fridge. No bread, milk, meat, cheese, nothing to sustain a person past dinnertime last night, and it was breakfast now, on the third morning, and there were six of us.

At the breakfast table behind me Greg Baxter sat folded forward with his head in his arms, his shorn, affronting head. He'd come down by himself while I was surveying the food, grunting a hello and slumping down into his seat, and it was then that I noticed the disappeared hair.

I placed a quarter-full bowl of dry Cheerios in front of him, wordlessly, and sat down with my own bowl.

"Thanks," he said, looking up bleary and unfocused, unshowered. When he saw me staring he said, "I needed a change. We're also out of shampoo."

The caterpillar brows looked starker than ever in the sudden moonscape of his upper face and head, pale white, with only the faintest shadow of former hair, the sloping forehead running up into an almost geologic baldness. It gave him a startled look.

"What?" he said.

"Did you Bic it or something? It's impressively smooth."

"Not much else to do around here, is there?"

I thought I might have heard an accusation, a tremor of fear in Greg's voice, but I ignored it.

"The skinhead look," I said. "Very classic."

"Don't be so predictable," Greg said.

I set to my bowl of stale Cheerios, but slowly—you had to make it last.

"A king in the morning, a pauper at night," I said. "Do you know that phrase?"

Greg didn't answer me.

It was the dietary folk wisdom of some Latin American

country—Peru, maybe, or Venezuela. You ate heartily in the morning and lightly, poorly at night, if you wanted to keep thin. And solvent, of course. This was the political subtext some writer had picked up on and expounded. "It might have been Trotsky, or maybe not," I said, holding forth to Greg in his waxing, weighing silence. He could see the object lesson in ideology, though, couldn't he? Out in the rural hinterlands where bread and milk and coffee cost less than the typical dinner foods, you learned to do your real eating in the morning, and you learned to valorize this, looking down on the fat late-dining rich in the big cities. In the same way, medieval Catholics learned to look up to Lazarus, wretched on earth, like them, but now rich and sitting at a heaped heavenly banquet—*Ave Lazarus*, patron saint of political quietism. In certain moods I could almost admire the elegance of this sham thinking—

"This is sand," Greg interrupted me. "These Cheerios just collapse into sandy sludge the second they hit your molars. I can't eat this shit."

"Yeah, sorry," I said. "It's no good."

"Why are you sorry?" said Greg, taking me in squarely now.

"Huh?"

"Why are *you* sorry?"

A long silence filled the kitchen.

"Why don't we just go out and buy some more food?" Greg said. "There's a novel idea."

"Do you think we should? Alex is probably right that we should be lying low, don't you think?"

"Do I think we should starve? No. I don't think we should starve."

"Well, how much money do you have? Because that's the other thing. I've only got twenty-eight dollars to my name, and twenty of it is in an account I can't access without an ATM."

"We can go to my ATM," Greg said. "Are you coming? I could use the help carrying the bags."

Outside, I squinted with what felt like my entire face—I felt the warmth of the sun on my teeth. I shook at the knees, sometimes dipping like a lunge stretcher when a step didn't hold and I had to struggle for balance. An instant oil was covering my face, and the eye flutter was back, sudden grabs and contractions that I couldn't predict or control. We made it to the Chase ATM, Greg and I, and continued on toward the Korean grocery in the blue shadow of the 7 train's hulking tresses. I found I kept calmer with my eyes on the sidewalk, the sun skittering off the little deposits of shine in the cement, going dull at the gum spots, in the sudden shade of a box tree. I saw the people of the city from the waist down: suit pants, jeans, shorts, skirts, a color-wheel menagerie of bony knobby hairy lower legs ending in running shoes, high-tops, loafers, sandals, high heels, boat shoes. One lower leg in particular arrested my attention, pale and hugely swollen at the ankle, the white sock stretching to hold its bulbous load. I left the ankle behind at the edge of a crosswalk, following Greg's New Balance trainers until a bass voice shouted, "Hey, hold it! Stop right there!"

I jerked up instinctively to see a plump traffic cop holding his palm out to us. A trio of men in green reflective vests and white hard hats bent over an open manhole behind him. Into the subterranean darkness I could see a hooked stepladder descending alongside a dirty segmented yellow hose, wriggling wormlike with strange pressures. It suddenly horrified me to think that a grown man had to go down there, tucking in his shoulders to get past the hose, breathing in the tangy decayed stench that came up to us a step delayed. We were back on the sidewalk now and I was suddenly nauseous.

Afterward, in the Korean grocery, I leaned my head into a freezer case. Greg asked if I was okay.

"Did you make eye contact with that cop?" I said.

"No, I don't think so. Why?"

"That scared the shit out of me. I haven't caught my breath."

Quickly, unobtrusively, we split up to fill hand baskets with the kind of food that could last us a week, two weeks, a month if we needed it to—bunker food. Pastas and soups, beans, canned vegetables and fruit, a goldbrick stack of ramen noodles, rice, bread, peanut butter and jelly, a trio of on-sale boxes of cornflakes, milk, a flat of bottled water that I tucked under my arm and labored toward the front of the store with. Greg intercepted me and reasoned that the water was too bulky to carry home and not exactly indiscreet, either, if that's what we were going for. I granted the point, but instantly I thought of the electric-looking orange water that stank in the bowl after my recent urinations. ("You're supposed to pee pale," Jen had told me—another intimacy.) I went back to scour the shelves until I found a box of Kool-Aid powders to help the tap water go down.

"Apparently I'm eight years old," I told Greg outside. "You sport a blinding neo-Nazi haircut for the cause and I can't even drink plain tap water."

Greg snorted a little, surprising me. A car slowed as it passed us in the street, pulling up to the curb, idling, a pair of brown legs getting out and a female voice calling "Yeah, you're good," apparently to the driver. It took me half a block to restart my breathing.

Greg said, "It'll be nostalgic. Like summers of old."

"What?"

"I used to drink that sugary crap every day."

"Oh, the Kool-Aid. Yeah. Thanks for buying that," I said. "Thanks for covering all this."

"Sure," Greg said, but now he was the one hesitating. At length he asked how much longer I thought we'd be lying low. I said I didn't know. He asked about the House's plans now that things with Bosch had obviously changed. A ponderous weight on that last word—"changed."

"I really don't know."

"Well, what are Alex and Sam saying about it?"

"I don't think they know either. I haven't actually asked them. Have you?"

Greg snorted again, but now it meant something else. I realized he and I were in the middle of the longest conversation we'd ever had—mostly I regretted it. The sun, late morning now, came down like a physical presence, a hot hand on the nape of my oily neck, the prickly crown of my head. The moving shadows that moored to the feet and legs of passersby crisscrossed on the sidewalk. Certain nips of quartz or marble, shiny somethings in the gray poured concrete, caught the light and seemed to lift from their places into the lower air, hovering, like fireflies, or the spirits of the dead.

"Can I ask you something?" Greg said.

"Okay," I said.

"And you'll answer me honestly?"

"Why wouldn't I?"

"Did we have anything to do with this?"

"No."

He looked across at me. "You're sure we had nothing to do with this? None of us? None of them?"

"No," I said.

"No you're not sure or no we had nothing to do with it?"

"Fuck you, all right? You asked your question, I answered it. I think I liked you better in bow ties, Gregory, your fucking cardigans—at least we knew where you stood."

"What's that supposed to mean?"

"You asked your question, I answered it."

We kept on toward the House with our grocery bags heaped in front of us, weighting us down. A few blocks shy of the House I started to feel it in my legs—not the groceries, not the first stint of exercise in three days. It was a sort of muscular dread that came over me, a resistance, a force field that the House put off and that my body couldn't penetrate. Ocean surf in my ears again, and underneath it a reedy whine like you'd hear after a loud bang. Something swooped at the corner of my eye and the eyelid clutched horribly. You felt the drag of surf against your ankles and legs, thighs, stomach, chest, slowing you now, floating you out past the breakers, out into the currents that carried you away from land. I could just hear Greg's voice coming over the sound of these swells, these *vagues* that pushed me back—

"All I'm saying is that if any of us are involved, in any way, or even if we're not, staying put is not necessarily a good idea. An investigation like this starts at the scene and goes out in concentric circles—family, friends, neighbors, anybody in the area who may have harbored a grudge, anybody, let's say, who may have gotten arrested on a disorderly at a Soline protest in Phoenix—"

"You seem to know a lot about this," I heard myself say, but distantly, drifting back.

"Yeah," Greg said, "I do. My stepdad's a cop. Okay?"

I was drifting back, wavering, floating away from my life and somehow dreading it at the same time. What I know is that I stopped short of the House's high cement stoop, set the groceries down on the sidewalk, and made an excuse to Greg. It wasn't a convincing one, I'm sure. I didn't need it to be.

When I was little, my parents embarked on a fitness regimen that consisted largely of charity 5Ks, a little gym work, and their first outings to the local high school's complex of under-kept tennis courts. To these last I tagged along. The thick grain of the courts came from a mixture of sand and other anony-mous grit that the court makers must have added to slow the playing surface down, or perhaps just out of thrift. In any case, it suited our family's debutante needs, keeping the ball high and hittable. We darted and swooped around the courts on Saturday mornings (I was aping my parents then, a preteen's carefree prerogative), pretending not to care what happened to our shots, reveling only in the fun of it, the exercise, suppos-edly, and the fact that we really were debutantes now, twirlers of tennis rackets bought at a proto–big box store called Pilgrim's Progress. We were playing the gentry's game not far from the spot where the *Mayflower* spilled its first WASPs! I recall my mother in bright red cargo shorts—the late eighties must have had another name for them. My father wore gray sweatpants and an Andre Agassi–esque windbreaker, a study in greens: neon, olive, pine. The courts were far from pristine, as I've said, and my parents looked much too much of their time to really threaten the timeless Wimbledon-white purity of the game, yet here was Dad unselfconsciously experimenting with top-spin and here was Mom, on my side of the court, hopping back to return the shot with a laughing *yip!* She regathered herself, mimicked a skirt-pinching curtsy as the yellow ball dribbled into the net.

"I say, Joseph!" Mom called in her best grande dame. "A cracking shot!"

"Oh you flatter me, Susanne-Anne!" Dad said.

My mother's name is Sue, my father's Joe, and in this memory they're laughing with the color high in their faces, the wind in their ridiculous outfits. Merciful forgetting has spared me any notion of what I must have worn on those outings, but I do recall the feeling of confidence gathering in my strokes as I hit the ball flat, then obliquely, then with slice (I caught on to the sport faster than either of my parents), and I also recall the uneasy dawning sense that my parents' rapport had come before me, developed independent of me, and perhaps had survived a little in spite of me. I was quickly very serious about tennis and often glum, throwing rackets and shouting what curses I'd learned in middle school. Not long after this my parents eased off on the family-style tennis dates, enrolling me in private lessons and sometimes jogging the perimeter of the courts together while I sweated and grunted and swung from my shoelaces.

It wasn't until the advent of my idea of myself as an intellectual that I learned to take pleasure, fitful pleasure, in sports. My first girlfriend, born in Korea, adopted into a family of looming Irish Catholics, believed she saw things differently from most people, and I believed her. She was certainly an unabashed scofflaw at Plymouth High, if the law there was to take Eagles football and basketball seriously, as it was. I recall Stephanie's ringing voice in the cafeteria: "Oh my God, will the ball go in or will it not go in? Will the ball cross the net/line/fence or will it not? The suspense is killing me!"

And this blasphemy was heightened by the fact that Steph, in the year we dated, danced in the JV cheer squad that took the court or the field during halftime and hurled its members high into the air—they looked like solar flares in their orange skirts and tops—and afterward returned to the bench or the sidelines to cheer on the boys. "All that clapping and rah-rah-rah-ing is just contractual," she often said. A contrarian by nature, she reveled in the eclectic image she knew she presented: short shorts that rode high on her white thighs, dizzyingly high, and the navy blue NPR tote bag that slapped against her side like a bulky constant companion. Years earlier, before I knew her, she'd made the local paper by exhaustively estimating the weight of our town—buildings, houses, cars and trucks in driveways, driveways, streets and roads, graveyards, the putrefying dead, trees, forests, rivers, beaches and marshes, and a hundred-odd-square-mile layer cake of topsoil and subsoil, roots, aquifers, sand, all the way down to Plymouth bedrock.

With Stephanie, in other words, you had to find a way to *justify* sport—pure purpose and grace in action, I argued on the shoulders of Aristotle, not so different from the pleasure of seeing a gymnast-dancer tossed in the air. In college I darkened and expanded this view with the help of Nietzsche and Schopenhauer, Derrida, Stevens, Larkin and Hardy, Woolf and Plath, and a handful of others who persuaded me, indirectly, that sports were no more or less meaningful than anything else. If all was *vanitas*, I would latch on to the things that advertised their emptiness, their artifice, the things that took a certain healthy pride in their self-created image—literature mostly, and games. My deepest scorn was reserved for the institutions and virtues that refused this kind of honesty. I mean religion, of course, but also, a little later on, "work" as a faux religion— its various altars to "value," "productivity," "efficiency," etc. I began sprinkling my breakfast cereal with scare quotes, seeing them everywhere, seeing them riding on the backs of every dust mote, every particle of "reality." After several brief but involving love affairs with Marxist writers ("Food first," Bertolt Brecht wrote, "then morality"), it seemed I'd become a Marxist myself.

It's a common enough rest stop if you're trying to take the long way around nihilism. You see the alternative there through the trees, flickering and turning like a sunless lake. You start to wind up and up through pine forests, high mountain roads made entirely of words, and wills, a vertiginously high mountain that you build yourself on the way up it. A wrong move, a sudden buffeting wind, and it's darkness all the way down. One night in the loosening of nerves just before sleep I'd asked Sam what he thought we'd really accomplished in killing Larry Bosch. "Maybe nothing," he said, and a part of me shuddered with recognition.

I got these thoughts down in note form in my phone, in the absence of my notebook, with the intention of transferring them later on. I'd need to go back to the House for the notebook at least, a change of clothes, a few other essentials—I was waiting outside Jen's work, but waiting with the manic, rattling feeling of a man who can see a giant countdown in the noonday sky.

Nada y nada y pues nada—from the Hemingway story, I noted down. The sky's whiteness blinded and obliterated. It meant nothing. I couldn't feel my right leg from the position I'd taken on the stoop. I didn't care enough to move. When Jen finally came down on her lunch break I lurched after her down the street like a zombie, a Frankenstein—or Frankenstein's monster. I meant the monster.

"Good grief," Jen said, turning. "You're out of line, Eli."

"I really need to talk to you."

"This is totally out of hand."

"I just really need to talk to you, Jen. Please, okay? I just really really really really really need to talk."

Jen started away from me, turning onto Canal Street, weaving through the fissures of onrushing humanity, running me off them expertly. She wore the pale yellow sundress with black polka dots that I'd loved her in, the pink shoes on her feet quick and light like ballet flats. I couldn't keep up with her, and now I heard that I was crying. I was streaming tears in the middle of Canal Street, crying in loud gasping jags and shouting Jen's name.

"Please, Jen! It's not what it looks like. Please! Oh my God, Jen, please!"

Abruptly she slowed and stopped, sidestepping into the lee of a McDonald's entranceway, but now I couldn't get the words out. She looked embarrassed for me, sour and squinting, confused, angry, repulsed, uncertain, all at once. She brought me into the suctioned-off airlessness of the restaurant's breezeway, the noise of the city dropping off as the outer door resealed.

"What? Eli, I can't . . . What?"

I was blubbering.

"I can't understand you."

I collapsed into her arms—literally. It wasn't a ploy, a coy gesture. My legs simply gave out in that quiz-show glassed-in

booth that looked out on the bristling passersby, the Hieronymus masses of Canal Street. I met their eyes as Jen swung me
around, struggling under my weight. The jury of my peers.

"My life," I stammered.

"Here, here . . ." Jen propped me up against the glass, put
her hands on my shoulders to pin me there. "Speak slowly. Slow
down."

"My life is over."

I said it again through halting breaths. I really felt it now. I
knew it in my body.

"Your life isn't over, Eli."

"I think it is."

"Look, hey. Look," she said, dipping to meet my eyes. She
swam up in my vision—beautiful Jen through my tears, with
the auburn bangs falling into the white round face, the smear
of freckles.

"You can't follow me anymore," she said. "You can't do it,
Eli. You understand that, don't you? Eli?"

On the other side of the breezeway a tableful of teenagers
sat staring at us, cupping their enormous drinks—

I felt like a worm slit open and pinned to the tray of the
world.

When I got back to the House I saw the brown paper grocery
bags slumped haphazardly on the kitchen counter, with one in
particular bowed and wavering with a dark low water stain. I
discovered the gallon of milk gone warm to the touch inside
it. Sam was already screaming at me—he'd followed me from
the door—but I went about calmly putting away the milk and
other perishables in the fridge. Where the fuck had I been?

Sam wanted to know. What the fuck was my problem? Where was Greg?

I said I didn't know where Greg was. I said, "Don't sweat the groceries, huh? Don't mention it. Your gratitude is so obvious," I said, but my voice was shaking now.

Sam took my shirt in fistfuls and threw me back against the fridge door, scattering magnets and papers all over the floor. A printed photo slid to rest upright: Alex and me and a gaggle of others in stages of pale undress, in the packed dark sand of a Long Island beach. We crouched around a giant FUCK THE POLICE that Alex had spent the better part of an hour carving out of the sand with a child's sand-castle trowel.

"This is funny to you?" Sam said.

"Yes," I said, "yes it is. Isn't it to you? Not even a little bit?"

The strength of his grip surprised me. I felt the hard sharp knuckles of his fists going into my sternum, pushing the breath from my chest, but I laughed all the same. I couldn't help laughing now. A late Saturday afternoon at the beach with Alex and some of our ISO cohort, with the beige wafer sun low in the sky since we knew our limits, UV-wise, or at least I did—Alex tanned, of course. It must have been her first outing of the season because her legs above the invisible shorts line looked almost milky in their whiteness, the tone below them starkly different, as if my girlfriend of only a few months at that point had been dipped halfway into a giant vat of root beer. It was an afternoon of swimming, reading, and half-assed sand-castle building until Alex hit on her whimsy and we just sat back and watched her work, laughing, shaking our heads, giving occasional pointers. Who had brought their phone? She wanted the angle of the photo just right, politely but insistently prodding a zinc-nosed man to try it again, if he didn't mind, a little wider, try to get us all in if he could. In this one the FUCK was partially cut off, in that one the POLICE. Would he mind trying one more time?

From that afternoon to this—could anyone have plotted it? I was almost crying for laughing.

"Hey! Hey!" Sam said, marking time with my shoulder blades against the freezer door.

"Okay," said Alex, "that's enough." She was just behind Sam now, bending to pick up the photographs of flyers and postcards on the floor.

"What are you going to do, Sam? Are you going to do to me like you did—"

His eyes warned me off it. He tightened his grip on my shirt and pressed hard until Alex said again, "That's enough." With the stack of papers and magnets in her hand she tapped Sam on the shoulder, gently, a gentle little gesture to embarrass him out of violence.

Tiffany and Jamaal, like plaintiffs at the bar, had come up to the chest-high island that opened onto the kitchen.

Alex's face was close to mine at the fridge, intimately close, unreadable, stoic. The words leaked out of her mouth. "Where were you, Eli? Where's Greg?"

"Gone, apparently," I said. "You know as much as I do."

"And you have no idea where?"

"No."

"Okay. Okay," she said, speaking softly, seemingly unaware of the audience drawing in around us like a buoy line. I answered the next questions with the forethought of only a few seconds. I'd gone to see Jen, yes, but only to say goodbye. On our walk home from the grocery store Greg had convinced me that we needed to move, all of us, that the best way to ensure we didn't get caught unfairly in the police dragnet was to get as far as possible away from it. I said in retrospect it did seem curious that Greg should empty his checking account to buy a few groceries.

"Only in retrospect, huh?" said Sam.

He turned on Tiffany and asked where Greg would go. He was from Connecticut, right? Where in Connecticut?

Unprepared, startled, Tiffany flinched a little, her face bowed. It was the effect Sam had on all of us lately—you couldn't not sense it: his new volatility, the dry-leaves crackle he gave to the air as he passed. Certainly Greg had sensed it.

"Where in Connecticut?" Sam shouted.

"Greenwich area? I'm not sure." Tiffany mouselike, resentful, shrinking back.

"Didn't you say you guys used to fuck? And you don't know where he's from?"

"He just always said the Greenwich area. I never went with him there."

"Fine," said Sam, "fine, fuck it. Fuck everything."

He took the stairs with bounding steps that we heard overhead like furniture crashing. When I went to the bedroom half an hour later I saw that some of the furniture really had been crashed—the black scarred chair overturned and the desk on its narrow side, the single drawer lolling out of it like a dead black tongue. On the floor Sam had spread all the papers and books Greg had left behind, rummaging roughly through them. In the middle of this mess I found my marble-covered notebook gutted and torn, all the pages ripped out, all the notes I'd made to remember Jen and the other good times, the bad times too, memory's ungovernable overflow, all of it lying like the dirty end of a ticker-tape parade on the bedroom floor. I'd reached down to gather what I could when Sam's scarecrow form darkened the doorway—I turned on it viciously. Sam shoved me back into the room, shouting at me. What the fuck was I thinking putting all that incriminating evidence to paper? What kind of a fucking sentimentalist was I? I charged at him. He waved me past him like a toreador and ran me headfirst into the wooden bunk-bed frame. For a second my vision exploded black and spotted, my legs gone limp. Sam caught me in his arms. He laid me down on the lower bunk bed like a father, or a lover.

When I woke up all the way it was morning and everyone's bags were packed.

In other versions I'm back at the gravel lot. Sam is there by the open car door tucking the black blocky thing into his waistband when I come up behind him and grab it away. I empty the clip into the gravel, one loud sharp bang after the next after the next after the next—

Or else I empty it into Sam.

I was in my bedroom in Plymouth now. My childhood bedroom.

A new notebook lay open on the blue-painted writing desk where I'd spent my first derivative efforts in high school, where I'd stared long and blankly into the thin wood-paneled wall that let in the ground moisture and the winter cold. It was supposedly summer now. Above the desk a small window gave on to a half pane of loamy soil, a buzz cut of pale green grass. You could see the tops of the spare beachy trees where my neighbor used to hide a Rubbermaid container full of ripped-out pages from his father's *Penthouse* stash. For five dollars he showed me where it was and for the space of a summer an equivocal friendship was born. One day Sean was righteous with anger over another boy in the neighborhood, Tim Sheehan, a grade below us, a small runty fighter who would wield just about anything, even his bike, as a weapon. Sean had the red livid marks on his calf to prove it, a bright perforated line where the tire treads had bit. "This *fucking* kid—he doesn't know when to stop," Sean said, thrilling to the word we'd both started adding to our sentences to season them, mature them. The woods behind my house connected through a long sloping rise to the Sheehans' property. One of the last things we did in that shape-shifting summer, Sean and I, was steal the offending one-speed and throw it down a broken cistern.

My *Confessions*. This was how I thought of the notebooks now, not that there was anything particularly Rousseauean in my tone or purpose—no dogma, no redemptive plan informed the scenes and memories I instinctively reached for. Into the notebook went Sean and the weightless falling bike, the leaf-composted bottom of the old cistern receiving it like a dark orange maw. Into the notebook went Bosch too, eventually, but not yet. I was getting down the life as I lived it, living to get it down—the other stuff would keep, the sequenced explosions that had sent me down into this bomb-shelter basement for cover. There was a hoary dampness to the light I now wrote by, a permanent evening suffusing the air. The room had been meant for a finished basement suite, I should mention in fairness to my parents. I believe they envisioned it as a potential rental space, but at fourteen years old I was desperate and pushy, impatient to be out of the upstairs bedroom that shared a wall with my parents' master. It wasn't their proximity to *me* that discomfited—I have no unsubtle love sounds to report, no Freudian primal scenes. No, it was much more about my proximity to them. Fourteen is a strangled peat fire in the stomach, and lower, of course. It didn't matter that several odd-shaped squares of industrial gray carpeting had yet to be cut and laid for the downstairs room's perimeter. It didn't matter that the new drywall partitioning the old flooded basement into a bedroom and an entertainment room remained unsanded, unpapered. What mattered was that I be left alone with the lurid pages I'd filched from Sean's filched stash. What mattered was the twenty-inch TV-VCR in the entertainment room and the Lentz family copy of *Schindler's List*, cued up to the brief early sex scene (such was my pre-Internet blasphemous desperation). Within a few years Henry Miller, Joseph Heller, Updike, Roth, and all the other artful bawds had rather koshered my libidinous fugue state, elevating it into art—the art was the art, rather, and I was brought to this limb-littered table, a starveling, to feast. Was it any wonder that I managed to ignore the damp musty smell that hung like a curtain in the room? Or the slick chill patches of wetness that seeped up into the bare cement corners in the mornings and startled my bare feet? Small sacrifices, really—small then, small now. I just needed the privacy. A few words to my buzzing stricken confused parents and I was back in the room where I'd spent my burning years, as I thought of them now.

In terms of the notebook chronology, I came first to the scene with Hahn and the craven petition for money on the way out of town. Travel funds, we called them, emergency funds. Sam was there to ensure my compliance. He sat beside me on Hahn's stiff couch, the brown high curtains drawn in mourning, I assumed, giving the room a cave-like air. Stephen had passed just two days before, Hahn informed us. The apartment looked swept and bare, as if it hadn't been lived in for weeks—a pile of mail crowding onto the fireplace ledge. I remember feeling touched and a little disoriented by Hahn's choice of words: "passed." A greeting-card word, a word for Congregationalist pastors. Where had this lifelong atheist passed on to, and where did this surviving atheist, a fresh widow, imagine he had gone?

"I'm so sorry," I said. "I had no idea."

"Our condolences," Sam said.

Hahn nodded with her lips tight. Behind her glasses with the dim light playing on them, striping them, her eyes were unreadable. Quiet hands on her lap, overlapping—a ridged vein stood out on her top hand and ran up through the fragile wrist.

"It was a long time coming," Hahn said, setting her tone down like a subject at a norming session, transitioning to a new subject. "What can I do for you two?"

She had no illusions about our presence there.

A strange formality filled her face, narrow as ever, framed by the dark blond bob grown nearly to her shoulders—and the sort of light I'm tempted to call *metaphysical* limned her features, the face's dips and prominences, the faint parenthetical creases at either side of her drawn mouth. It was a dim light, crosshatched with shadows, and it coaxed her out subtly, gently, like a Rembrandt subject.

In the end Hahn asked very few questions and led us down to an ATM at the corner of her street. She took out three thousand dollars, the maximum her bank allowed, and placed the neat stack of hundreds in Sam's outstretched palm, demurring his quiet thanks. I couldn't say anything.

At the foot of her apartment steps she hugged us goodbye, each in turn, and wished us good luck. I asked Hahn when the services would be and she told me. "Services"—another God-tainted word, smelling of camphor, old men's robes.

"You'd better have asked about that just to be polite," Sam said, lifting his arm out on Fifth Avenue to hail a cab. This wasn't the least inconspicuous mode of transportation, perhaps, but it was the fastest.

I didn't answer Sam's threat.

"Eli?"

"Don't worry," I finally said.

"Now I am worried. You can't just show up at a public funeral, Eli. I'd think that's pretty obvious."

"Don't fucking worry."

"Are you going to Hahn's husband's funeral—yes or no?"

"No."

"Don't turn liability on us."

"Wow."

"What?"

"Wow," I said.

In the cab back to Queens we were silent, angled away from each other and looking forlornly out the windows, each to his own side. I was forlorn on my side, anyway, slack and glassy instead of twitchy—detached, floating ghostlike past the blurring rails up FDR Drive, the East River a broad tarnished china plate. It took me a minute to realize we'd turned off onto the Midtown Tunnel and by then it was too late. I touched Sam's narrow knee. He flinched, looked up, squinting.

"I think this guy's taking us the long way," I whispered, almost mouthing the words.

"So let him take the long way. We're good for it." Sam turned back to the window—the city had pivoted to the left, running off behind us. To the right stretched the skinny docks and low red warehouses, the green park-inlets waving up the Brooklyn coast. "City of Whitman," Sam said.

"That's right," I said. "That's right—you're a poet."

There was wonder in my voice. I meant no sarcasm. It's just that it was easy to forget how we'd first met, where Sam and I had come from. He'd rarely talked about his poetry back then, and when he did it was with an embarrassment and a sort of guilt that his baptism into Marxist politics only sharpened, intensified. He'd been thieving all along from the common stock, he said, gobbling up Pell Grants, subsidized loans, and for what? A few tepid sonnets, a villanelle sequence, everything metered and cozied and rhymed. He was a fucking *formalist*, he said, with self-loathing. But he was too hard on himself—I can say this now, definitively, with Sam in the ground. He had real talent, grace of line, enough earnestness to choke you sometimes, but sometimes it did fill you up.

The one poem of Sam's I still have he read one evening, appropriately enough, at KGB Bar in the East Village—red-light-district decor, Soviet schmaltz on the walls, high stools around a cramped gleaming bar, and a patchy PA system, of course. I didn't catch the title of the poem the first time I heard it read, but the rest of it I liked enough to ask Sam for a paper copy afterward.

The Good Life

I despair about where/if it is, this mushroom land,
dun carpet in a stand

of dunny trees
(nutrition in a sun-blocked world)

I feel quite stuck in cosmic waiting
rooms,

the brooms of systems sweeping me out
with dust toward dust. I must

get my shit together, I must come good
after twenty-eight years of grace, period.

But who do I ask for directions?
The gurus are cheats, assholes,

exes,
and I've never really known my Father.

I've only my two thin hands to break brush with.
Tell me: should I bother?

At the House Sam divided up the money five ways. We all exchanged curt hugs before retreating to our separate cars—Sam and I to his old broad Buick, Alex and Tiffany and Jamaal to Alex's Honda. No one knew where the other was going, exactly, and no one asked, though we all had our ideas.

"Do you think we'll see Jamaal or Tiffany again?" I asked Sam in the car.

"I hope not."

"They have their suspicions, you know, just like Greg did."

"Let them suspect. They don't know anything, and they're scared. Productively scared."

Sam dropped me at Grand Central with my single lean garment bag—amazing how little you really need, in the end, how much of a life can be abandoned—and I started away toward the station. With a shy honk Sam called me back to the passenger-side window he had leaned across to crack open. Not then, but on the Amtrak home I recalled the day more than three years earlier when I'd slipped a Marxist primer through the cracked-open window of the same front seat, though on that morning the conspiratorial shtick had been just that—a little shtick, a joke. What a horrible joke that Sam and I should be playing out this scene in nervous earnest now, cutting our eyes left and right, lowering our voices.

"Where were you on that night?" Sam said, testing me. "What were you doing?"

"Sam, I've got it."

"What were you doing?"

"Diner, fishbowl, long way home—I've got it."

"What diner?"

"The Peter Pan."

"And when the rain got bad, where did we pull off?"

"Sam, I'm going," I said, and I headed for the bank of brass-gleaming doors without turning around.

During the three days I spent at my parents' house I surfaced to the main floor only reluctantly. Base appetite had driven me to my basement lair years earlier—only appetite could drive me up again. I made ham and cheese sandwiches in the kitchen, quickly, efficiently, or else PBJs (my taste buds regressing to high school too, apparently), trying to ignore as best I could the professional speculators piping in from the TV in the living room. Nancy Grace had the story now. I tried to block out the segments squeezed cheek by jowl between Pepto-Bismol ads, Viagra commercials, shills for the newest heart medication. Mostly it was Bosch's name, that primal noise, that broke in on me—*Bosch . . . Bosch . . . Bosch*—like explosions from a distant battlefield.

Since when had my parents watched so much twenty-four-hour news, anyway? How had they learned to watch Nancy Grace?

"Oh, you don't really watch it," Mom said. "It's just a noise to keep you company."

"It's *unbearable*," I said. I felt my eye, the insistent something under my eyelid beginning to jump and grab with each *Bosch*.

"Is it unbearable? We're so used to it by now."

Apparently the "news" as a kind of aural nightlight began shortly after I'd left for college. I'd never complained about it on visits home before, Mom told me. I'd never seemed to notice. Dad, especially, coming in from the corporate cold of an insurance brokerage in downtown Boston—asshole boss, tetchy clients, bad commute—didn't care for the added insult of an existentially quiet house. Mom needed the constant burble less. Thirty years into her high-school math teacher's stride, she'd started singing in an ecumenical choir that met several nights a week to practice Bach masses, old Negro spirituals, the whispery haunting pieces that you couldn't quite locate in time or space.

"Why not play some of your music?" I said. "Why not run the fucking dishwasher? It'd be better than *that*, surely."

"I could turn it off if it means that much to you," Mom said, moving toward the set.

It was the second week in August and she would soon be back in school. She had the rosy capillary blush about her cheeks that suggested inveterate drinking in some Irish, but in my mom it just meant a recent visit to the beach. She'd lost weight where my father had gained it—at the sucked-in cheeks, at the under-chin with its sharper smoother drop-off. When she showed her white teeth they looked whiter, wider, with a plasticky tensile sharpness in the lips. Her nervousness made her look younger by several years. Yet I sensed that any conversation with her reappeared son made her feel older, too, more fragile, as it did me.

I heard familiar music coming out of the TV, then Maria Nava's voice.

"Wait," I said, "that's okay. You can leave it on."

It was the Bank of America ad Sam had showed me on YouTube. I hadn't heard the sincerity, somehow, the genuine relief in Maria's voice the first time I'd seen the ad. Now Maria spoke through her wide soft face into my mother's living room, shots of Aida and Luís horsing around on the grass. "I was afraid," Maria said. "I really was afraid for me and my family when all this was happening. I was looking around for any help I could find. I didn't think I'd find it with someone at a bank, you know, but then I met Ned." Cut to Ned, hair parted at the side, anodyne, friendly-looking. He looked harmless. Ned began to talk about the "debt-forgiveness plan" he'd created with Maria. Hey, he had a family too, he said, and he knew how hard these times were for hardworking people like Maria. I realized I was watching a more extended version of this commercial, an ad that was also a penitent genuflection that was also and always an ad. The cozy acoustic guitar came up on the young family gamboling around in the green green grass—fade to white and the final tag line in black: "Caring. It's what we do."

I waited for the old ire, the sense of rightness in my cause—I suddenly wanted it, needed it—but it wouldn't come. Nancy Grace filled the screen, with a harry of legends and tickers and crawls all around her. I'd caught a little of this loop out of the corner of my eye before, but now it assaulted me head-on: pictures of Bosch and Bosch's family, and now Nancy Bosch at a lectern with two adult children at her side, all of them red-faced, swollen, as Nancy struggles to read prepared words about a loving husband and father, a good man, who never deserved this. Cut to another snippet of video as the suited executive squints and raises his hand against the strobing gale of camera flashes—cut to a large black Escalade pulling past a corridor of metal police barriers that holds back the angry protesters with their signs. The chasm widened in my stomach and I began to fall through it, Alice-like, falling into nothingness, blackness. I rushed back to the kitchen counter and grabbed my plate, scurrying back downstairs to eat alone.

"Son?" Mom called after me. "Eli?"

At the writing desk all my recollections read back like horrible stalls, feints, repetitions. I'd started practicing my statement to the police, too, writing it out like the fool I was.

Where was I on the night of August 21? Out for a little drive with friends, Officer, and I think a stop-off at a diner— what night was that again? A Thursday? It must have been the Peter Pan Diner, and I must have ordered from the breakfast menu since I remember the hash browns tasting like wood chips soaked in oil. An overrated place, we all agreed, and yes, cash only—we paid in cash. Then we took the long way back to the city, pulling over to the side of the road when a rainstorm made a mockery of our windshield wipers . . . Then we drove the rest of the way home without incident.

What a fool I was! What a rank coward to cling so hopelessly to this thin little filament of a chance! If the police came digging, circling back, prodding my story for inconsistencies,

I was supposed to volunteer that we'd actually stopped off in those dark rainy woods to smoke pot, fishbowling the car. This was Sam's invention, his pièce de résistance—it explained why we'd taken the toll road up (they'd have the footage available) and the out-of-the-way way back. It also gave off a little whiff of criminality, ergo plausibility—ergo problem solved.

I confess that I'd briefly felt flattered that the group should choose me for this subtler role—the fool!—this character who withholds a minor infraction, then confesses it shaking and racked. And then I felt genuinely racked, genuinely shaky to learn that Sam had been keeping weed in the bowels of his old-school glove compartment all along. (If the cops checked for traces there, he assured us they'd find them.) The fact astonished me: All the time we'd been out on "junkets" in Sam's Buick, chasing and tailing Bosch around the city, or out trawling around for unguarded cell phones, laptops, iPads—all this time Sam had carried the classic pretext for an arrest in his glove compartment.

This moving target of a man—when had I lost the bead on him? And had I ever really had it?

In the late afternoon I heard someone on the creaking stairs descending, hesitating. The wooden planks lulled their song momentarily, but now the song resumed and gathered tempo and purpose. I was at my bedroom door before Mom could get into the entertainment room. She saw me, startled back.

"Oh," she said. "I was just coming to talk to you."

"I figured."

The room glowed bluely with light from another cutaway window against the wall, a lighted band of blue-white sky above a narrower band of dark loam. The house was set at an angle, you remembered, dug into a slope that slowly rose toward the back of the property. In heavy rain I used to watch the black dirt gel and burgeon at my bedroom window, half daring the earth to come through the glass and bury me, sink me struggling in that black grainy sea, a white hand sticking out in sudden desperate protest—*Of course I didn't really mean it!*

"Do you have a minute?" Mom said.

"Actually," I said. "Maybe not quite yet."

"Let's pretend you do, okay? As a favor to me? Call it a trial run."

"A trial run?"

"You pretend you're the kind of son who still comes to his mother when he needs help, I'll pretend I'm the kind of mother who can still help you. Okay? A trial run."

She sat at one end of a plaid couch against the wall and patted the spot next to her with her small white hand. She wore blue argyle socks and the gray corduroys, narrow-waled, that Dad liked to run his fingernail across at speed, making a sharp little *zeep* sound. A thin black sweater, narrow with white stripes, like a fashionable take on prison garb. She'd cut her brown hair to curl tight around her ears and upper neck, having taken inches off her pageboy too. She opened her mouth to speak but changed her mind, dropping back into a not-quite smile.

"Why am I here, right? That's what you want to know?"

"We assume you're here because you need to be here," Mom said, "but yes, a little detail would be nice."

I leaned my back against the armrest, slipping my feet under Mom's warm thighs as I'd done throughout childhood, the two of us reading, say, or watching TV, with Dad off in his study or away on business. Sealed away in our respective minds but close, connected, touching.

I started into the lie I'd prepared for this conversation too, another alibi—things souring with Jen, the engagement called off, the ultimatum from Hahn to finish my dissertation or else, the job I'd gotten, the job I'd lost, the money I'd borrowed from them and all but squandered . . . I could see the concern in the long smooth lines of my mother's face, but I couldn't tell whether or not she believed me. For some reason I felt that the money was the sticking point—ten thousand dollars wasn't easily sneezed away. I described what I'd spent to appease the people I'd crashed with for too long, how quickly large sums can disappear in New York. I said I was sorry—and I was.

"I'll pay you back," I said, "I promise. I want to pay you back."

"How much of it do you have left?"

"About four hundred."

The money was Hahn's, but the figure was accurate.

Unfazed, Mom nodded, but then she said, "Who are these friends you owe money to? You owe them rent, you said?"

"I don't owe them anything anymore. I didn't mean that. They're not really my friends, either."

She looked calculating now—doing the numbers, carrying ones across multiple lanes of numerical traffic. You saw it happen at parties sometimes, family gatherings, a vacant look while she went somewhere behind her eyes and peeled back the weeks and months and years of your time on this earth. Tell her your birthday, she'd tell you the day of the week you were born on—a trick she'd learned in graduate school.

Mom said, "Is one of these friends you owe money to Alex? Your old girlfriend Alex?"

I looked at her without cover, without preparation.

"She called the house this morning while you were in the shower. She asked if you were here."

"She did? What did she say?"

"She just asked if you were here. I said you were but you weren't available, could I take a message. She didn't have one. I think she might have been calling from a pay phone. It was a strange call."

"You're sure it was Alex?"

"I recognized her voice. She seemed shy to be talking to Eli's mother. Do you owe her money, Eli? Does she need money from you?"

"Does Alex need money? How should I know?" I said. "What the hell are you talking about?"

"I'm just asking you a question," Mom said. "Are you in trouble?"

For the rest of the afternoon I waited for Alex to call again, or text—or something. What did she want from me? Why was she calling my parents' landline? I waited through the evening and late into the night, cycling through the old CDs still arranged in the sideways wooden cubby on the brown dusty ledge above my bed. The old bulbous CD player still worked, with the cutout picture of Robert Plant, curled at the edges, yellowing with age, hanging on the wall with a red thumbtack through one of Plant's iconic golden curls. In the picture he is quiet, eyes closed, holding the microphone tenderly with overlapping hands as if he just might kiss the thing instead of sing into it— an older man's gentleness, his face lined. "Going to California" was on the player now, 3:00 a.m. by the red glowing numbers of the clock display. I sang along to the chorus distractedly, as I had fifteen years ago, more—

> *Made up my mind to make a new start*
> *Going to California with an aching . . .*

The words stretched on Plant's ghostly tenor like a canvas, an otherworldly skin. Perhaps it was here that I'd picked up the crooner style Mal chided me for when I tried to sing Mahler.

I'd never been to California. I'd only gone as far west as Maria Nava's backyard in Phoenix, Arizona, it occurred to me now, and now I thought I didn't stand much chance of completing the journey to the coast. Eastward, against the course of empire, I'd gone as far as Europe after college—London, Paris, Brussels, Munich, Berlin, Vienna, Florence, Rome. For a month you run along rail lines and rutted tourist trails like a neuron passing unthinking through the automatic brain, the vast cerebellum of western Europe. The sameness of desire is humbling, occasionally comforting—very occasionally. When I think of that trip now the first thing to resolve out of the gray blur of monuments and mansard blocks and other generic beauties is the talismanic head of Karl Marx, at his gravesite in North London. You wend back through the unpruned greenways of Highgate Cemetery and suddenly there it is, looming up hero-size—Marx's great gray bust on a high granite base. The forehead sat hugely above prow-like brows, great recessed pits for eyes, the round nose riding high on a prodigious seafoaming wave of mustache and beard. He looked like Poseidon, Zeus, a menacing Santa Claus. Years later when I sold my car to fund a weeklong trip to Florence with Alex, I made a special arrangement for an eight-hour layover at Heathrow so that Alex could visit the grave too. The afternoon was misting, I remember, and Marx looked changed, less inspired and inspiring, his eyes prosaically visible in the gray even light. He seemed to be looking down on us, weighing us in the balance.

"Done ticked this box, haven't we?" Alex said in a sudden chirping cockney.

I couldn't tell if she was joking to mask her disappointment or to lighten mine, or maybe both. *Done tixed is box, aven't we?*

The gilt lettering of "WORKERS OF ALL LANDS UNITE!" looked faded and a little chintzy, but Alex posed underneath it and smiled in her pink zippered hoodie that doubled as a raincoat, the water beading and pilling on the soft fabric.

I tried to keep these memories with me as I journeyed into sleep, fitful sleep, but I couldn't hold on to Alex or rainy disappointing London for long. In the morning I walked outside into birdsong and bright light, letting myself feel shocked. I walked up the long sloping rise past the Sheehans' property, past the stand of thin trees where Sean and I had huddled over crumbling pink body parts, the limbs shoveled haphazardly into our gaping id furnaces, the doors of superego standing wide . . . Eventually I looked around me and saw that I'd wandered far beyond the woods near my house, uncertain of where I was anymore, with no bread crumbs in sight. Then a woman on a horse cantered into view, slowing to a walk as she approached me. What a tall, broad-chested, proud-maned animal she rode! I gave the horse a wide berth as it passed, the woman high in her saddle in white riding pants and a light brown shirt with a darker silhouette of a palm tree on it. She looked distinctly out of place in Plymouth, Massachusetts, but she did match her horse, mocha-colored with white streaks in its mane and lower legs so that it might have been wearing tube socks. I nodded a hello to the woman, who looked off beyond me, battening down her eyes in sudden confusion.

"Me?" the woman called out, pointing. "Or him?"

I knew it was Alex before I'd turned around. A hundred yards off, not far from where two trails joined in a sandy confluence, a small figure waved her arms against the brightness of the trail mouth. Familiar in her tank top and shorts, familiar in the voice she lifted up against the tree sounds and wind—I saw Alex's Honda, too, parked a little ways behind her in a cul-de-sac. A pickup with a horse trailer attached to it curved into view as I picked up my pace, running. A strange sense of calm was coming over me, an inevitability like the movement of an airport conveyor belt. When I got into the car beside Alex I tried to get her attention, putting my hand on her hand as she reached for the ignition.

"Hey," I said. "What are you doing here?"

Alex started the car. "We should go. We're drawing attention to ourselves."

"You weren't exactly discreet a moment ago."

The woman on horseback came to the trailhead, descending her mount with a swift athletic swing of the legs, holding the reins at her cheek like a child with balloon strings. Alex and I must have looked like quarreling lovers in our dumb show, my body at right angles to hers. I needed to know what was wrong.

"What's wrong?" Alex said. "What's wrong? I don't know, Eli, what could possibly be wrong? I was looking for you!"

"Why were you looking for me?"

Alex pulled away at speed. Mailboxes shot past us, cracked driveways, modest white houses through the trees.

"Where are you going?" I said. "Do you even know where you're going?"

"They questioned Sam," Alex said. "The police questioned him."

"What? When?"

"The other day."

"Yesterday?"

"Fuck, Eli! How should I know? He didn't give me a detailed timeline on the phone."

"He called you? From jail?"

"He didn't call me from *jail*, moron! You think he'd call me from jail?"

Alex jerked her head back and forth, back and forth again, as if trying to shake off my naïveté, my preening moronic questions. Yet I didn't know anything. How *had* he called her? Where was he? How had the police found him? Where had he gone?

"I don't know any of that," Alex said. "I just know we have to find him. He's obsessed. We have to find him."

"Wait," I said. "Wait wait wait wait wait wait—"

Through the window the shapes and colors of my childhood spun past—past Ames Way, tree-lined Marshland Street, past Carolina Road, past the O'Briens' and the Delanos' and the Sheehans'. The fixed point of the mailbox at the top of my family's drive rushed toward us—past us.

"Alex," I said. "Alex, where are we going? You just passed my house. What are you doing?"

She was shaking her head again, muttering bitterly through tight-set teeth.

"What?" I said. " 'Fucking' what?"

"Fucking amateur! He goes to his parents' house to hide!

Probably the easiest place in the world to find you, Eli, and that's where you go."

A blue minivan shaped like a great sleek nose sped up Standish Drive as we shot down it, a brief sucking *boom* as we passed.

"Jesus Christ, Alex, will you slow down?"

She leaned forward and to the right with the sudden swinging pressure of the car, arcing us left onto Webster at the bottom of the hill, barely slowing at a three-way stop.

"Oh the discretion!" I sang. "The discretion!"

At the next stop sign, a four-way intersection, Alex slowed just enough for me to jimmy up the power locks and jump out of the car. A crazed operatic scream chased after me, the noise stretching and yo-yoing back as Alex turned the car around and tracked my progress up the hill, making a running recitative of abuse through the open window: "Goes straight to the first place anyone would fucking think to look, the shit for brains. Get the fuck in the car, Eli! This is serious! Do you doubt it?"

When I looked up again she was showing me the gun. It was shinier than the other one, all-around shiny, snub-nosed.

"Wait," I said, slowing. Alex's Honda kept pace beside me.

"Just trust me when I say this is serious," Alex said. "Okay?"

"That's not the same one, is it?"

"What do you think?"

"No."

"No, it isn't."

I broke around the back of the Honda and flew up the little bank of grass that the Teague family never kept mowed—past the fishing boat on its side in the side yard, the lichened blue aboveground pool that Mr. Teague once threw me in to teach me how to swim, my rigid little body like a mute white stone sinking straight to the bottom. The oldest Teague girl broke into our house a year later and stole petty cash, a little jewelry, leaving a sort of calling-card note on our fridge's message board—the cops compared it to the handwriting on her homework. Half a mile straight ahead, then, through backyards and driveways and copses, clouds of ghosts, bursting through them like a cannonball through its smoke. I came out of these last woods with a crosshatch of thin red lines down my arm, a long pearling streak down my leg. The skin of my face felt tight, the sweat prickling at my hairline. I saw Alex's car in the driveway, Alex's form through my fogged-in glasses going soft at the edges as she stepped into my house, my mother holding open the front door.

When I got upstairs I did nothing to hide my heavy breathing, the red stripes and scourges on my arms and legs from the neighborhood's brambly woods. Mom blinked at me. I was bent over my knees.

Alex said, "Speak of the devil . . ."

We told my mother we were going out for an early lunch to hash some things through—vague like that, and I think she sensed we were lying.

She said, "Is this the type of lunch place that charges money for their food?"

I put a hand on Alex's shoulder as we dropped down the stairs, to make a better show of it. When we turned the corner away from the front door Alex muscle-bucked my hand away.

"Where'd you get the gun, Alex?"

Back in the car she volunteered a little more information about Sam—less affronted now, driving slower. He'd hung back in the city looking for Greg while the rest of us returned to the leafy suburbs we'd spawned from, apparently. Not that Sam had shown much acumen, either, asking around about Greg at ISO meetings, around the Randolph campus, sleeping at the House or in his car—but that was Alex's point: Sam was losing it, a danger to Greg, a danger to all of us now. He'd kept it together enough to tell the cops the story we'd agreed on—he was out again, not enough to be held on—but now he was probably out redoubling his search for Greg. An obsessive, a liability.

"So he called you from a pay phone?" I said.

Alex nodded.

"Do you know if he mentioned the fishbowl thing to the cops?"

"I don't."

"What were the questions they asked him? How did they find him?"

"I don't know," Alex said. "I don't know any of that. It was two minutes on the phone and most of the time he was asking *me* the questions, trying to find out where Tiffany or Jamaal had gone, if I knew anything about Greg, anything about you and where you might have gone."

"Me? What have I got to do with anything?"

"We just need to find him," Alex said, "or find Greg. Find Greg and maybe we'll find Sam. He won't be far behind."

"And you have no idea where he is?"

"You mean Greg?"

"I mean Sam! Your boyfriend Sam!"

"Is that what he is?" Alex said softly, a little amused. Then she said, "Why don't you tell me where he's gone to—he's your best friend, isn't he? No? You don't know?"

She appeared to take brief satisfaction from this little touché, if that's what it was, but now her face dropped back into olive-sallow slackness, her hair wet and luminously dark from the shower she'd taken in the downstairs bathroom, the first she'd had in three days. I'd showed her how to work the wonky taps in the shower, the bathroom unfinished like my bedroom, unadorned, the shower stall a mere plastic husk of a stall, a placeholder, the white bowl of the sink sticking out of the wall with its gray throat exposed—provisionality abandoned to permanence.

Past Alex's window a row of light-topped silver stanchions ticked by like the measure lines of a sonata, a sudden pastorale. Green within green again, a scrim of trees running behind the unlit car dealership at the edge of town. Up ahead I saw the interstate and signs for Middleborough, Taunton, Norton, each name an echo, a ghost limb. There were years when those place-names would have brought nothing to mind so much as the locker rooms attached to the high schools in them, the dark linoleum hallways after school hours, the spread of fenced-in tennis courts we played on, the meager crowds, mostly parents. Now the names put off a fresh-cut grass smell, reeking mulch, the hiss of sprinklers, the sensorium of suburban wealth that got weaker as you moved out of Boston's powerful orbit, stronger again as you came into New York's.

On the interstate the sky lowered like a shade, darker grays within gray, suddenly, the furrowed white brow of a thunderhead pushing out here and there from the newly installed mass. We were headed toward Greenwich and the millionaire ZIP codes of neighboring Westchester County. Somewhere nearby Bosch's ghost would be hovering in the air, like a seagull on the wind, a plane in a holding pattern over JFK or Newark. I was up there with it now, seeing the bodies from a bird's-eye view when I saw them, the eye of memory slowly turning in the air, hovering, half presiding over the bodies, a man's and a dog's, in their final loneliness.

I realized that the car—coming back to earth—was bending away on an off-ramp.

"We're getting off?" I said to Alex. "Why are we getting off?"

I saw her subtly check her phone. I noted the blue illuminated bars showing gas levels on the console stacked four or five high above the glowing red E. A group of faded, sad-looking picnic tables slid by on our left, a widening apron of grass. Then the low-slung rest stop came out from behind trees, a group of small brown shacks with a lodge aesthetic that the gas stations and fast-food chains roughly matched: a restrained set of golden arches, a Dunkin' Donuts sign in muted earth tones . . . The main building's low roof ran up shallowly, its peaked overhang like an amphitheater shell to an audience of cars. The sun was still behind clouds, but enough light seeped through to reflect the slate sky in the prodigious span of windshields coming into view on our right, recalling a super-image spread across a bank of tight-packed TV screens, the sky in the million microdomes of a bug's eye.

"This is the lunch stop we promised your mother," Alex finally said, parking. "To hash things through, right? I'd love to know what you told her."

Inside the main building a line of vending machines and a grimy blue pay phone filled the space between the men's and women's bathrooms. I came out before Alex, scoping the layout—a convenience store in the right-hand trench, a fluorescent food court–style expanse at the left, white square tables and chairs all welded together and bolted to the floor as if road-warped travelers might try to pry them up for souvenirs. Just then Alex came in through the front entrance again, the glass doors sucking shut behind her.

"I thought you were in the bathroom," I said.

She nodded at the small leather carryall looped over her shoulder. "Forgot this in the car," she said, and disappeared into the ladies' room.

For a good twenty minutes we sat across from each other eating Quiznos at a table in the corner, a casualness sinking into our skin, like exhaustion, and at the same time, with our guard down, an old-times intimacy coming up, an old-times routine.

"Guy in the corner," I said. "Other corner. Don't stare! It's like riding a bike, Alex. How are you so rusty at this?"

"In the Patriots jersey?"

"The very same."

"Half empty or half full?"

"Whichever you prefer."

"Whose jersey is he wearing? Is that Brady's?"

I craned my head to try to make out the numbers spread across the man's spreading gut under the table. I couldn't quite see them, but then I wouldn't have known Brady's jersey number anyway—my taste in sports ran admittedly to the genteel.

"Not mine," Alex said. "I'm a woman of the people. I know all about the Boston Football Patriots."

"Of course."

"Actually, I do know a little about Brady from the tabloids. Let's assume for the sake of this exercise in"—she hesitated, neck bent, squinting—"in glass half fullness, let's assume the gentleman in the corner, our friend Rick, let's assume, is wearing a Tom Brady jersey. Now, understand that Rick isn't one of those big-boned stocky guys of—what, English stock? Irish?—who seeks some vicarious existence in his favorite righty quarterback. Brady's right-handed, right?"

"No idea."

"Pretty sure he is. Rick is too. But here's the thing: Rick doesn't get off on thinking he *is* the quarterback Tom Brady, fucking the same supermodels and paying out the same giant alimonies when he gets tired of them—or maybe it's child support? I can't remember. But Rick's not interested in that. He just likes the way the guy passes the ball, the way he runs out of the pocket, the way he squeezes a water bottle a good foot above his head on the sidelines, very casual-like, you know? Rick loves that. He loves Tom Brady, but he doesn't actually want to *be* Tom Brady. Tom Brady doesn't get to just relax and eat a Big Mac at a middle-of-nowhere rest stop. Tom Brady can't eat Big Macs at all. Tom Brady probably has to suffer through an endless stream of minimally plated nouvelle cuisine dinners, often working to make conversation with people he doesn't know or particularly like. See, Rick doesn't want that. He likes being alone with his thoughts—he can handle that. Do you see him checking his phone every two seconds? You don't. He likes to relax and enjoy a Big Mac, which he enjoys a lot better, frankly, than whatever bastardized European fare they serve at those overpriced bistro pubs, whatever the fuck a bistro pub is. If there's a meaningful distinction between a bistro pub and any other mid-price restaurant with a liquor license, our friend Rick doesn't see it. He doesn't get taken in by marketing, he's not one of Pavlov's slobbering dogs. The man likes his Big Macs, so what? He likes a shamefully rich football player playboy who's probably delinquent in his child support payments, so what?"

With a grimace-smile I raised my index finger like a referee's yellow flag.

"Too much projection at the end there?" Alex said. "Okay, I'll withdraw it."

"Why should he feel the need to defend football and Big Macs?"

"A little splash on the entry, granted, but pretty good otherwise, no?"

"Eight out of ten."

"Who's rusty now?" Alex said, slapping the table. "Okay,

your turn. Who who who who who?" she said, roving her gaze across the room.

In Florence Alex and I had played this game daily, obsessively, at every meal, every snack stop. The first half of our trip was filled with glass-half-full speculations about soft-eyed gelato-shop owners, amateur artists with their easels at the banks of the glittering Arno, French tourists in their stylish dress, uncomfortable-looking shoes. Then came the midweek announcement that Alex and Columbia were finished, the academic life she'd lived, goodbye to all that—and with it, curling silently, sourly in the air, the suggestion that she and I were probably finished too. From then on the trip had all the lilt of a funeral march and all our speculations about the people we saw went glass half empty, decidedly. The pruned woman kneeling down with her eyes closed at the cordon line before Ghiberti's golden door? A religious zealot first, an art lover second or third or tenth, or not at all. The glum-looking man at an alfresco café table, staring at the tourists over his thin empty glass? Stood up on a date, or maybe just out of work, swallowing his savings one grappa at a time. The classical guitarist with the long dark braid that hung down her chest like a ferret? Unemployed too, basically. A hobbyist. What else did twenty years of careful study in just about any art make you? I recalled for Alex a line of Saul Bellow's: The best humanists would be called in to pick out the wallpaper for humanity's crypt. The guitarist was good, too, very good, subtle and soulful in her playing, and lonely. She set up nightly on the steps of a little stone church a few streets from the Ponte Vecchio. In the distance you could hear the more popular buskers with their acoustic-electric American Top 40 on the famous lit-up bridge. We'd passed these talentless young men before, seen their open guitar cases glittering like treasure chests. How simple it was, sometimes, to hate the world. You just opened your eyes.

On the other side of the table Alex had come back to herself—playtime over, apparently. Clouds moved in over her face, her eyes unblinking through narrowed lids. At her neck a tendon stood out like a long fin, running down through the clavicle and making a line against which the gentle bait in her throat dropped and rose again.

"You see that pay phone up front?" Alex said, nodding. "That's our ticket."

"Ticket to what?"

"Don't say anything incriminating on the call, just find out where he is. Do you have his number?"

"Sam's?"

"Greg's. He's the priority. We need to warn him, but we obviously can't do that over the phone."

"Warn him against what? What's Sam going to do?"

"How would I know that?" Alex said. "All I have are worst-case scenarios."

She took her phone out of the carryall, a pen, an old grocery receipt, and copied down the number for me to call. She'd tried herself several times but Greg hadn't picked up, and frankly she didn't blame him. She was linked in Greg's mind with Sam, and Sam hadn't exactly been subtle in his suspicions of Greg, his late hostilities to him. I was different. I'd earned Greg's trust enough to elicit advice from him, borrow money from him—I'd been the last to see him.

"I tell him it's important that we talk to him, but we have to do it in person," I said.

"No 'we,'" said Alex. "Don't even mention me."

I took a handful of quarters to the pay phone by the entrance. The doors behind me rang open and sucked shut, sounds of sneakers on the floor mat, the thwack of flip-flops, the traffic noise from the interstate rushing over the cement partitions and coursing in on the breeze. For long seconds I heard no dial tone, no meaningful clicks—I was on the point of fingering down the receiver when a staid single beep signaled Greg's voice mail. I said the words. I tried to keep my voice low and calm, but a tremor of genuine worry must have ghosted through the message. I don't like to consider where that fear came from—that Alex's concern, a concern about what all this might mean for *us*, is what accounted for the frightened vibrato feathering the edges of my words. Yet it's also obvious, isn't it? Self-interest presided over all this, that bugaboo of Marxism and all utopianism, that black beating heart of all genuine interaction under capitalism. *Of course I mean it! It involves me!* Maybe Greg heard something of this in my message to him—I can't be sure—but a few minutes later when I tried him again I heard his voice on the phone, his live voice, tinny and far away, trembling, breathless, cowed.

It had to be in person, I told him. "Not over the phone. In person. Trust me, okay?"

He gave me the address. I wrote it down. I lied and said I was calling from New York. Two hours, I said, maybe a little under. It was that simple.

I returned to the table, smiling, an idiot vanity on my lips, idiot vanity on my face, the way it pulled up my brows like a marionette's, the puppyish, golden retriever's pride in my eyes . . . That was me. That was the face I wore to the cliff's edge.

"You got it?" Alex said.

I pushed the paper across to her. "You should have timed me," I said.

"Maple Court, huh? In Stamford? That sounds about right—the obligatory tree fetish. I'll bet he's at his parents'."

"Maybe so."

"Quite a group we put together, isn't it?"

"What did you expect? We're a bunch of grad school dropouts."

"It's okay," Alex said, standing, looking quickly past me. "It'll be okay." She crossed to my side of the table and hugged me tight around the neck, leaning into my ear, saying, "Please don't be mad at me, Eli. This'll all be okay. Okay? You know I love you," and she pushed her lips hard into my cheek.

I wheeled around, tracking her sudden steps to the door. Sam was just inside the entranceway, tall and pale, his thin frame loose in the soiled white giveaway T-shirt that hung from his shoulders as if off a coat hanger, the concave chest, the sharp jaw that bent to receive Alex's hasty kiss. He pulled her to him, holding her in an embrace, the subtle exchange of the receipt, and now Sam's eyes were on me. He carried a sagging blue JanSport backpack over his right shoulder as he stepped into the harsher light of the food court, an overhead light that filled him out, lit up the pits and hollows of his face. He was nakedly what he was.

"Don't be mad at Alex," Sam said as he lowered himself down across from me. I retain the image of a green wispy road-runner on the front of his T-shirt, an impressionist figure sliding past—I was staring straight ahead, making a fixed frame for Sam to drop into.

"Eli?"

"You needed the address?" I said. "Is that why I'm here?"

"For what it's worth, Alex didn't want to do it this way, but it had to be done. It was my idea."

I looked up at Sam. "All you've got weighing down that backpack is your dirty laundry, I assume?"

A faint smile crossed Sam's lips, minnow-like—there, then gone.

"And what's to stop me from walking out of here right now?"

"And hitching a ride back to your leafy Boston suburb?"

"Or anywhere."

"Common sense," Sam said, rising slowly back out of the frame. The runner in stylized outline, his limbs like wisps of green smoke, rose too—low cacti in the foreground, a few deft lines to hint at canyons in the background. "Cedar City 10k—Fun in the Sun Run," the shirt said. It moved out of view and trailed after it a belated fug of body sweat and overmatched Old Spice. Sam whispered in my ear, soft and low, dovish, like Alex from a moment ago.

He loped to the front entrance and turned and waited for me there, feigning interest in a Coke machine that he almost matched for height. He wore the tight dark jeans I'd rarely not seen him in, the ones with the white threadbare outlines in the fabric like salty leavings from his front-pocket wallet, the rectangular cell phone he still used in a pinch, I gathered, and here we were in a pinch. He wore the same flat loafers, too, that he used to slip on after tennis, furred and moccasin-like with wear—or if not the exact pair, a close descendant. He was not one to change styles quickly, Sam Westergard. A man of deep habit. A man of action with the habit of repeating his ac-tions again and again, clinging to his talismanic routines. I later learned that Sam had made a near nightly ritual of his trips up to Bosch's neighborhood, sometimes late-night trips, sometimes trips that must have shaded into very early morning, the pale light in a few of the tollbooth photos covering Sam's tan Buick in a purple shroud, covering over the car's dents and rust spots, taking years off it, but never quite obscuring the license plate or the jagged New Jersey–shaped hole shaping the glow of the left brake light. The sexual politics of the House's upstairs bedroom being what they were, I never really wondered why Sam should move from mattress to mattress, rarely waking in the same one consecutively, as if the darkness of night hid nothing so much as a silent game of musical beds. Upward of forty trips, I learned at the trial. An obsessed man, Alex had called him—and I'm convinced that that much of her performance was genuine. I could see the burning points of Sam's personality emanating off him by the Coke machine, unfurling like plumes, like a peacock's spread of manifold shimmering secrets. For the bird it's an automatic gesture, an upwelling out of deep, primordial springs. I wonder how much different it was for my friend Sam.

At length I let him catch my eye. I let him nod me to the door. Outside in the lot the tan Buick overhung the parking spot just opposite the one Alex's Honda had been in.

Sam spoke once we pulled back onto the interstate. He told me we were doing the right thing, the smart thing.

"I'll be the one to talk to him," I said. "That's a requirement. You don't even come near us. Promise me that or I'm out right now."

"Of course," he said. "That was always the plan. Why do you think we needed you?"

"You don't come within a block of the address. I keep the address, actually. Hand it over."

At length Sam did as I asked.

"You drop me at a place where I can get a taxi. He thinks I'm coming up from the city—it should look that way."

"Of course."

We dropped back into silence while the green overtook us at either side, closing in on us. It dulled the senses, doing to the eye what the tires' steady keening through the car's thin floor did to the ear—white vision, white noise. I remember perking up as the steepled clock-tower sprawl of New Haven came and went, the red-brick city like the miniature landscape in a model train set. I perked up more when the road dipped down and hugged the shore and a great infinitesimal light danced over the water—a late sun had come out—and curved Connecticut, staring, ran out across the molten Long Island Sound. It occurred to me that Sam was probably a fugitive.

"Let's not get dramatic," he said.

"Let's not get dramatic? You were just questioned by the police about a murder, weren't you? Are you supposed to be crossing state lines? Aren't the cops keeping tabs on you?"

"It's not a drunk tank, Eli. They don't take your keys."

"What did they say to you? What did they ask you? What do they know? Sam? Will you cut the fucking sphinx routine already? Aren't I basically your accomplice now?"

"Relax," said Sam. "Relax. I don't know what Alex told you, but you can relax, okay?"

It was suddenly all I could do not to leap across the wide leather console and yank that grief-counselor calm off Sam's face. He knew everything except how to keep us out of prison! He knew everything except how to put out the fire we were presently dying in, our bodies chucked in for meaningless tallow. Sam told me again not to be so dramatic, almost whispering the words now, shaking his head—I was shouting—staring ahead at the paying-out road and shaking his head like a disappointed father.

"Tell me everything the cops said to you, right now," I shouted, "and I'll decide whether or not it calls for drama. Right now, you sphinxy fuck! Aren't I here? Aren't I in the car with you? Haven't I given everything to your fucking suicide march?"

"Not everything," Sam said. "Not everything. You can't pretend you haven't had divided loyalties."

"What the fuck does that mean?"

"In the world, sometimes, but never really of it, huh?"

"Will you put your fucking New Testament Greek away and speak—English!"

"You were a member of the House but never all the way. You were there on a trial basis, a need-to-know basis—it was all over your face. It still is, Eli. And what you need to know now is that the cops found me. Somehow they found the House. How did that happen? Do you know?"

"I have no idea. That's what I'm asking you."

"Oh I have an idea," Sam said. "I have an idea. His name is Greg. Your buddy Greg. Anything physical, anything solid and the cops would have never let me go. They wanted to talk about the Bosch protest, in Phoenix—two years ago and on the other side of the country? How would they know about that?"

"You think Greg informed on you? You're saying *he* sent the cops to the House? Why would he do that?"

"I'm not saying he did that. I'm not saying that."

"What *are* you saying? What are we doing right now?"

"I'm just saying it'll be good to talk to him. I just want to talk to him. Maybe he's confused. Maybe he's scared. Maybe he thinks he knows something he doesn't."

"*I'm* talking to him," I said. "I'm doing the talking."

"Sure," said Sam. "Of course, sure. We just need to remind him that he doesn't know anything. None of us do. We hold our nerve, this goes away. That's the message, all right? Stamford five miles." He nodded to the sign.

He took out his phone and handed it across to me. We could use it to navigate the last stretch, he said. He was planning to destroy it anyway.

"Shouldn't we stay off cell phones altogether?" I said. "Don't you have some kind of map in here?" I reached for the glove compartment's handle that didn't give, noticing for the first time the small round lock in the handle's corner.

"No map," said Sam. "Sorry."

"You're sure?" I said. "I could check it for you. Which one of these opens door number one?"

Sam arrested my hand, violently, just shy of the ring of keys hanging off the ignition. "There's no map in the glove compartment," he said. "Trust me on that. And look—let's be realistic for a second." Slowly Sam unfastened his grip on my wrist, the blood surging. "I'm going to need to know where you are, and I don't think tailing a taxi into quiet residential streets is a good idea. Just put the address in the phone, Eli."

"Let me out," I said.

"No."

"Let me out. I'm serious, Sam."

"You're welcome to try—that'd be, what, the drop and roll at seventy miles an hour?"

I was suddenly desperate. "Sam, please, come off it. Let me out! Please let me out!"

"And where would you go?"

"I'll hitchhike. I'll go to a bus stop. You'll never hear from me again."

"I need to talk to him," Sam said, "and I need to make sure it's done right, okay? Say you're worried about me—say I know where he lives, I could be close, say I'm crazy and unhinged and all the stuff you probably do say about me. Say you'd feel a whole lot better if you two were on the move—a talk in the car. Or maybe you're paranoid about wiretaps, whatever. Say whatever you need to say to get him in a car and away from his house. Okay? Then you park somewhere—maybe you need to pee or you thought you saw a cop. Make him park and I'll take it from there. That's the plan. That's all you need to do, Eli. Then you're free. Okay?"

In the taxi now, numbness spreading—

Nothing twitched or grabbed anymore, nothing troubled the glassy surface. It was a new phase in the sensorial Tilt-A-Whirl of the last several days. Now the surgeon put the knife in but all you sensed was the blunted pressure of it, the smell of blood like copper in the air. It could have been anyone's blood.

I felt the dull weight of the gun through the JanSport bag in my lap. I'd insisted to Sam that I bring it with me—not that I'd use it, not that I knew *how* to use it. It was a lucky rabbit's foot, merely, a dark charm, the prospect of rhetoric by other means. This is what I'd told Sam—Sam in his loose road-race T-shirt, in his police-evidence car, with something locked away in the glove box, Sam with the whitish dark rings under his eyes like pats of butter melting down his face.

Through the broad tinted windows of the taxi I could make

out Greg's town unspooling like a straight solid line. The manicured hedges, the narrow drives, dormer windows cut out of the gray shingled roofs, the ineffectual white wooden fences and stacked stone walls—it was Norman Rockwell's America, privilege koshered by quaintness. I'd seen this town before. I'd seen it before I'd ever laid eyes on it—a sin, yes, a violation of etiquette, but not a falsehood. You're brought up to believe that the world will always slip your stereotypes of it, resist your generalized ideas about it with the force of its *thingness*, each snowflake unique, etc. How disappointing to realize that this myth too has been debunked—I think of the Cheever story in which all the husbands and wives of a town turn up to a costume party in football jerseys and wedding gowns. A whole slew of humanity playing to type, uncoordinated, unplanned. It's all they can do to laugh about it.

And my type? What was the role I was trapped in? I walked down the slight decline of a driveway to the house I'd written down the number for, the numbness lifting, dispelling like a sun-chased fog, a certain brightness churning out of the motion of my legs. The taxi hummed off up the road, and underneath it I thought I heard Sam's Buick cutting its engine through the trees. A stone wall rose in sliding scale with the driveway—it ended at the garage at the side of the split-level green-shuttered house, pine green against the whitewashed clapboard. You could have taken my parents' house in Plymouth and set it down some two hundred miles away and there you'd have it. Here you had it. A mulched garden at the level of the retaining wall with pods of green topiary bushes, a black-brown wooden fence at the side yard, dark with weather and age, a line of maples and oaks foreshortening the backyard, mooring to their shadows that stretched like prison stripes across the roof. I rocked myself up into the garden, noticing the inset stairway only a few feet ahead, feeling the gun at the bottom of the JanSport rebounding against my back. A sudden rapping from somewhere behind me—a storm-window rattle. I backed up enough to see the twin glass slits in the white garage door, like robot eyes in their darkness and narrowness. A moment later a jack-o'-lantern light came on in the windows and there was Greg's face looming up baldly, smoothly, wide-eyed in the left-hand glass.

I could hear the heavy breath coming out of him as I scooted under the lifted garage door. I saw the boat shoes he wore, the navy khakis capping thick white legs, an almost comic self-impersonation.

"What's with the paranoia routine, captain?" I tried to sound bluff.

"What?" said Greg. "What you said on the phone, the way you sounded—"

"I know, I know. Okay, look. Why are we in a garage?"

Particleboard lined the walls, a suite of power tools hanging off hooks in the switchboard of holes. There was a small gray Jetta with rounded edges like a cocoon just behind Greg, who faced me again.

"My little sister's upstairs," he said. "I'd rather talk down here."

"Whose car is that? Is it yours?"

"Not really. I use it when I'm here."

"Okay," I said. "I want to show you something."

I brought the JanSport bag around to my front and peeled open the zippered compartment to Greg's view. Like a wounded man, I uncovered my spleen to him, dark and shining, lit at odd angles—a spill of black blood, it could have been, a squid's ink filling the bottom of the bag.

"What is that?"

"It's what you think," I said. "It's not mine, it's Sam's, all right?"

"What are you doing with it?"

"I need your car. I'm not stealing it—I just need it." I closed up the bag. "Listen to me."

When I laid my hand on Greg's arm he flinched dramatically, thrown back against the car's back window, a stuntman's reaction.

"Hey," I said. "It's okay."

"My sister's upstairs," he whispered.

"I just wanted to show you what we're dealing with. Sam's nearby, okay? I need your car. I'm going to leave it at the train station—look for the keys under the wheel well. Sam wants to talk to you but you don't want to talk to him—trust me. As soon as I'm gone, lock your doors. Call the police. Tell them everything I just told you, okay? Greg?"

He stared past me, a sudden porcelain doll, the white skull and forehead and cheeks, the great brown Marxist eyebrows unmoving. I wondered if he'd heard me, if he'd taken any of it in. Then he whispered, "In the ignition. I leave the keys in the ignition."

"Call the police," I said.

I took the turn out of Greg's driveway smoothly but at speed, expecting a certain restraint from Sam, a discreet following distance that would have kept my hapless passenger in the dark, if I'd had one. I was the passenger now, the passenger and the driver, the doubter and the doubt—I was the lure. And discretion had never been Sam's style. The big rattling boat of the Buick came up in my rearview as the town quickly gathered the line it had cast—picket fences blurring by like clouds of spirit, the spirited measure-marker progress of lampposts and telephone poles, the trees, the sky, everything, all of it respooling.

Sam was half a block behind me. When I looked in the mirror I could make out his mute stern features hovering there, his face like the face scrawled onto a balloon floating above the steering wheel. It gave nothing away. Could he see who was driving? Could he tell that the passenger seat was empty? The Jetta's windows tinted the last of the daylight through the car, making a vacuum of deeper purpler dusk inside—was it hiding me, protecting me? Could Sam really not see what was happening? What was to stop him from just turning around?

I paid little heed to a stop sign out of the residential blocks, turning onto a larger hilly street that still looked small, quaint in the way the stores and red-brick buildings cozied it, but big enough for a traffic light at the bottom of the hill—red, of course. I was a mile from the train station, more—*Keep straight*, an automated female voice directed me from my phone. Maybe Sam couldn't tell I was alone from a distance, but now his Buick nosed up and over the same hill, cresting it like a Viking ship over a gray wave, a steady speeding up as gravity did its work. With the crossway traffic speeding smoothly through the intersection, Sam's face filling the mirror again, bearing down on it—just as the front of Sam's car disappeared into the back of mine, the mirror's trick, I stuck my hand out the window and hooked it right, over the roof, pointing largely, frantically, gesticulating with all the subtlety of an air traffic controller, all subtlely abandoned now. I peeled right onto the shoulder to avoid a speeding car, the Doppler wail of its horn as it swerved into the oncoming lane to pass me. I cut left and into the rush of traffic, cutting off a green sedan and another car behind it—a moment's relief—before Sam could make the turn. I didn't know where I was going, where this road was leading us. Panic filled up my veins, made my chest thin and weak. When the green sedan dropped off behind me it was to turn into one of the long, obscured driveways that sudden remoteness had scarced—we were in deeper woods now, green covering everything, thickening everything. Sam was coming up behind me. The other car had gone. I felt the gravity lift in my stomach as the Jetta turned hard and we slalomed, the car and I, down the first narrow street that came to hand. Why I sought out this isolation that could only jeopardize me—a sandy clearing up ahead on the left, an abandoned construction site set back from the woodland houses stretched like grimy gray pendants on the little string of road—I couldn't say. I couldn't access self-preservation just then, or maybe I was still trying to keep up the ruse.

I was out of the car, in any case, before Sam could cut his engine. A reddish mound of heaped crusted earth stood off to one side of the clearing, a scatter of tree stumps like excised moles on the rocky land around it. Something was supposed to have been built here, but who knew how far back that supposing stretched, how many years of waste this clearing represented—I think of this now with a coroner's objectivity.

"Playtime's over, Sam," I was shouting, "playtime's over." I had the empty JanSport slung over my shoulder, the gun in my hand. "Give me your keys."

In the wedge of the open door Sam shook his head woefully. "You stupid fuck," he said.

"Fuck *you*, Sam. Give me your keys."

"I was talking about myself," he said. "*I'm* the stupid fuck. He's not in there? Just to confirm?"

"Give me the keys, Sam. This is ridiculous."

"Maybe I'll see you around, Eli," Sam said, and he got back in the car.

"I'm pointing a gun at you!" I shouted.

"That's right. You are." Sam sprang up and out of the front seat, a sudden lilt in his movements, in his voice.

"Why don't you give that back to me," he said. "It doesn't belong to you. You really don't want it."

"Give me the keys," I said.

The snub-nosed pistol trembled horribly in my hand. Looking around I saw a snatch of a shack-like house through the trees, an old car on blocks—strange rustification.

"You look ridiculous with that thing," Sam said. "I should have listened to Alex. You're an amateur."

"Give me the keys."

"You're going to shoot me, Eli?"

"Give me the fucking keys!"

"Might want to rack the thing first, you fucking amateur."

I pulled the top of the gun toward me like you see in the movies—a sudden terrifying *clack* filled the air.

"You might also want to load the thing," said Sam, stepping toward me, his palm outstretched. "There's no ammo in it." He said again, "Give me the gun, Eli. This doesn't involve you anymore."

He lowered his head and shook it once, disgustedly. When he lunged for my arm the gun bucked and Sam folded forward like a briefcase. He dropped to the ground bent forward and holding his side, screaming. He was screaming my name. It took me a long time to understand it but the noise, a blue peal in that clearing, was forming itself into words. I could make out my name. "Eli! Fuck, Eli! What did you do?" The ringing came up in my ears then, in my emptied-out bell-struck skull, the ringing canceling out everything, pushing me back, staggering me back toward the getaway car.

"Where are you going, Eli? Eli!" Sam shouted.

I was driving by pinpricks, just trying to avoid the trees, aiming only for blankness. I could hear Sam's screams reach a new desperate pitch behind me, rising up through the ringing like an aria. "Eli, help me! Come back! Eli! Eli! Eli!"

This is the picture I'm left with. This is the scene I come back to again and again, more helplessly, more joltingly than the one with Bosch. I've presented it here by way of reconstruction, a first-time recording—my notebooks leave off just before Alex's arrival at my parents' house in Plymouth.

Anyway, you don't forget something like that. At the trial Sam's death at my hands was taken for a kind of confession from us both, a bodily confession, with the signature in Sam's blood like a long rough stroke from where he'd dragged himself back to the Buick. He called an ambulance but didn't know where he was, didn't know who'd shot him. On the 9-1-1 tape they played at the trial his voice is weak already, drained: "I didn't recognize him. Never seen him before. Please hurry." The lead prosecutor, a vain man despite his lumpy baldness and rough, pitted cheeks, argued for an interpretation of events that made Sam look amateurish, thoughtless, careless, stupid, blind, and very lucky. The state wanted it both ways—Sam was a bumbling, raw, instinctual Raskolnikov whose obvious left-behind clues required a table of crack lawyers in smart suits to decipher them. When a reporter asked this same prosecutor, post-trial, how the three of us had evaded capture for nearly two weeks, he replied, "Beginner's luck."

Nothing I have to say here will match that for crassness—I regret everything we did. I regret the deaths, of course, but more than that, prior to and larger than that, presupposing it, enabling it, I regret Sam's projection that incubated and grew, with our help, and became flesh and blood. The zealot's heaven imposed on earth, in the little patch of dirt where Bosch lies turning and turning still. For what it's worth—and I do know how little it's worth—I wish Bosch were still alive. I think Sam wished that too. Whatever access of panic or nihilistic drive overcame him in that moment by the lake in the woods, I have to believe it was momentary, unplanned, and uncharacteristic. I want to believe that. I had seen Sam's gentleness overlaying his sharpness, the lubricating skin, the kind gestures, the gentlemanly niceties. And weren't they more than mere gestures, mere niceties?

On the Long Island Rail Road train into New York that night, with Greg's Jetta left behind at the station just as I'd promised it would be, I saw a text message from Sam. It must have come in only a few minutes after the 9-1-1 call: "You didn't mean to, did you? I believe you didn't. S." It took me almost an hour to respond—was he all right? was he in the hospital?—and by then he wasn't responding at all. Alex, too, got a message from Sam that night. She admitted as much at the trial, but no more. "It was of a personal nature," she said in the affectless tone she adopted during those weeks, her brown eyes flat and withholding, and not once meeting mine. The evidence of the message was buried along with Alex's cell phone in the East River silt. Sam's phone had been destroyed with a well-placed bullet to the memory card—an arduous task. All that blood swathed over the Buick's leather seats, the thick console, the wide glove compartment that he finally unlocked to take out the gun. The rest of the evidence in the car remained intact, preserved carefully, lovingly, a diorama of Sam's guilt—he was a Christian to the end. His final recidivism was to try to take upon himself all the punishment, all the sin. In the Buick's trunk: another handgun, an unscrubbed laptop, a scatter of books, and a handwritten note that read "I alone killed Lawrence Bosch on the night of August 21. —Sam Westergard."

There were four guns in all, and all of them purchased through an Armslist page sourced to western Pennsylvania. Sam's name and details had been changed for the purpose, the seller's too, presumably, but the IP addresses matched. The story about Sam's sister and the new baby, the hunting tagalongs with his brother-in-law—all bullshit. A lie for my benefit, and apparently for Alex's too.

One of the books found in Sam's trunk was *The Urban Guerrilla's Handbook*, perhaps the most incriminating of the documents he'd taken from the House. It was complete with Sam's careful underlinings, his sparse but telling notes. "Yes," he had written at one point, a simple *yes* floating up the margin like a trial balloon, the word tied to a double-underlined sentence about how the imperialist giant is known by his toe, how that single prominence foretells the great gathering bulk behind it. "Start your attack, therefore, at the toe . . ." Sam had written at the bottom of the page. On another page he'd written: "Phoenix as our Moncada?"—Moncada, the military barracks where Castro's forces had suffered a defeat that paved the way to future victory. All this was introduced as evidence at the trial—Sam's pipe dream, apparently. His pipe-bomb dream. I can see that now. I think I might have seen it then—had I chosen to see it. At the time I pushed any hard-stop realities out of my mind—we were only talking, weren't we, no matter how earnest or daring the talk, how thrilling? Also, I had no idea Sam was building up a small arsenal. The section in the *Handbook* on munitions was particularly well underlined.

Four guns. One to Sam, one to Alex, the gun I had taken with me to Greg's, and the gun in the Buick's incriminating trunk. The black blocky pistol Sam had shot through his phone with was the same one he'd shot through Bosch with—it bore only his fingerprints. When the paramedics finally arrived they found Sam's dead body in the driver's seat, with the glove compartment unlocked and hanging open like a mouth, its secrets spilled.

I still don't know what to make of it all. What was this threatening "talk" Sam had planned for Greg, and would he have done more than just talk? Why *should* that gun have been loaded? Or did Sam know the jig was basically up—playtime was indeed over? He'd pre-prosecuted himself with the left-behind clues, cast the narrative of his guilt (*I alone killed Lawrence Bosch . . .*) in the amber of his ancient Buick. At the trial the police photographs of the car looked Hollywood-ized, klieg-lit, flooded with annihilating light—for each line or feature the photographs carved out, another was lost in the glare. Sam's giveaway T-shirt was deep crimson down to the bottom hem, the jeans stained and wet through the crotch. His face, as I can't help but see, had the same death wanness I'd seen on Bosch's face, the vital color drained from it, the skin like parchment. I can see the slaked tilt of Sam's head and neck against the car's side beam, and the long, sharp, locked jaw—all lurid. And all of it for nothing. You wonder if Sam's Christ would have climbed down from his blood-slicked cross if he'd known just how little his sacrifice would matter. The state wanted its heads in the end, live ones, and only Alex and I had ours to offer. Thirty years for Alex, thirty-five for me—parole on the distant edge of that horizon, on "good behavior," but what does that mean? What does it mean today, or tomorrow, or twenty years from now? Twenty years is an epoch, an endlessly receding mirage, like Sam's heaven.

But I have gotten ahead of myself.

On the train back to New York, with Sam's text message catching me up more breathless than I already was, a sudden spasm, a contraction of the lungs like you see with whole cars getting flattened like beer cans—I looked out at the night and saw only my reflection in the glass, dull, haggard, shocked. I fixed on the long regress of my glasses reflected in the window reflected in the glasses . . . I suddenly wanted to see Jen. I needed to see her. I remembered that Stephen Hahn's memorial service would be held tomorrow morning—I wanted to see Hahn too, and I wanted to see tomorrow morning. The night slid darkly by beyond the window, darkness foreshortening the world and framing me inside it, a complicated image, diffuse, spirit-like, as if the soul I devoutly doubted had slipped from my body to hover over and observe me, judge me, sending invisible currents of thought and disdain from that world to this, a synaptic tentacling. In high-school physics it was Dr. Zeke who'd lit up a pale crystal ball like a miniature sun. It radiated spikes and zigzags of energy until you laid your palm on it and drew all the molecular action to yourself—narcissism at the level of biology, at the level of the cells. "Chemists want to be biologists," Zeke often said, loose with his students, seigneurial, smelling powerfully of the Marlboros he smoked in the room's equipment closet. "Chemists want to be biologists, biologists want to be physicists, physicists want to be gods."

Strivers everywhere. "That's the hierarchy," Zeke said. "That's life." Endless striving. I thought how odd it was to be through with all that, through with life in the middle of life, in my body and out of it, observing. All I wanted now was to see Jen, then Hahn, then I'd lift my hand from the buzzing ball for good—I would turn myself in. This plan in its seeming modesty reassured me as I stepped out again into the open air. New York City surrounded me, the great masses with the neon lights covering them in a fish-tank glow, the Hieronymus masses with their plain handsome wide narrow black white faces passing, a strobe effect of them, shifting, merging.

The cabdriver on the way over to Brooklyn spoke to me in his deep sonorous accented voice, from Elsewhere. He asked me where I got my news from.

"My news?" I said.

"All the mainstream outlets are owned and operated by one company only, did you know that? You have to go online to find the real truth."

I'd never heard of the website this earnest chatty man mentioned to me—I've forgotten it now—but the worldview he espoused was instantly familiar. I could have been listening to a member of the Group, unsung, unremunerated, a professional truth teller who'd heard and answered the call. Multinational corporations were set up above governments, whole countries, shaping world events to serve their quarterly profits. Russia, Ukraine, Israel, Palestine, Egypt, Sudan, Syria—all of it could be resolved in a month if a handful of billionaires got together in a room and decided on it. But why would they? It went against their vested interests. The military-industrial-technical complex, the haves and have-nots, depressed labor, rarefied tax evasions, elections bought and sold.

I tipped the man handsomely—I had $300 of Hahn's money to my name, in cash—but on the sidewalk outside Jen's apartment I felt coated in something, some new contaminant. The taxi pulled away down the dark empty car-lined street trailing its brake lights, turning and disappearing. A cold blue light filled the window in Jen's living room, the white pleated curtains riffling softly in the air conditioning. It was cool now, but I remembered how hot Jen's apartment could get in late summer. I felt the weight of brackish river water in the air, an expectation of fall. When I buzzed the number, it was Mallory's voice that answered—to my relief, I realized. She came downstairs in black formal pants, high to the navel, and a white blouse that billowed and overflowed the waistband like a pirate's shirt. Mal pinched and released the excess fabric and said, "Work, Eli. Damned work. I just got home."

"I see."

She stepped out onto the gray cement stoop that a canvas awning overhung, dividing the shadow from buzzing streetlight. Mal's face was in the gloom, the finer features obscured, but I could make out easily enough the look of chagrin rising up, the preemptive apology.

"Is she here?" I said.

"I think maybe you should come back, Eli. Or could you call?"

"Is he here with her?"

She nodded.

"I'm in trouble, Mal. I need to talk to her."

"You're in trouble?"

"Please tell her it's important. I know it's awkward for her."

"Not just for her."

"I'm sorry," I said.

"Well," Mal said, holding open the door behind her, "you might as well come on up. Make a clean belly flop of it."

In the open living room Jen sat on the mint green sofa cushion. Her crossed legs were drawn up like an ascetic's, her arms hugging her knees, her upper body pressed forward under the kneading hands of her boyfriend on the longer couch. Macduff looked harmless and smaller than I remembered him, boyishly intent on his ministrations, a pink bud of tongue sticking out of the side of his mouth. He saw me first—surprise and caesura, interrupted in the middle of this quotidian intimacy, *quotidius interruptus*. If I'd had the ability to feel pain at this scene, a silent shard sliding into the palm I held up to the man—I still didn't know his name.

Now Jen looked up at me, making sense of the change in the room's atmosphere. She wore blue Randolph gym shorts, mesh and loose, pooling like water at the base of her white thighs. I'd have ached to see this, too, though not with desire. Wasn't it months into our relationship before she'd felt comfortable enough to lounge in this gym-rat comfort in front of me?

"Mal?" said Jen, looking over to her friend. She had her palms out too, pleading helplessness.

"I'm sorry," I said. "I am sorry. I made her do it." I addressed all three of them.

For a moment Jen's face was uncertain, wavy—concern overtaking the anger. How wrong had she been about me? Was I dangerous? Her mute eyes slid slowly past me like a satellite dish readjusting. She exchanged silent signals with Macduff. "What are you doing here, Eli?" she asked, not looking at me.

Nothing could have sounded hollower than the vague euphemisms I'd prepared about "trouble," "mistakes," "consequences"—like a high-school guidance counselor to a truant. I chose silence instead.

Jen looked up at me and repeated her question. Her summer-light hair was parted casually and fell in waves past her shoulders. She was waiting. The room felt suddenly cavernous, running away from me—I caught myself against the doorframe. Mal reached out her hand. Was I okay? I fought something back for a long minute.

For all this, Macduff kept silent beside Jen. I felt suddenly grateful to him, indebted. How easy it would have been to cut me down, to make some macho taunt, but instead he followed Jen's lead.

Finally I said, "Professor Hahn's husband, her husband, Stephen—he died. The memorial service is tomorrow morning."

"I'm sorry to hear that," Jen said.

"I have nowhere to stay."

Macduff was on his feet now—not abruptly. He rose with an attempt at casualness. He might have glanced at his watch.

"Derek," Jen said.

"It's fine," he said. "I'll call you tomorrow morning, okay?"

I stepped aside to let them pass together out of the apartment, sending another apology like a weak paper airplane down the stairs. It fluttered, sank. Childishly, sheepishly, I clung to the wall inside the door with my hands behind my back, the loose diamond of my elbows, slouching, avoiding Mallory's eyes.

At length she said, "What kind of trouble, Eli? Are you not going to tell me?"

"If it's all right with you, I'd rather not say."

"Of course," Mal said. "Of course. Don't put yourself out for me." She went back to her room.

When Jen came upstairs I was alone on the couch, staring at a rerun of *House Hunters International*, another comfort measure it had taken Jen longer than this, I thought, to begin in my presence. At first it was all PBS opera broadcasts, art films, classic musicals—it all had to *mean intensely*, as I think Robert Browning put it. That was our model, whether we knew it or not—the Brownings, the *Sonnets from the Portuguese*, Mahler and Mozart, high love and high art rising together like a winding staircase. Only later did we let down our guard and take off our finery around each other, confiding guilty pleasures in pop country music (me), Agatha Christie novels (her), reality TV shows (both of us). For a while our favorite after-dinner fare was the show that flashed aquamarine and pale-sand white across the screen just now: young Americans, mostly, grand locales, big dreams and plans and sometimes the budgets to make them happen, mostly not, but we never tired of it—that blue-and-white dream field, that vicarious expanse.

"You sent Mal away?" Jen said to me.

"No, no. Not really. I didn't mean to."

Without breaking her stride she passed out of the living room and returned with a load of bedclothes—sheets, a pillow, a red-and-orange Mexican blanket we'd once picnicked on in Central Park, I remembered. I thanked Jen again, apologized again, looking off at the screen now, past it, out of cowardice.

"Do you remember this one?" she said from behind me. "I'm pretty sure we watched this one. Young couple leaves New

York to live simple in Costa Rica. They want to live by the beach."

"But they can't afford it. They're crestfallen with the prices. I remember."

On the screen a curving wedge of hourglass sand ran up to meet the couple in their pastiness—the young husband in a Hawaiian shirt, the young wife in a loose pink blouse flapping behind her like a sail. The next scene shows the couple in a low darkish room with the windows cut directly from the stucco; the room has the stoic, unformed air of a monk's scriptorium, but with green spiny palm fronds waving from outside. The Hawaiian-shirted husband is slouching, squinting as he takes in the space, the kitchen, living room, and dining room all combined, apparently. Can they make it work? The woman is shorter by a head and a half, her sail-shirt sagging. What does she think of the place? It's hard to know. The couple is unfailingly polite in front of the plump man with rawhide skin, a bone-deep tan, and a real estate license on the side. If they have hesitations they whisper them, careful of the agent's feelings, perhaps, but careless of the conventions of reality TV. There was a flash-forward to the next segment as the show went to commercial—another apartment, cleaner edges on the inside, a more traditional floor plan with the kind of built-in bookshelves that Jen and I had always oohed and aahed over. Then a shot of the couple out in front of the apartment, squinting into the gale of downtown traffic.

"This isn't the one where they make a shoe stand out of the bookshelves, is it? And the guy forbids his wife a piano because it takes up too much space?"

"You think these two would do that?" said Jen, taking a

seat on the edge of the couch, the bedclothes sitting chaperone between us. "I don't think they're capable of that. Maybe this is a new one?"

Her glass half full for these strangers—of course. It was Jen's default mode. How I'd missed this woman! How I'd miss her again. I decided to tell Jen everything, and plainly, but not yet. I'd tell her on the way to Hahn's husband's memorial tomorrow morning. I didn't want this moment to die too, fragile, flickering in the light of a car commercial.

As it happened, I dressed in a pair of Derek's gray khaki pants the next morning—I'd survived the night—khaki pants and a navy blue button-down that he'd left behind at Jen's apartment, the items pinching and pressing at my chest and middle. It felt like a final insult that our proportions should more or less match, but with the *more* on my end. I'd tried to trim my edges with tennis, hone myself, make myself a proper vessel for something, but not even the House's privations could thin me much. Out on the street I told Jen the story all at once—or I tried to, but she kept telling me to go back, wait, was I serious? Waiting for the punch line that never came, slowing to a stuttering walk, almost to a standstill.

"You're serious?" she said again. "You're serious?"

Against her somber outfit, a black skirt and a black, unseasonably thick sweater, her face looked parchment pale, drained but impervious, refusing to take in the vital facts. I didn't help with my delivery, I suppose, speaking the words automatically, distantly, as if they had nothing to do with me.

Finally Jen stopped altogether on the sidewalk, turning me

to face her. People I have no memory of pressed by on either side. We were feet from the stairs of the Greenpoint Avenue subway station, a great cavern underneath us.

"Are you serious?" Jen said to me. "Are you being serious?"

"I'm just trying to tell you what happened," I said.

"And what are you saying happened? Tell me again. Tell me slowly, Eli."

I told her again. Then I said, "I'm writing it down for you."

You get more used to it over time, but never all the way. No image of your dead brings them back to you, of course, or changes what happened to them, and yet you can't help searching out the magic icon, the potent imagining. Take the effort to remember Stephen Hahn before he shrunk down so vividly into his wheelchair. It's just that—an effort. You feel the uselessness of it in the strength of your wishing for it. That's God, too, I think. That's any heaven you can pin the name on.

I do regret that I didn't get to attend Stephen Hahn's memorial service, or see Hahn again. Jen took me directly to the Ninety-fourth Precinct building off Lorimer Street, a gentle frog march. She insisted on calling around for a lawyer for me. She held my hand at the intake desk.

I would have liked to apologize to Hahn that morning, however obliquely. Any outright disclosure would have only added to her grief, but a hug, a grateful word in her ear . . . I can imagine the gathering: an older, dignified, gray-haired group, with a smattering of students and perhaps a few former patients, all of us in nighttime colors under Hahn's high ceilings, a photograph of Stephen, pre-sickness, handsome and gently arch, smiling out from a frame on the fireplace mantel. Maybe

Hahn can bring just such an image to mind when she thinks of Stephen—I hope so. My image, as I said, is set. How could any framed photograph compete with the live man trembling at the top of a minivan's ramp, listing to one side in his motorized wheelchair, the face gaunt and plastic, the body at the edge of a great darkness, with only the eyes showing clear? And how, for that matter, could any other picture of Larry Bosch dislodge the last one I keep of him, that bird's-eye view of his body on the path, the legs twisting away, trying to take him somewhere but never actually moving him?

And yet I find I can picture Sam as I want him—small mercy to have driven away from his death so blindly. Small mercy to have known him best and least. Perhaps at his core, in his essence, I didn't know him at all—perhaps he eluded himself in that way—but bodily I knew him. Bodily I can conjure him—his long, pale shape, his square jaw cutting the air, cashiering out against the backdrop of a green tennis court. I can see him at the service line, long and gaunt but somehow doughy, too, in his giveaway T-shirts, his baggy basketball shorts, his pale unmuscled legs descending out of them like gym ropes. Where does all his power come from, his speed and agility? He is beating me easily now. He is rounding into form. The arm rises to the toss, crane-like, regal, the spinning yellow ball in the air like a sun at its zenith.

ACKNOWLEDGMENTS

John Adams never wrote a piano piece called "The Radicals," but I'd like to think my made-up John Adams piece isn't too out of tune with the austere, hauntingly beautiful works he has written—*Hallelujah Junction*, *Shaker Loops*, and *The Gospel According to the Other Mary*, to name just a few of the pieces that coursed around in my apartment or in my head as I wrote. Also, while New York University students did stage a protest a little like the one Eli describes, it didn't get as violent and it didn't take place in the post-Occupy moment I placed it in. And these liberties appear just in the first chapter or two—I've taken many others, of course, incurring many debts along the way. Books like Mark Rudd's *Underground* and Larry Grathwohl's *Bringing Down America* helped me riff and extrapolate a little more intelligently, as did many of the writers and pamphleteers the characters in the book read and reference.

For their conversation, critique, and kindness on and off the page, I'm particularly indebted to Hugo Aguayo, Aimee Bender, Vanessa Carlisle, Gil and John Gould, Paul Heideman, Officer Tom Loughran, Mike Turner, my agent PJ Mark, my editor Alexis Washam, her assistant Jillian Buckley, and of course Sharon McIlvain, first and best reader, without whom nothing of this—nothing at all.

RYAN McILVAIN's first novel, *Elders*, was longlisted for the Center for Fiction's First Novel Prize in 2013. His work has appeared in *The Paris Review*, *Post Road*, *The Rumpus*, the *Los Angeles Review of Books*, *Tin House* online, and the *Believer* online, among other venues. A former Stegner Fellow in Fiction at Stanford University, McIlvain now lives with his family in Tampa, Florida, where he is an assistant professor of English at the University of Tampa.